PRAISE FOR
The Last Mile Between Us

"I was originally attracted to this series because of the setting and the author's ability to bring Alaska to her readers. However, Heidi McCahan's regular release schedule, her willingness to connect with reviewers on social media, her mastery of many tropes, her personality-rich, flawed characters, and the way her stories continue running in my head long after I'm finished, keep me reaching for her next publication. She's quietly nudged her way to the top of my auto-read list!"

— The Literate Leprechaun, Goodreads

"I don't know how Heidi does it but every book is different. Jude and Caroline's characters have completely different personalities than her other characters. The situations they find themselves in keep you reading to see what happens next."

— Ruth, Goodreads

"What an awesome read about second chances and forgiveness. *The Last Mile Between Us* had chemistry and tension between Jude and Caroline. The characters were relatable with their own struggles and shortcomings, the plot was engaging, and the story has faith elements."

— Allyson, Goodreads

The Last Mile Between Us

Welcome to Redemption, Alaska

The Other Side of Goodbye
The Long Way Back to You
The Last Mile Between Us

WELCOME TO REDEMPTION, ALASKA

The Last Mile Between Us

HEIDI MCCAHAN

The Last Mile Between Us
Welcome to Redemption, Alaska - Book 3

Published by Sunrise Media Group LLC

Print ISBN: 978-1-966463-34-4

For more information about Heidi McCahan please access the author's website at the following address: HeidiMcCahan.com.

Published in the United States of America.
Cover Design: Sunrise Media Group LLC

For the men and women who work tirelessly
to keep Alaskans safe and healthy.
Thank you!

"In their hearts, humans plan their course,
but the Lord establishes their steps."

Proverbs 16:9 NIV

One

JUDE MERCER HADN'T PLANNED TO TORCH HIS career in front of the television cameras, a panel of veteran judges, and bleachers packed with devoted fans. Cheating had always gotten under his skin though. And this time had been no different. Yeah, okay, maybe he shouldn't have confronted Myles Griffin at the finish line. But what was he supposed to do? Let him leave the venue and destroy the tiny device tucked in his ear? Jude was ninety-nine percent certain Myles had used it to communicate with his coach during the biathlon. He hadn't been about to overlook the blatant illegal activity.

But somehow in his quest to make things right, their interaction had gone horribly wrong. Myles had walked away unscathed. Well, mostly. And Jude had gotten suspended. Unsportsmanlike conduct, making allegations without proof, and creating a disturbance detrimental to the competitive environment.

A week had gone by, and the whole mess still made his blood boil.

And a trip to Alaska to film a commercial hadn't eased his frustration one bit. He stood inside the doorway of his rental cabin in Redemption, Alaska, and stared through the screen door. A monarch butterfly dipped and bobbed over the freshly mowed lawn. Four little kids played a game of tag under a trio of spruce trees. May sunshine glinted off the metal roof of Redemption Resort's main building.

Turning away, he pawed through his duffel bag until he found bug spray, sunglasses, and his trail runners. The single-story log cabin smelled like cedar and laundry soap. He hadn't asked for much detail when he'd booked the reservation. Mainly because he didn't have the luxury of being fussy. The huge bathtub made up for the bare-bones kitchenette, but the place was rather basic. Not that he was here for the amenities. This trip was more about exile.

He grabbed his CamelBak, along with his shoes, and stepped outside. The screen door creaked and slammed behind him with a hollow *whack*.

His phone buzzed. Of course it did. He groaned. "Not now."

He fished the phone out of his vest pocket, half tempted to leave it on the cabin steps when he saw the name on the screen.

Braxton Dale.

Agent. Babysitter. Voice of reason.

Sighing, Jude thumbed the green icon, then pressed the phone to his ear. "Well? What's the latest?"

"Hello to you too," Braxton's deep baritone rumbled. "I wish I had good news."

Jude rubbed his forehead with his fingertips. "Lay it on me. Not like things can get any worse."

But the silence on the line said otherwise.

He sat on the green plastic Adirondack chair on the porch, then shoved his feet into his trail runners. He needed to move. He needed to *run*.

"The energy-drink people just bailed," Braxton said.

"High Voltage? Why?" Jude sat up straight. "I'm *exactly* the kind of guy they need representing their brand. Bold. Fresh. Not afraid to say what I think."

Braxton cleared his throat. "Right. Except a guy who knocks over a camera and nearly takes out a camera operator isn't quite the on-brand message they're looking for."

"He was in my way."

"In your way to *what*?"

"I had to get to Myles before he got to the locker room and tampered with the evidence."

Braxton sighed, a long exhale that said he'd had this conversation far too many times. "Listen. At some point we're going to have to address your unconventional conflict-resolution strategy. It's—"

"What about it?" Jude pinched the phone between his ear and his shoulder, then tied a double knot in his shoelace. "Somebody had to call Myles out."

"As the ruling body tried to point out, there's a time and a place and proper channels established to voice allegations," Braxton said.

"Whatever," Jude scoffed. "They're ignoring the cheating that's going on right under their noses. I can't pretend I didn't see that earpiece."

"At what cost, Jude? You've lost almost all your endorsement deals, and you're suspended from competition."

"Thanks for the reminder." Jude stared up at the sky and let the silence stretch. "Everybody needs to calm down. They overreacted."

"Regardless of what you think you saw, this community doesn't respond well to unsubstantiated allegations." Braxton's tone turned flat. "Myles's coach is pushing for a stiffer punishment."

Jude's stomach pitched. "Such as?"

Braxton hesitated. "I'll keep you updated if anything substantive develops."

"Okay, fine. What's next? Who else? Forget High Voltage. How about those meal-kit people? The ones that deliver straight to your door? I'd be perfect for that."

"Uh-huh." Braxton didn't sound convinced. "How about you

focus on working out, blowing off some steam, and filming that commercial."

"Braxton, wait—"

"I gotta be honest, my guy. If you don't pull it together—"

"Whoa." Jude pushed to his feet, adrenaline spiking in his veins. "Whose side are you on?"

"Yours, of course. But I'm also not kidding. You're not getting any younger. You need to behave. Get your head right."

Jude kicked a pine cone across the grass. "What's that supposed to mean? There's nothing wrong with my head."

"Really? Then how about running a race without accusing people of cheating? And what if you competed and you didn't care what other people did? You just focused on winning?"

"It's tough to ignore the competition when they're cheating."

But the line went dead. Braxton was already gone.

"And I'm always focused on winning." Jude stared at the screen, then squeezed the phone until his knuckles turned white. His hand ached, but it wasn't enough to distract him from the pressure mounting in his chest.

He wanted to hurl the phone into the woods. Instead, he popped back inside the cabin and tossed the thing onto the blue upholstered love seat. Then he unzipped his fleece vest, shrugged it off, and left it beside his phone.

Get your head right.

Braxton's horrible advice echoed in his head.

Jude might be frustrated. Misunderstood. Ridiculed.

But calling out that cheater Myles wasn't wrong.

For now, he'd focus on filming the commercial and getting back in the good graces of the public. He double-knotted the laces in his other shoe, adjusted the mouthpiece on his CamelBak, and took off down the trail the front-desk clerk had said made a five-mile loop. Perfect. He'd redirect all of his aggravation toward Myles into gutting out the next five miles.

As he jogged into the woods, a raven cawed from a tree branch overhead. The breeze picked up. Moss squished beneath his feet. Pine needles whispered with every step. The rhythm of running was familiar—like the start gate at a biathlon course, the moment before the gun went off and everything faded except his breathing and getting to the targets.

A memory stabbed through him. His dad giving him a lecture after a bad race. The same lines. The same tone. Always circling back to *You let us down, Jude.*

But what about when people let him down?

How could he win and perform at the highest level if the other competitors cheated? Between doping, cheating via earpieces, smart contact lenses, and hidden devices or using drone surveillance to spy, some days he wondered if any biathletes weren't sidestepping the rules to gain an advantage.

Some days he wondered if he should join them.

No.

He banished the thought. Biathletes were wired different. *Built* different. He didn't need to cheat to win.

He'd prove to Braxton, to Myles—to the entire competitive community if he had to—that following rules mattered. This most definitely *was not* the beginning of the end.

The trail forked. He stopped, took a sip from the tubing, then stretched his quads again. The left fork led deeper into the trees. That's what the woman at the desk said—*hill at the far end.*

Excellent.

He turned left, picked up speed. Every pump of his arms, every crunch of gravel underfoot was a push against the voice in his head: *You're not getting any younger.*

His knee twinged. Back muscles ached. More of Braxton's words looped like a bad playlist.

Behave.

He hit the base of the hill and charged ahead. Legs burning.

Lungs tightening. Sweat dripping down his back. The trail narrowed. He reached the top but barely noticed the view. Someone had built a crude bench overlooking a small pond. Wildflowers bloomed in the tall grass.

He didn't stop.

Instead, he took another quick sip, wiped the sweat from his brow, then headed down the hill.

Pebbles skidded under his shoes. He stumbled, and his stomach lurched. Arms flailing, he lost his balance. Then his body pitched forward, and he hit the ground on his left side. His hip and shoulder protested. Grunting, he clawed at the hard ground. But there wasn't a single blessed thing in sight to grab onto. He rolled like a log down the embankment.

A guttural sound ripped from his throat as white-hot pain exploded in his left quad. The world tilted, blurred, and then he stopped with a sickening thud.

He lay there gasping, limbs sprawled in the dirt, pulse thundering in his ears.

No. No. No.

He didn't move.

His leg—

Lord, please. I know we're not speaking right now, but a little help here?

Spots danced across his vision. His breath came in short, ragged bursts. The pain felt sharp and unrelenting. Different from anything he'd fought through before.

He'd faced down world champions. Outskied a herd of caribou. Come back from a compound fracture that nearly ended his career the first time.

But this?

This felt like something else.

This felt like his leg had ripped open.

There wasn't one single mention of moving back home anywhere on her vision board. Because accepting a job in Redemption wasn't even plan B.

Caroline McGuire balanced a small cardboard box on her hip and shoved the brand-new key into the lock. The deadbolt clicked. She turned the knob and pushed the door open. The hinges creaked and the smell of fresh paint and new drywall greeted her.

Moving into a small apartment above a sporting-goods store and working in the same clinic where she'd had all her well-child checkups, sports physicals, and X-rays sounded like her worst nightmare.

But she'd taken the job because it was her only offer. So now she'd smile through the pain. Pretend this was exactly what she wanted. Because there was no way she'd admit to her family that she didn't want to be here.

Her mom stopped behind her in the hallway, carrying a plastic bin filled with cleaning supplies. "Oh, look at those windows," her mom said, squeezing her shoulder. "You are going to be so happy here."

"Yeah, so happy." Caroline stepped inside, letting the box drop to the floor with a soft thud. She pulled her phone from the back pocket of her denim shorts and opened the notes app where she kept her never-ending to-do list.

"Are you taking a picture of your empty apartment?" Mom scooted past her and crossed to the windows. "Come check out this view, hon."

"I'm adding 'measure for curtains' to my list of things to do."

"Oh, don't buy any," Mom said. "We have five bins of fabric in storage. I'll make you some."

Caroline hesitated. Homemade curtains were not exactly what she had in mind.

Bright sunlight poured through four huge windows overlooking Redemption's Main Street. Outside, baskets of petunias hung from the new lampposts, their purple, pink, and white blooms spilling over the sides. People wandered along the sidewalks, stopping to chat in front of the Copper Kettle coffee shop, where the doors stood propped open. A sandwich board near the entrance advertised Mocha Moose Tracks in chalky blue letters.

Caroline's chest tightened. It was a perfect May Saturday, but the unease twisting in her stomach wouldn't let her enjoy it.

Her sneakers squeaked against the ash-gray luxury vinyl plank flooring as she crossed the room to survey the rest of the space. A granite-topped counter with space for two stools—maybe three if she bought basic ones—separated the kitchen from the living area. She peeked inside the stainless-steel fridge to make sure it had been turned on. Cool air soothed her flushed face. Exposed wooden beams stretched across the ceiling, and the gas fireplace tucked into the far wall added a cozy touch. It was a great apartment. A great opportunity.

So why did it feel like a consolation prize?

Her mom set down the cleaning supplies in the middle of the empty room and crossed to the half bath situated just off the kitchen. "I doubt the people working in the store downstairs will get too rowdy, so it should be nice and peaceful for you."

"Yeah, and Redemption Outfitters isn't opening for another couple of weeks, so I've got plenty of time to get settled." Caroline forced a smile when her mother came out of the bathroom. "Come on, let's go help the guys with those boxes."

They headed down the stairs, the echo of their footsteps bouncing off the narrow walls, and pushed through the heavy door at the bottom. Out on the sidewalk, her dad sat in his wheelchair, offering tips as her brothers Ethan and Luke unloaded the pod that contained all of her belongings and furniture from Colorado.

They wore jeans, T-shirts, and work gloves, sweat gleaming on their foreheads under the midday sun.

"Wow, look at you," a woman's voice chirped.

Caroline froze mid-step. Slowly, she turned. "Hi, Mrs. Dawkins."

The older woman stood on the sidewalk in a leopard-print cardigan that hung to her knees, a beige T-shirt, and faded black jeans. Her black slip-on shoes were scuffed, and her curls—springy and almost entirely white—framed her face like a halo.

"Did you just come from the salon?" Caroline grabbed a box from the neat stack Ethan had created beside Dad's chair.

Mrs. Dawkins patted her hair and grinned, revealing a smudge of lipstick on her teeth. "I sure did! How could you tell?"

Caroline forced herself to keep her voice light. "Oh, just a feeling. It looks good. How are you?"

Mrs. Dawkins's smile faded, her expression shifting to something sharper. "Well . . . I'm a wee bit concerned."

Caroline's pulse quickened. She braced herself.

"You've got big shoes to fill," Mrs. Dawkins said, her tone dripping with faux sympathy. "If Dr. Wallace is really retiring, are you sure you're up for it? Lots of folks think you're a little . . . well, a little too new, sweetie."

A hot flush climbed Caroline's neck, burning her ears. She could feel her family watching, their silence amplifying her humiliation. Her dad's disapproval radiated toward Mrs. Dawkins like heat off asphalt.

Caroline cleared her throat, forcing herself to meet the woman's hawkish gaze. "I graduated near the top of my class. I'm board-certified. I've done all my clinicals and gained a ton of experience. Everybody has to start somewhere, right? But I think I'll manage."

Mrs. Dawkins scraped at a pebble on the sidewalk with the toe of her shoe, her mouth pinching into a tight line. "I guess we'll see. Have a great day."

Caroline exhaled as Mrs. Dawkins turned and shuffled away.

Her mom leaned in and whispered, "It would've been nice if she'd offered to carry a box or three."

"Actually," Caroline said, "I don't want that woman inside my apartment. Ever."

Her mom gave her an encouraging pat on the back. "You handled that well, dear."

Oh, she wasn't so sure. The words clung to her, heavy and sticky. There would always be skeptics here. People who doubted her. And she certainly didn't need anyone to point out that it had taken her three attempts to get into PA school. Redemption loved its second chances, but it loved its judgment even more.

She drew a deep breath, shook off the awkward encounter, then carted her box toward the stairs.

She was halfway up when her phone buzzed in the back pocket of her shorts. Setting the box down at her feet, she swiped to answer. "Hey, Tate. What's up?"

"We've got a problem," her brother said.

"Uh-oh. What happened?"

"One of our guests fell on the trail, and he's hurt pretty bad. I tried calling Doc Wallace, but he's not answering. I'll call 911 if you want me to, but . . . do you think you could come take a look first?"

"Of course." She didn't hesitate. "I'm on my way."

She ended the call, put the box inside, then hurried back down to the sidewalk. "Bad news. I need to run over to the resort. Can you carry on here without me?"

"What's wrong?" Ethan asked, his brow furrowed.

"Someone's injured. Tate asked me to check it out."

"What about Doc Wallace?" Dad rolled his chair closer. "He's good about coming by whenever we need him."

Ouch. Thanks for the vote of confidence. Caroline swallowed back the terse words. "He didn't answer his phone. When I saw his wife at the post office yesterday, she said he was going fishing today."

Mom took a bottle of water from the portable cooler she'd brought along. "But I thought you didn't start until Monday?"

"You're right, my official start date is Monday, but that doesn't matter. If someone needs help, I'm not going to blow off Tate's request."

Luke tossed her his keys. "Take my truck. Your medical bag is still in back."

"Thanks." She caught them, then jogged down the street to where he'd parked.

Caroline climbed into the driver's seat of Luke's truck, double-checked that her bag was still wedged behind the passenger seat, then started the engine. She adjusted the rearview mirror, checked for traffic, and pulled out onto Main Street.

Redemption unfolded around her like a postcard, picturesque and vibrant. Sunlight shimmered off the bay to her right. Emerald-green water rippled in the breeze. Two kids stood on the sidewalk in front of the bank, licking ice cream cones that were already melting. One of them tilted his cone too far, and a chocolate scoop plopped onto the pavement. He froze, staring at it for a moment before bursting into laughter, his friend joining in.

On the bike path that ran parallel to the road, a couple pedaled bicycles. A golden retriever on a leash trotted beside them, its pink tongue lolling. The scent of fresh-cut grass drifted through the open window as she passed a roadside park where a man walked with a tiny, energetic dog on a neon-green leash. The dog barked at a flock of seagulls that had gathered near a picnic table, scattering them into the air.

Wildflowers bloomed along the edges of the road, splashes of yellow, purple, and white standing out against the deep green underbrush. In the distance, mountains rose up from the sea, their peaks capped with patches of snow that hadn't yet melted.

She tightened her grip on the steering wheel, her thoughts spinning as she turned onto the gravel road that led to the resort.

The crunch of the tires on the loose stones was a familiar sound, one that tugged at memories of growing up here—lazy summer afternoons exploring the trails, bonfires in the field, and the way the air always smelled like pine and saltwater.

But today, none of that offered comfort. Her stomach churned as she replayed Tate's words in her mind. Someone was hurt. Badly. Sure, she'd trained for emergencies. But this wasn't a clinical rotation under a mentor's watchful eye. This was real. And it was on her to help.

As she approached the resort's main building, she spotted clusters of guests outside. A family gathered at one of the picnic tables on the lawn. Three kids played with a Frisbee while the adults unpacked a cooler. Two young couples unloaded luggage from the back of an SUV, their friendly banter filtering toward her.

Caroline parked the truck in the closest open spot and grabbed her bag. Slinging it over her shoulder, she hurried toward Tate, waiting for her with an ATV parked near the end of the building.

"He's on the trail by the ridge. Something's stuck in his leg."

Caroline's chest tightened as she climbed onto the ATV behind him. "Who is he? Do we know?"

"Elite athlete. He's here filming a commercial. Guess he decided to go for a run."

When they reached the ridge, Caroline grabbed her bag and rushed toward the injured man. He lay sprawled in the dirt at the base of the embankment, his body twisted at an awkward angle. A jagged stick jutted from his thigh. Blood trickled from the wound and soaked the fabric of his shorts. Dust clung to his skin, and bits of grass and dirt marred a scrape along his left arm.

His CamelBak lay on the ground beside him, and the drinking tube rested on his shoulder. His T-shirt was damp, and his shoes, which looked expensive, were scuffed. His chest rose and fell rapidly. Grunting, he flung his arm across his forehead. Was he in shock or just agony?

Then her eyes locked onto his, and everything inside her froze. No, it couldn't be. The last time she'd seen him, he'd made a hasty exit out of her life in Colorado.

Well, he wasn't running today.

"Jude," she whispered.

His stormy hazel eyes flicked up to meet hers, pain darkening their depths.

"You're the last person I expected to see," he said, his voice tight. Chagrin rippled across his pinched features.

Her resolve faltered, her memory replaying a montage of how he'd looked at her that night in Colorado. And the way his lips had brushed against hers, slow and deliberate. She also remembered the silence that had followed. For days, weeks, and months.

"Yeah, well—" She hesitated. "I'm your best hope right now."

His eyes lingered on hers. Something unspoken flickered behind them. An apology, maybe? Or regret?

It didn't matter. Her hands shook as she tugged on her disposable gloves. She'd already learned the hard way that Jude was lousy at apologizing.

Two

LYING ON A GURNEY IN A SMALL-TOWN ER WITH a stick impaled in his leg wasn't how Jude had envisioned spending his Saturday afternoon.

He stared up at the fluorescent lights buzzing overhead. The sharp, metallic scents hanging in the air made him restless. Not to mention that the sight of blood always made him feel lightheaded. His leg throbbed and the pain got worse whenever he shifted, no matter how carefully he tried to stay still. That darn stick pressed into his skin, a constant, humiliating reminder of how far he'd fallen.

Turning his head a fraction of an inch, he stole another glance at her.

Caroline McGuire.

She sat in a cheap plastic chair in the cramped cubicle, scrolling through her phone, her face calm and unreadable. Of all the people to see him like this—bleeding, broken, and mad as a hornet—why did it have to be her?

"You don't have to stay, you know," he said, his voice rougher than he intended.

She didn't look up. "I'm not going to leave you."

"How considerate."

"I try."

Determined to get a reaction, or maybe because waiting made him cranky, he tried to get a rise out of her. "If I'd known you'd be the one patching me up, I might've aimed for a paper cut instead."

Oy. There he went again, running his mouth and saying things he didn't really mean.

She lifted her head, those stunning blue eyes boring into him. "If that was supposed to be an insult, I think you can do better."

He barked out a laugh. Ouch. Huge mistake. Pain flared in his leg, sharp and unforgiving. He groaned, his head sinking back against the thin pillow.

"See?" Caroline said, her tone dry but tinged with amusement. "Don't be sassy and that won't happen."

She stood, honey-blonde ponytail swaying as she crossed the cubicle and pulled back the curtain to peek into the hallway. The sound of muffled voices filtered in, mixed with the squeak of sneakers on linoleum and the hum of carts rolling by.

"Aren't you a doctor or a surgeon or something now?" he asked, trying to adjust his position without jostling his leg. Sweat slicked his palms. "Why don't you just yank that thing out and we can be on our way?"

She turned slowly, propping her fists on her hips. "I am a physician assistant, and I don't technically start until Monday. So for insurance purposes—and to keep the hospital administration happy—it's best if I function as a Good Samaritan. Think of me more as a representative of the resort and less as a healthcare professional."

Her expression softened, and he hated that it made his chest tighten.

"It stinks that you have to wait," she said, glancing at her watch.

"But Dr. Wallace is out fishing for the weekend, and Dr. Monroe is delivering a baby. I hope it won't be too much longer."

He nodded, swallowing the lump of mortification lodged in his throat. It wasn't just the injury or the small-town ER that made his gut churn. It was her. The way she sparred with him, an appealing sparkle in her eyes that reminded him of the night they'd kissed in Colorado.

And, wow, what a kiss it had been.

He looked away. The kiss wasn't the problem. It was how everything had clicked. Her soft lips against his, the warmth radiating from her skin when he'd cupped her face in his hands. He'd thought about their encounter more than he'd wanted to admit. And then he'd ghosted her. Like an idiot.

"Jude."

Her voice snapped him out of his thoughts. Heat crawled up his neck.

"Yeah?"

"How's your pain? Scale of one to ten."

"Three."

Her lips twitched. "That's cute. Try again."

"Okay, fine. Honestly? Seven."

"Sorry to hear that. Now, sit tight. You're not bleeding out, so you'll live."

He snorted softly, shifting his shoulders against the thin mattress. Out in the hallway, someone brushed past the curtain, making it sway. Caroline's citrusy fragrance lingered as she reclaimed her seat, and it was maddening. Distracting. He hated distractions.

"When did you get here?" he asked, hoping to steer his thoughts away from his pain.

"I was unloading boxes when my brother called to let me know there was an emergency. I flew in a couple days ago, and my stuff just got here."

"Huh. Are you glad to be home?"

Silence.

"Oh, so that's a no, then," he said.

Her eyes widened. "It's not that I'm not happy to be here. I love my family. This is a great town. But . . ." She leaned forward, balancing her elbows on her knees. "I had, um, thought about moving farther east."

"How far east?"

"Virginia."

"Really?"

She frowned. "They had a fantastic position available in the ER in Richmond, but I didn't get it."

He studied her, noting the way her fingers tightened around the edge of the chair. "But you grew up here. This is your turf. You'll pretty much know everybody, right?"

"Exactly." She sighed, leaning back and massaging her forehead with her fingertips. "Listen, could we, um . . . could we keep that between us?"

"Ooh, like a secret?"

She shook her head. "Forget it. Forget I said anything."

"Caroline." He hesitated, then lowered his voice. "I get it. You don't want your family to know you're not thrilled to be back."

She exhaled and gave him a look he couldn't quite decipher. Popping to her feet, she started to pace. "I just don't want my family to know, okay? They've been so excited about me moving back. I think they'd be really bummed to know this wasn't what I had planned. So just keep this little heart-to-heart between us."

"My lips are sealed." He reached out, extending his pinky. "Pinky swear."

She arched a brow, clearly unimpressed. "I haven't done a pinky swear in decades."

"Well, now's the perfect time," he said, a faint grin tugging at his lips despite the fire burning in his leg. "Pinky swear, or I'm going to tell everybody I meet."

"Fine," she said with a huff, hooking her pinky around his and giving it a shake.

He didn't let go right away, savoring the warmth of her hand longer than necessary. Her cheeks turned the faintest shade of pink, two splotches of color spreading across her skin.

"Now that we've bonded, can you ask somebody how much longer this is going to take?"

Rolling her eyes, she tugged her hand free. "Look, I have to work here, so no. You're just going to have to be patient."

"Well, maybe they could send somebody to find a doctor who's fishing," he said, his tone laced with exaggerated annoyance. "Drag him back. My legs are kind of important, you know. Some might say they're my livelihood. He can fish another day."

"Huh," she said. "You're just as patient and easygoing as always."

"What's that supposed to mean?"

Before she could answer, the curtain was pulled back and a woman in teal scrubs entered the cubicle. Her salt-and-pepper hair was woven into a long, thick braid that hung over her shoulder.

"Hi. I'm Dr. Monroe," she said, giving them a warm but efficient smile. "You must be Jude."

He nodded. "Mm-hmm."

She immediately moved to the small sink under the cabinet, washing her hands with practiced ease.

"Hey, Caroline," she said over her shoulder. "Good to see you. Excited to have you start on Monday. You getting settled?"

"Uh . . . trying," Caroline said. "My friend here interrupted when he decided to fall down and land on a stick."

"That's unfortunate timing." Dr. Monroe dried her hands with a paper towel and turned to face them. "Would you like to assist?"

"No." Caroline circled around to the opposite side of the bed. "I've been told I can't."

"Oh, rats," the doctor said with an amused pout. "Well, you're here for moral support, then?"

"Yeah," Caroline said, her tone wry. "And to make sure he doesn't bleed all over your ER."

"Well," Dr. Monroe said with a chuckle, "I'll do my best to make sure that doesn't happen."

Jude groaned, his patience wearing thin. "Ladies, I love this little coffee talk you're having, but could we get on with it, please?"

The women exchanged glances, and Caroline's lips twitched.

"As much as I don't care for your attitude, you're correct that we shouldn't delay this any longer." Dr. Monroe pulled on a pair of gloves and wheeled a cart with a sterile tray closer to the side of the bed. "Listen, I know you've signed all your consent forms, but just a reminder—there is a risk of potential damage to surrounding tissue and blood vessels."

"What?" Jude glanced at Caroline. "That was so not on the form, Doc."

Dr. Monroe gave him a reassuring nod. "We'll be as careful as possible."

Her gloved hands moved with precision as she examined the wound. Caroline stood a step closer, her arms crossed but her eyes tracking the doctor's every movement.

"So, Jude," Dr. Monroe said as she worked, "I understand you're an athlete?"

"Yes," he said through clenched teeth. "Biathlon—cross-country skiing and rifle shooting. But obviously, it's spring, so I'm here to cross-train and shoot a commercial."

"Oh, great." The doctor's voice was light, but her expression was serious. "Well, this might set you back a little bit."

"I think it already did," Caroline said.

Jude's jaw tightened. "This will pretty much ruin my summer, then. Great."

Caroline tilted her head. "Not your whole summer."

"Um, hello," he growled. "Things couldn't get much worse. I'm injured. And suspended. It's going to be hard to bounce back."

"Don't worry," Caroline said with a gentle smile. "It's all going to work out."

Her gaze held his, steady and sure, and for the briefest moment, the tightness in his chest eased. Now, see? There she went. Being kind. Reassuring. Her smile slicing right through his resolve to stay mad.

"I'm going to call a nurse in here to assist since Caroline, technically, is benched," the doctor said, poking her head around the curtain.

Caroline held out her hand. "Do you want to hold my hand?"

Yes.

"No," he said, shaking his head.

"All right." She shrugged, amusement flickering in her eyes. "Just thought I'd ask."

Instead, he gripped the cold metal handrails on either side of the bed.

"When she removes the object, you have to be still," she said, her voice softening just enough to make him glance her way. Again.

"Noted."

The curtain swished as a nurse entered—a tall, willowy young woman who looked like she wasn't a day over eighteen. Jude clamped his mouth shut, resisting the urge to make a sarcastic comment. He'd already popped off too often tonight, and he was starting to feel like a trapped animal, cornered by his own bad attitude.

Dr. Monroe nudged the cart closer, her expression focused and professional. "Okay, Jude, here we go. Caroline, last call for hand-holding."

Caroline stepped closer to the gurney. "I offered but the patient declined."

"I'm fine," Jude said through gritted teeth.

The doctor worked quickly, preparing a syringe loaded with

clear liquid. "I know needles aren't fun, but I can't move forward without numbing the area."

"Understood."

"Perfect." The doctor's voice was calm but firm. "You'll feel a little pinch."

He nodded. The pain from the needle's injection was minor compared to the white-hot pain he'd experienced when he'd landed on the stick.

"Good job." Dr. Monroe disposed of the needle in the red plastic container mounted on the wall. "We'll wait a couple minutes for the medication to take effect."

Jude didn't answer. His mind had already circled back to envisioning worst-case scenarios. What would this injury really mean for him in the short term? Would he be out of commission for a couple of days? Or weeks?

"All right. Ready? Three . . . two . . ."

Before she even hit *one,* Jude let out a pathetic yelp and grabbed Caroline's forearm.

"What's the matter?" Caroline hovered over him. "Your upper leg is supposed to be numb."

"It's the sound—like slurping or something." He could barely form the words. His vision tunneled. *Oh no.* He couldn't pass out. Not now.

"You're okay." Caroline's expression grew serious as her eyes roamed his face. "Focus. Deep breaths. You've got this."

"Okay, done." Dr. Monroe held up the offending stick. Long and jagged, speckled with blood, dirt and bark. "Wow. Looks like a trail marker."

"Yikes," Caroline whispered.

"Your family might want to look into that," the doctor added.

"I'm sure they're aware." Caroline's gaze shifted to find Jude's. "You okay?"

The nurse pressed sterile gauze pads against Jude's wound, and he winced, letting out a shaky breath.

"Breathe, Jude," Caroline said, leaning in closer. Her ponytail spilled over her shoulder, the ends brushing the bare skin of his arm.

"I *am*," he ground out, though his breath felt shallow and uneven.

"Look at me," she said firmly.

He let his eyes slide to hers, drawn in by the calm steadiness there.

"Slow breaths," she said, her voice low and soothing. "You know how—just like you breathe before you aim at your target. In for three, hold, out for three."

He tried to focus on her words, ignoring the tightness in his chest and the way his vision blurred at the edges.

"We can't have you passing out now." She grabbed his hand. Her fingers were warm, and the contact sent a flicker of something sharp and unwelcome through him.

"Jude, you're a rock star," Dr. Monroe said, her voice muffled in his ears. "I'm going to stitch the wound closed. You'll be done in no time."

He nodded faintly, his jaw clenching as he fought to stay present.

"Thanks for, you know, not letting me bleed out," he muttered, turning his head away as the doctor prepared the sutures.

"That's what we're here for," Dr. Monroe said. She worked quickly. "We're almost finished, Jude. You're handling this like a champ."

Yeah, a real champ. Yelling like she'd amputated his leg or something. And barely staying conscious. More like a wimp.

He closed his eyes and went to his "happy place," the tire swing hanging from a majestic tree in his family's backyard in New Hampshire. The scene he always imagined when he felt overwhelmed.

Funny thing—this time, it wasn't brought on by a mountain or a ski trail. It was Caroline, smiling at him like she had in Colorado, snowflakes clinging to her hair.

Dr. Monroe finished treating the wound, then tugged off her gloves. "All right. I'll fill the prescription for pain meds and antibiotics. The pharmacy should still be open for a couple more hours. Someone will be in with your discharge papers shortly, okay?"

"Got it. Thanks again," he said, his voice low.

Silence filled the room as the doctor and nurse left.

"You doing all right?" Caroline asked, leaning down to examine his leg.

He glanced at her, the tension in his body easing slightly.

"Looks like you got seven stitches," she said. "Dr. Monroe did an excellent job."

"Caroline."

"Yeah?"

"About Colorado . . ." His throat tightened, and he swallowed hard. "I'm sorry."

She didn't respond right away. Her expression shuttered, her guard slamming into place like a fortress door.

"I'm going to get Tate," she said finally, her voice cool. "He'll make sure you get back to the resort."

Before he could say anything else, she turned and left, pulling the curtain shut behind her.

He squeezed his eyes shut. "Mercer, you're an idiot," he whispered.

It wasn't her job to worry about him.

Caroline tamped down thoughts of Jude sitting in the ER struggling to manage his pain. She slammed the door on the truck she'd borrowed from her brother Luke and crossed the parking lot to

Homeport. Seagulls cawed overhead, and a family of four stood at the railing overlooking the harbor. Flowers spilled from two terracotta planters on either side of the restaurant's aqua-blue door.

She stepped inside, and the smell of salt, fried batter, and a faint hint of something lemony, cleaner maybe, enveloped her. The place had been freshly painted, probably after the tidal-wave damage. They must have worked fast. Framed photos in shades of aqua, gray, and royal blue popped against the bright white wall. Each photo featured the best of Alaska—commercial fishing boats, birds, flowers, and wildlife. Reclaimed wood tables and nets with blue and green glass fishing floats added to the coastal vibe. Somebody had strung fairy lights crisscrossing the ceiling, and country music filtered through a speaker nearby.

She scanned the chalkboard menu overhead, pretending to study it even though she'd already decided she'd be ordering fish and chips. So maybe there was at least one good thing about coming back to Redemption—dinner at Homeport.

"Caroline."

She turned, hesitating near the young teenager waiting behind the counter to take her order. Her high school friends Abbie and Emma were already seated in a booth in the corner. Emma wore her red curls pulled back in a loose ponytail, gesturing with her hands as she talked. Abbie held her soda in her hand, smiling.

"Hey." Caroline waved. "I'll be right there." She stepped up to the counter and placed her order for halibut, fries, a side of fruit, and iced tea.

Then she worked her way through the tables until she reached her friends. Both women stood and hugged her.

"I'm glad you're here," Emma said, pulling back, her bright green eyes scanning Caroline's face.

"And I'm glad you scored a booth." Caroline scanned the crowded dining area. "This place is packed. Didn't they just reopen last week?"

"Yes. Thankfully," Abbie said, sliding over in the booth to make room. "There's literally nowhere else to get decent fish and chips in town."

Caroline sat down beside Abbie, blew out a long breath, and slouched back against the beige cushioned banquette. "I hope you haven't been waiting long. Dr. Wallace is out fishing, so I had to help Tate take a guest from the resort to the ER."

"The ER? Already?" Abbie shook her head. "You just got here."

Emma's thin brows sailed upward. "What happened?"

Caroline fidgeted with the strawberry charm she'd clipped onto the handle of her handbag. "It's no big deal. Just a guy who fell and jammed a stick in his leg."

"Ooh!" Emma shivered. "Yikes. That grosses me out. Sorry I asked."

"Hmm, a guy." Abbie smiled, then nudged Caroline's shoulder with her own. "Is he cute?"

Caroline gave her the side-eye, but her cheeks flamed, betraying her feelings. "That's not the point."

"Oh, it so is the point." Emma grinned as she nudged her drink aside. "I see the color on those gorgeous cheekbones of yours. Do not even try to deflect."

"Wait." Abbie held up her palm. "I heard there's an infamous athlete in town. My husband mentioned something about him. Jude? Jack? He's here to film a commercial."

Caroline swallowed back a groan. Of course. News that juicy wouldn't be kept under wraps. "His name is Jude Mercer."

"So you do know him," Emma said. "What's the deal with the two of you?"

Caroline twisted around in her seat. "Where is our food, anyway?"

"Oh my word, you're stalling," Abbie said. "So is there a deal?"

Sighing, Caroline faced her friends. "Fine. Yes, we have a history. Sort of."

"Sort of?" Emma clasped her hands under her chin. "Details, please."

Caroline glanced around the busy restaurant, half hoping someone would interrupt or deliver their order. Anything.

Nope.

She relented with a resigned shrug. "We met last November in Colorado. He was in town for a race or something, and I was doing a rotation with the orthopedic surgeons who provide team coverage. Anyway, a bunch of us went out after the race and sang karaoke. There was just this amazing chemistry. Afterward, while I was waiting for my Uber, he came out behind me and we had . . . a moment."

Abbie reached for her water. "What kind of a moment?"

Warmth bloomed in her chest at the memory. The way Jude strode toward her, weaving through the people mingling on the sidewalk, thick wet flakes falling from an inky night sky. His gaze locked on hers. Fierce. Determined.

Caroline hesitated. "We kissed. Impulsive, I know. But it was magical."

Emma twisted the paper wrapper from her straw through her fingers. "Then what happened?"

"Then he ghosted me."

Emma's mouth drifted open. "No way. Why?"

"I wish I knew. Someone posted a picture of us kissing, and when he was asked about it in an interview, he said I was no one."

"That's terrible." Emma frowned. "I'm so sorry that happened."

Abbie grabbed her phone. "Is this the same Jude Mercer that just got kicked out of some major competition for losing his temper? I thought I saw a post online."

Caroline shrugged. "After what happened between us, I've tried my best to not pay any attention."

"Wait. Jude Mercer." Emma tapped her fingernails on the table. "Biathlon champion. Possible Olympic hopeful?"

"Yep, that's him," Caroline said.

"Oh dear." Emma reached over and grabbed Caroline's hand. "I don't think you want to be involved with him. I don't care how cute he is, you deserve someone who will show up for you. Not disappear after an epic kiss."

"Agreed," Caroline said. They'd exchanged numbers. He'd known how to find her online because they'd both been tagged in the same photo on social media. There really was no excuse for how he'd promised to reach out but never had.

"It's fine," she insisted. "I've moved on."

"Have you though?" Abbie tilted her head, eyes narrowed. "Because here you both are in Redemption together."

"We're not together," Caroline said. "I mean, seeing him today and helping him out in the ER was weird, but it's not like I'll fall in love with him or anything."

"You don't sound convincing," Emma said.

Abbie's expression grew serious. "Are you all right? That must have stung a little."

Caroline gave her a small smile, then waved her off. "I told you, it's fine. Just awkward."

"Especially since you'll probably run into each other a lot. I mean, he's staying at your family's resort, right?" Emma scrunched up her nose. "Super awkward."

Before Caroline could protest, their numbers were called, and they retrieved their meals from the counter. Caroline slid her orange plastic tray onto the table, then scooted back into the booth. The aroma of fried fish and crisp french fries made her stomach growl. It had been hours since she'd eaten.

"Enough about him." Caroline reached for the tartar sauce. "What's going on with you two. Abbie? How are the kids?"

Abbie twisted her brown hair up into a messy bun, then secured it with a ponytail holder she'd worn on her wrist. "Exhausting, adorable, and counting down until the last day of school. I almost cried this morning when I realized summer break starts in twenty-three days. I'm not ready."

"Have you signed them up for summer camp? Or vacation Bible school?" Emma squirted ketchup into her basket of fries. "There will be plenty of activities for kids at the festival."

"True." Abbie cut her fried fish in half with plastic utensils. "Except that's only one day."

Emma shrugged. "Just trying to help."

Abbie sighed. "I know. Thank you for that. It's just a little overwhelming to think about filling a whole summer without school or preschool. They both thrive with structure and a routine."

"Don't we all," Caroline said. "I'm happy to hear the festival is still on. Wasn't sure how that would all shake out after the tidal wave."

"Now that we've confirmed there's a handsome biathlon champion in town, maybe I should rope him into volunteering," Emma said.

"Please put him in the dunk tank," Caroline said, pointing a fry at her. "I'll be first in line to buy all the tickets."

Emma and Abbie burst out laughing. Caroline couldn't help but join in. For the first time in ages, she felt lighter. Like she still belonged with these ladies. Sure, she'd had friends in Colorado and plenty of outdoor activities and a brutal schedule to keep her occupied, but nothing measured up to reconnecting with friends she'd known for most of her life.

As she dug into her fruit, her mind drifted back to Jude though. That cocky smile. The way he'd bantered with her in the ER. And the memory of that one incredible kiss she couldn't quite forget.

Three

C'MON, MAN. DON'T BE A BABY. IT'S ONLY SEVEN *stitches.*

Jude lay sprawled across the double bed in his cabin, sweat dampening his skin even though the air blowing in through the cracked window carried a chill that made him shiver. His leg throbbed. A deep, insistent pulse that hadn't let up since Tate had driven him home from the ER a few hours ago. They'd sent him limping on his way with little more than extra-strength ibuprofen, antibiotics, and instructions to rest. But the meds barely diluted the burning pain in his thigh, and worse, he was starting to feel off. Lightheaded. His stomach twisted.

Fever? He dragged a palm across his hot face. No. Not happening. He could handle this.

He tried to roll onto his side, but the movement sent a sharp jolt up his leg. He groaned, then gritted his teeth against another wave of pain.

Don't be weak. Just get through the night. You've battled worse.

He'd raced in subzero conditions, fought through injuries that should have sidelined him. He wasn't about to let a dumb sharp stick take him out. Except . . . what if he was making it worse? What if something had happened at the ER? What if they'd accidentally sewn a gauze pad in there or given him an infection?

He shook his head. That couldn't be right. The wound wasn't that big.

Breathing slowly, he counted each inhale, then exhaled through his nose. He needed backup. But who?

He fumbled for his phone on the nightstand, his fingers sluggish as he scrolled through his contacts. His agent, Braxton, was asleep. It was close to 4:00 a.m. on the East Coast, but Jude paid him plenty to take middle-of-the-night calls. Still, from the other side of the continent, he wouldn't be much help.

He thumbed through his recent texts. Tate McGuire. They weren't friends. He'd just met the guy. But he seemed decent, and he'd made sure Jude got something to eat and settled into his cabin. Probably not the kind of guy who'd make a big deal out of a late-night phone call.

It's not even dark outside. Text him. You're not asking for a kidney.

He hesitated, deleting three different messages before settling on:

Jude

Hey, are you around?

Tate responded quickly.

Tate

Yep. Everything okay?

Jude winced, then pecked out another message.

Jude

Not really. Might need a little help.

The dots bounced. Then a new message arrived.

Tate

On my way.

Jude dropped his phone onto his chest and closed his eyes. Shame burned almost as much as the fever creeping through his body. Man, he hated needing help. Hated feeling weak. Hated that Caroline's brother was the only one he felt like he could call. Because Tate was probably going to put two and two together and ask Jude what in the world he'd done to set Caroline off, and he was not ready to talk about it.

A sharp knock sounded on the door.

Jude pushed himself upright, swallowing back a groan as pain flared in his leg.

You'll be fine. You can do this. Answer the door.

Limping, he staggered to the door, undid the deadbolt, and tugged it open, breathing heavily.

"Whoa." Tate stood there, an electrolyte drink in one hand and a first aid kit in the other. He surveyed Jude with a critical eye. "Man, you don't look good."

"Thanks so much," Jude growled. "Super encouraging."

Tate stepped inside, closing the door behind him, and set the drink and first aid kit on the table. "I can go back to the resort and get you a thermos of hot tea."

Jude snorted. "Do I look like the kind of guy who drinks hot tea?"

Tate shrugged. "I don't know. Right now, you look like a stubborn guy who didn't take enough of his meds."

"Yeah, you're probably right."

"Why don't you sit down? Or lie down. Whatever. Let me take a look."

Jude hesitated, then sank onto the end of the bed and slid his mesh athletic shorts up, exposing the wound. Carefully, he peeled back a corner of the elastic bandage holding the nonstick gauze pad in place.

Tate's frown deepened. "It's red. Swollen. You have a fever?"

"Maybe." Jude glared at the angry, stitched-up wound on his quad.

"Okay, here's the deal." Tate put the bandage back in place and stood. "You probably need medical attention."

"I already got medical attention," Jude said. "Stitches. Antibiotics. Ibuprofen—the horse-pill-sized ones. I'll be fine."

Tate's eyes narrowed. "Right. That's why you called me."

Jude looked away. "What do you think I should do?"

Tate pulled out his phone. "Caroline?"

"No."

Tate raised an eyebrow. "That was fast."

"Not happening. I already saw her. She didn't help. Something about not officially being an employee yet."

Tate pinned him with a long look. "I don't know what went down between you two, but my sister's skilled at helping people. And you need someone who knows what they're doing."

"It's too late to bother her." Jude leaned back on his elbows, wincing. That was a flimsy excuse, and he knew it. Of course he knew it. Tate was right. Caroline had probably spent years patching people up, diagnosing injuries, keeping hot-tempered athletes from making things worse.

And yeah, maybe he shouldn't have disappeared from her life like a spineless coward. But at the time, it'd felt right.

"So what's the problem?" Tate's fingers flew over his phone's screen.

Jude shook his head. "It's a long story. I really don't want you to deck me, and I need your help."

Tate glanced up from his phone. "You kissed her, didn't you?"

Jude went still.

Tate let out a low chuckle. "Yeah, that's what I thought."

Jude flopped back onto the bed, scrubbing a hand over his bristly jaw. "It was a mistake."

"You sure about that?"

No. But Jude didn't answer.

Tate exhaled. "You need help. So either let me call her, or I'm driving you back to the ER, and you'll probably see the same person who stitched you up."

Man, Jude hated every part of this conversation. Maybe he could just push through and pretend it wasn't that bad. Maybe some chamomile tea *would* help him fall asleep.

Or . . . he could face the one person who knew exactly how to get under his skin. Who wouldn't put up with his bravado. Not for a second.

He blew out a rough breath. "Fine. Call her. Text her. Carrier pigeon. Whatever. Find someone who can help me not feel like hot garbage."

"Got it." Tate nodded. "Good choice, friend."

"Yeah. We'll see about that."

So much for not worrying about him.

Caroline walked across the manicured grass outside the resort. The sun had dipped behind the mountain peaks less than an hour ago. A few wispy clouds, with their edges still dreamy shades of soft cotton-candy pink, floated in the pale-blue midnight sky. After spending the last six years in Colorado, eighteen hours of daylight would take some getting used to. She drew in a deep breath, savoring the cool, fresh air. The faint scent of pine needles mixed with the earthy aroma of grass. A gentle breeze rustled the evergreen trees behind the cabin, making them sway like dancers in a slow waltz.

She paused outside Jude's cabin door, her hand tightening

around the strap of her medical bag. Whispering a prayer, her voice barely audible, she said, "Lord, please give me strength and a heaping dose of patience."

She knocked once before pushing the door open and stepping inside without waiting for an invitation. The rustic charm of the log cabin greeted her: a small, contemporary couch sat opposite a sleek, compact kitchenette. A doorway led to the bedroom, where warm light spilled across the soft beige walls and polished wooden floors.

Jude didn't even stir. Sprawled on the bed, his gray T-shirt clung to his damp skin, darkened with sweat. His head tipped back into the pillows, and his flushed cheeks stood out starkly against his usual tan. His legs shifted restlessly under the blanket, and a faint groan escaped his lips.

Wow, he did not look good. Caroline set her bag on the floor at her feet, her professional instincts kicking in.

"Hey. How are things?" she asked, keeping her tone light.

Her brother Tate moved out of the shadows and closer to the bed. His arms were folded tightly across his chest, his jaw set.

"We'll all feel better if you can give him a quick look," he said, his voice low.

The worry carving a notch in Tate's forehead made Caroline's scalp prickle. What had he seen that freaked him out so much?

Jude's mouth twitched, a shadow of his usual cocky grin. "Florence Nightingale, is that you?" His voice was hoarse but laced with dry humor. "So glad you're here. Nothing like a snarky comment or three to bring me back to health."

"Florence was a brilliant nurse. I'm a physician assistant." Caroline pulled her digital thermometer from her bag. "I know you have trouble with facts and details sometimes, so that was a freebie. Have you taken your temperature?"

Jude held up his right hand, where a dark ring circled the fourth finger. "No, but my super-smart device here tells me things aren't great."

"Can't always trust the data from those. If you don't mind, I'll just get a temperature. You'll hardly feel a thing."

He didn't object as she moved closer, scanning the digital wand across his forehead. The device beeped, and the screen lit up: 100.2°F. She turned it toward him.

"Low-grade fever," she said. "Not good news, but unless it spikes higher, I think you can stay put."

Jude blew out a slow breath, somewhere between a sigh and a groan. "Just a little fever. Is that your diagnosis?"

"No, the diagnosis is you tripped and fell down a hill and collided with a sharp stick, which earned you a nasty gash plus some cool stitches." She put the thermometer away. "And perhaps you picked up a virus somewhere because I find it hard to believe you have a fever as a result of your wound."

"Unless he didn't take his antibiotics," Tate added.

"Valid point, but I did take them. They're nasty, by the way," Jude grumbled. "So, what's the plan, Doc? Wait it out?"

Caroline stifled her exasperation. "Again, *physician assistant,* not a doctor. Caroline will do. Miss McGuire if you're feeling especially chivalrous."

"Nope. Not tonight." Jude tunneled his fingers into his dark hair. "Check back Tuesday."

Tate smothered a laugh, turning away as Jude tried to push himself upright.

"Slow your roll there, big guy," Caroline said, placing a firm hand on Jude's chest. The heat radiating through his shirt made her pause—but not as much as the definition of his muscles beneath her fingers. The hem of his T-shirt rode up, revealing chiseled abs, and her gaze lingered.

Unfortunately, Jude noticed. His hazel eyes locked on hers, and a knowing smirk tugged at the corner of his lips.

Shoot. Caught. She cleared her throat and reached for her medical bag to cover her flustered state.

"I don't need any additional wound care, thanks," Jude said, but the muscle in his jaw twitched as he spoke.

"Let me just take a look, okay?" she said, her voice soft but firm. She undid the ACE wrap and the plastic zip-top bag of ice covering his stitches. The area was tight, red, and swollen. Her fingers moved gently over the wound, but Jude flinched.

"That is *not* necessary," he growled.

"Oh, and yet here we are," she replied, unbothered. "How long has the ice been on?"

Tate checked his phone. "Twelve minutes."

"Okay, let's go eight more and then you'll be good to go. Last time you took meds?" Caroline asked, her words efficient.

Jude scrubbed a hand across his face, fumbling on the bed until he found his phone. His hand trembled as he scrolled. "I took the ibuprofen they gave me at the hospital."

"It's midnight now. Did they give you any pain meds?"

Jude hesitated. "They gave me some oxy, but I don't want to take it."

"Okay, well, you can alternate ibuprofen and Tylenol through the night. That'll bring your fever down. You do need to be vigilant with the antibiotics. And it's time for your next dose."

"I've got a snack here, and I brought him a drink," Tate said, retrieving an electrolyte-replacement drink and a granola bar. He handed them over. "Here."

"Thanks, man." Jude sat up straighter, wincing.

Caroline adjusted the pillows behind him, careful not to touch his shoulders. "As soon as we get that fever down, you'll hopefully be able to rest."

"I've been resting."

"Arguing with me, moaning, groaning, and fighting a fever are not resting," she shot back.

Jude sighed, then closed his eyes. When he opened them, his gaze landed on her, and for a moment, a flicker of something she couldn't quite decipher flashed across his handsome features. "You didn't have to come."

"You're right, I didn't. But lucky for you, Tate is more persuasive than you deserve."

Tate held up a palm in mock surrender. "Let's settle down, shall we? I'm too exhausted to referee an argument."

Jude's gaze shifted between Tate and Caroline before he ran a hand through his damp hair. "You said you don't officially start work till Monday. Hope I didn't put you in an awkward position."

Her heart betrayed her, thudding too loudly as she remembered those full lips leaning down to claim hers. She shoved the memory aside. "Well, you're a guest at my family's resort, so the boundaries are getting a little blurry. And you're not exactly in control of what position you're putting people in."

He cracked open the bottle. "Thanks, I think."

"Did you just say thank you?"

Jude hesitated, the container halfway to his lips. "Yeah, and don't make me regret it."

"Annnd, I'm out. Keep me posted," she called over her shoulder as she headed for the door. Outside, she clutched her bag tighter and quickened her pace. Tate kept stride with her, his gaze flicking toward her profile as if he was gauging whether to press further. She could feel the weight of his concern, but she wasn't ready to unpack it—not now.

The cool air brushed against her cheeks, but it did little to calm the heat rising in her chest. Her mind churned, replaying the scene back in the cabin. Jude's flushed face, the way his eyes lingered on her, the stubborn set of his jaw when he tried to brush off her care. And that smirk—the one that always managed to fray her nerves in the worst way and yet, somehow, made her stomach flutter.

Tate broke the silence. "Care Bear, you're overthinking it."

"I'm not." She glanced at him, her words sharp enough to cut, but Tate didn't flinch.

"You are." He gave her a pointed look. "You always do this. You've been second-guessing yourself since we were kids. Remember when you thought you'd ruined Christmas because you accidentally broke Mom's favorite ornament?"

"That was different," she insisted, her voice tight. "This is someone's health, Tate. His career, his future. There's a lot more at stake than some glass angel."

"Maybe. But you're forgetting one thing." He stopped walking, forcing her to turn and face him. "You know what you're doing, Caroline. You're good at this. And if Jude didn't trust you, he wouldn't have let you anywhere near that wound."

She hesitated, the weight of his words settling over her. "He didn't have much of a choice."

"Sure he did. He could've told me not to reach out to you. He could've refused to let you in the door. But he didn't." Tate crossed his arms, his expression softening. "Look, I don't know what happened between you two, and honestly, I don't think I want to know. But whatever it is, it doesn't change the fact that tonight, you did your job. You helped him. That's all that matters."

Caroline exhaled slowly, her shoulders sagging. "I just—" She paused, her voice faltering. "I don't want to get it wrong, Tate. Not with him."

Tate tilted his head, studying her. "Why does it feel like there's more to that statement than you're letting on?"

"There isn't." She turned away and resumed walking, her shoes striking the ground with a little more force than necessary. "Jude's a guest at the resort. That's all. I'm just trying to do my job and keep things professional."

"Uh-huh." Tate's tone dripped with skepticism, but he didn't push further. Instead, he let the silence stretch between them as they passed the charred remains of the cabin that had burned down a couple months ago. Caroline averted her gaze, but the sight still gnawed at her, a stark reminder of how quickly things could spiral out of control.

Finally, Tate spoke again, his voice low. "You're not responsible for everything, you know."

She stopped in her tracks, her hand tightening around the strap of her bag. "I know that."

"Do you?" he pressed gently, his eyes searching hers. "Because sometimes it seems like you're carrying the weight of the world on your shoulders. You can't fix everything, Caroline. And you can't protect everyone. Not all the time."

Her throat tightened, but she forced herself to meet his gaze. "I know I can't fix everything. But that doesn't mean I shouldn't try."

Tate sighed, his lips curving into a faint, knowing smile. "Stubborn as ever."

"Someone has to be."

When they reached the resort's parking lot, Tate stopped again. "You good?"

"I'm fine," she said, though the tension in her voice betrayed her.

He hesitated, then nodded. "All right. Try to get some sleep. And Care Bear?"

"What?" She glanced over her shoulder.

He smiled. "You're better at this than you give yourself credit for. Don't let him get in your head."

She didn't respond, but the words lingered long after Tate turned and headed for his truck. Caroline stood beside the sedan she'd borrowed from her parents, clutching her keys.

The soft glow of the resort lights spilled from the windows. Stars twinkled in the baby-blue sky. Mosquitoes buzzed around her, spurring her to climb behind the wheel. But as she turned on the engine and set her bag on the passenger seat, the image of Jude's hazel eyes and that infuriating smirk refused to leave her alone.

She sighed, rubbing a hand over her face. How could one man irritate her this much yet take up residence in her brain so easily?

Not fair. Not fair at all.

Four

HE WASN'T BUILT FOR SITTING STILL.

Jude limped across the lawn, his legs like noodles. Drops of moisture clung to the blades of grass. Two squirrels zipped across his path, then scampered up a tree. A family of four stepped out of the resort and carried their suitcases toward a waiting van. Sunlight filtered through the trees, and a clear blue sky arced overhead.

What a great day for a hike, paddling a kayak, going for a long run, or even rollerblading. But the pain in his leg hinted that he wouldn't be doing much but watching Netflix and taking a nap. Thankfully, his fever had broken. Somewhere around five this morning. He had slept fitfully, leaving him feeling exhausted and grumpy.

The back door of the resort creaked open, and Mrs. McGuire stepped out.

"Oh, I was about to come find you," she said. "You look like you've had a rough night."

"It wasn't great," Jude said. "But Tate and Caroline were kind and helped me out."

"Glad to hear that." She smiled. "And you need breakfast. I've got eggs, sourdough pancakes, and coffee inside."

He hesitated, but his stomach growled. "Sounds tempting. I could definitely eat."

"Good. I meant to tell you that Caroline overslept. Otherwise she would have come by. We're all headed to church. Want to join us? After you eat, I mean."

He nearly laughed.

"Church." Jude rubbed the back of his neck. "Haven't been in years."

"Today's a great day to start. We have an incredible young pastor right now." Mrs. McGuire tilted her head. "Not like you have big plans, right?"

"Wow, Mrs. M. You know how to hit a guy where it hurts."

"Oh dear." Her brow pinched, and she gently squeezed his forearm. "I'm sorry. I didn't mean to overstep."

"I don't really do church."

"You don't have to do anything. Come sit. Listen. Be around people who care."

He scoured his brain for a decent excuse. She just stood there, though, smiling.

"Fine," he said. "But I'm not volunteering to chaperone any field trips or lock-ins. Can't lead a Bible study, that's for sure."

She grinned. "Nobody's asking you to do any of that. Come on in. I'll fix you a plate. We'll be on our way in about thirty minutes. Sound good?"

"Sure."

But he already regretted his decision.

Inside the dining room, he sat down at one of the long wooden tables and stretched his sore leg out under the bench. The rich scent of fresh coffee mingled with the sweet aroma of cinnamon rolls.

A few minutes later, Mrs. McGuire brought him a plate stacked with pancakes and a side of bacon.

"Here you go, Jude." She smiled. "Molly will be along in a minute with butter, syrup, and some fresh fruit."

"Wow." He spread a paper napkin on his lap. "Thank you. This looks incredible."

"You're welcome. Enjoy. On Sunday mornings, I try to provide a warm breakfast for guests. The rest of the week it's continental: muffins and fruit. Anyway, I'll be out by the front desk when you're ready to go."

Oh. Right. "I'll eat quickly, I guess."

She moved on, stopping to speak to guests sitting at the table behind him.

Molly passed by, slowing down long enough to drop off butter, syrup, and a small bowl of strawberries.

"Thanks." He reached for a piece of bacon, the edges crisp and fried to a russet red. Just the way he preferred.

Around him, a handful of other guests ate in quiet conversation. An older couple lingered over their meal, a teenage boy scrolled his phone between bites, and a mother cut up her toddler's pancake while her husband refilled his coffee. The low hum of morning chatter and the clink of silverware made the place feel alive.

Less than thirty minutes later, Jude rode in the passenger seat of Mrs. McGuire's SUV, wincing as she hit a pothole in the middle of the road.

"Oh dear." She shot him an apologetic look. "Sorry about that."

"Not a problem," he said, shifting in the cloth seat. Maybe he should've taken more ibuprofen at breakfast. The distracting ache in his leg hadn't subsided.

Outside the window, Redemption rolled past in a blur of dense evergreen trees, bright green leafy cottonwoods, and a bald eagle soaring over the tide flats edging the bay. Mountains loomed in the distance, still snowcapped.

"I'm so glad you came along," Mrs. McGuire said as she turned down the local Christian radio station just enough to talk. "I know visiting a new church can be . . . a lot."

He opened his mouth to say something, then changed his mind. She'd been so sweet to him. No matter how much he'd been wounded by people who turned their backs on his family after his mom's stroke, it wasn't fair to take out his resentment on Mrs. McGuire.

They turned a corner, and the small white church came into view—modest, with a tall steeple and a wooden cross. The parking lot was already filling up, and people milled under the portico outside the front door.

He moved slowly, trailing behind Mrs. McGuire. The church atrium was bright and open. Laughter punctuated the air as people greeted each other. This was everything he wasn't used to—warm, welcoming, and oozing with people who seemed happy to be here. He hovered near the wall, hoping to blend in. Or maybe summon a rideshare and hightail it back to the resort.

A teenage boy did a double take, then elbowed his friend. "Dude. Jude Mercer."

Jude pasted on a tight smile. The last thing he wanted was attention. But the boys approached, phones already in hand.

"Hey, we're huge fans. Can we get a selfie?"

"Sure."

The boys wore T-shirts with vintage National Park logos, cargo shorts, and trendy sneakers. They had shaggy, curly hair and probably weren't more than fourteen or fifteen. They posed on either side of him. Jude lifted his chin, angled his head, and willed himself to offer his most carefree expression. The boy on his left snapped the photo.

"Thanks," he said, grinning.

"Not a problem." Jude shook his outstretched hand. "Take it easy."

They moved a few feet away, then huddled together, fingers

flying across their screens. *Oh man.* They were posting that. His stomach tightened. Maybe he should ask them not to—

"Jude, ready to grab a seat?" Mrs. McGuire tipped her head toward the double doors propped open, leading into the sanctuary. "Would you like coffee first?"

"No, I'm good, thanks."

From the corner of his eye, he saw Caroline walk in. Wow. She looked beautiful. Her hair was twisted up in some kind of plastic clip, with tendrils spilling down, framing her face. She wore more makeup than yesterday and had on a green dress with tiny white polka dots. Flowers adorned the straps of her high-heeled sandals, making her legs look longer and—

"Jude, you ready? Service is about to start."

He blinked and turned back to Mrs. McGuire. "Sure."

Caroline didn't notice him. Or maybe she did and just didn't say anything.

He followed Mrs. McGuire down the center aisle, wooden pews on either side with Bibles and hymnals tucked into sturdy pockets. The air felt heavy, thick with the scent of old wood and paper. It brought back memories of childhood years spent at that massive church back home in New Hampshire. The thought of sitting still, surrounded by people singing old familiar verses, made his skin itch.

His phone vibrated. Then again. And again. Then one more time.

His gut coiled in a tight knot as he fished the phone from his jacket pocket and glanced at the notifications. People were already commenting on the post from those teenagers he'd met in the atrium.

> @StarWatcher87: Jude Mercer spotted in Alaska, running from his suspension. Guess church is where sinners go to clean up their PR messes. The guy should have been banned for life.

The words blurred together. His chest tightened, breaths coming in shallow gasps. It didn't matter that these were strangers. Didn't matter that they had no idea who he really was. The weight of judgment pressed in, stealing the air from his lungs.

He stood and limped out, working his way through the adults and kids still streaming into the atrium. His head pounded. His leg burned. Shame rose up, hot and suffocating.

Bursting through the doors, he sucked in the cool morning air, welcoming its sting against his flushed skin.

"Jude."

He turned, expecting Mrs. McGuire—but instead, it was Caroline.

"Hey, you all right?" Her smooth brow furrowed. "Is your leg bothering you?"

"No. I'm just not cut out for church."

"Did something happen?" She moved closer, and he caught the faintest hint of her perfume or body wash or something. Citrusy. Appealing.

He turned and limped farther away from the door. "I posed for a selfie with some kids. Then they posted it, and I got the notifications right when I sat down. Evidently the keyboard warriors don't take Sundays off."

Her heels clicked on the asphalt as she walked up behind him. "Sorry to hear that. People can be so cruel."

Jude stared at two geese swimming across the small pond beside the church. "I'm just not great at failing publicly."

"Who is?" She held out her hand. "Can I see?"

He shook his head.

"Please? Maybe I can help."

Heaving a sigh, he scrolled to the picture. The comments had multiplied—nearly sixty now. His jaw tightened as he read through them. Each one was like a fresh wound reopening. The last one made his insides churn like hot molten lava.

@TeaSpillCentral: I guess a washed-up athlete has to find redemption somewhere.

His gaze lifted, focusing past Caroline. He hated the name of this place already. Hated that it felt like a challenge. Hated that it made him wonder if a comeback was possible.

His phone vibrated again. A text from Braxton this time.

Braxton

Call me. We need to talk.

Jude shoved his phone back into his pocket. That wasn't good.

"I'm gonna catch a ride back to the resort," he said. "Tell your mom something came up."

"All right. I'll check in with you later. Is that okay?"

He shrugged. "Whatever."

He summoned a ride and waited, his thoughts twisting into a snarled knot. Somewhere along the line, he had forgotten what he believed about God. About knowing Jesus in a personal way.

At this point, redemption probably wasn't even something a guy like him could hope for.

But running from his problems certainly wasn't working either.

Day one. Here we go.

The next morning, Caroline flipped down the visor in the truck, applied her lip gloss in the mirror, then hung her stethoscope around her neck. She took it off and put it back on. Then off again.

Sighing, she tucked it back in her bag.

"Too much. You look like you're trying too hard," she whispered.

She flipped the visor up, grabbed her keys and her bag, and exited the vehicle. Gravel crunched under her rubber clogs as she crossed the parking lot. Light drizzle fell from a gray sky, misting her cheeks and coating her bright blue jacket in beads of moisture.

The wooden sign outside had been updated: Redemption Community Clinic.

But the building was exactly how she remembered—a modest single-story manufactured structure left over from the construction of the oil pipeline. A ramp had been added, but the same wide steps and squeaky front door remained, flanked by knee-high terracotta planters. Cheerful orange marigolds and yellow and purple pansies bloomed in both containers.

She opened the door and stepped inside. The smell of antiseptic mixed with the comforting aroma of coffee brewing somewhere welcomed her. A silver bell sat on the tall front desk.

A woman slid a piece of plexiglass to the side and smiled. Connie Riddle. She had once given Caroline a lollipop and a sticker after a flu shot.

"Well, hey there, Miss McGuire," Connie said, her warm smile unchanged. "Or is it Dr. Caroline these days?"

Caroline wiped her feet off on the rug. "You can just call me Caroline, Miss Riddle."

"Oh, please—call me Connie. Dr. Wallace is in with a patient, but you're welcome to come back and put your things in the lounge."

"Great."

She went through the door to the right of the reception desk. Linoleum floors, bright lights, and a short corridor with exam rooms branching off on either side greeted her. Connie scooted back in her rolling desk chair and limped toward her.

"You're limping. What's the matter?"

"Oh," Connie said, patting her ample hip. "I need a hip replacement. Not interested."

Her floral tunic was dotted with tropical flowers in shades of orange and turquoise. Her salt-and-pepper bob was stylish, and her blue eyes gleamed. A shiny red manicure caught Caroline's attention as Connie pointed down the hall.

"Here you go. You can tuck your things in a cubby in there. Grab some coffee if you want. I just brewed a fresh pot."

"No thanks. I'm good."

Caroline passed pictures of the clinic's small staff at town festivals and a few pieces of artwork painted by Sally Gibbons, the famous artist from the area.

"We don't really have an official onboarding process for new employees," Connie continued, "other than the paperwork I emailed you last week."

"Yep, got it."

Caroline tucked her bag and her coat into a cubby along the wall. She surveyed the small kitchen, with its round table and four plastic chairs. Well-used overhead cabinets lined the wall above a gray Formica countertop. In the corner, a dog-eared novel and a stack of medical journals sat on a table beside a leather recliner.

"If you want to speak to Dr. Wallace, you can pop into his office. It's just across the hall."

"Will do. Thanks."

She tucked a tissue and her stethoscope into the pockets of her white jacket, then stepped into the hallway.

Dr. Wallace stood there, studying his tablet, glasses perched low on the end of his nose. Was he humming an old Johnny Cash tune?

"Good morning, Dr. Wallace."

"Caroline!" He grinned. "So glad you're here."

"Thanks," she said. "Happy to be here. What's the plan?"

"Well, why don't you come along with me, get to know some of our patients?"

She hoped her face didn't betray her disappointment. Follow him? Shouldn't she have her own caseload? This wasn't the time to argue though.

"We have three well-child checks, a possible UTI, and a guy who's convinced he's got Lyme disease," Dr. Wallace said.

"Oh my. Self-diagnosed online, I presume?"

Dr. Wallace nodded. "Most likely."

They reached exam room one. He paused, hand on the door, and glanced over his shoulder.

"First day. Nervous?"

"No," she said quickly. "I mean, yeah, a little, but not for the reasons you'd think."

"Let me guess. You're worried people haven't forgotten what happened at Camp Midnight Sun."

She froze. Her pulse tapped a warning in her neck. "Wow. You don't mince words, do you?"

His brow furrowed. "You think I don't remember? Even though it didn't go like you thought it would, I watched you learn a valuable lesson."

"I made a mistake," she said quietly. "A dumb one."

"You were nineteen, Caroline. You cared. That's not the worst thing in the world."

"Tell that to Mrs. Peterson."

"Huh. Petersons have always been unhappy. They haven't liked a medical decision I've made since 1993, when old Mr. Peterson had to have a finger amputated by yours truly. People in this town love a good story. They like to talk. But after surviving a tidal wave, I feel like we're all a little more gracious these days. Don't let that summer define you."

"I just don't want to let anyone down. Not you, Dr. Wallace. And not this town."

He reached over and gave her upper arm a gentle squeeze. "Then don't."

Before she could respond, Connie popped her head out from the reception area.

"Miss Caroline? Dr. Wallace? We've got a walk-in. A young child fell down on the dock. Mom says he's got a gash and maybe something in his eye."

"Glad there's two of us then," Dr. Wallace said. "Ask Wendy to bring the child and the mom back and put them in exam room two. We'll get there as soon as we can."

They stepped into exam room one. An older woman in a hooded sweatshirt, jeans, and flip-flops sat on the end of the table.

"Dr. Wallace. Good morning." Her gaze slid to Caroline. "And you are?"

"Caroline McGuire, physician assistant. Nice to see you, Mrs. Hopkins. How are you feeling today?"

"I've been better. I'd really much prefer to see Dr. Wallace, if you don't mind."

Caroline's stomach dropped. She glanced at him.

Dr. Wallace washed his hands at the sink and offered Caroline an empathetic glance. "Maybe you could pop across the hall and see the walk-in?"

"Of course." She slipped outside, knocked on the door, and entered.

Wendy, the nurse, in lavender scrubs and with her blonde hair twisted in a bun, glanced up. "Hey, Miss Caroline. We were just getting settled in here."

"Hi." Caroline pasted on a polite smile, although Mrs. Hopkins's terse dismissal had her rattled.

The mom stood nearby, arms crossed and panic etched in her face. A boy, probably about ten, sat on the table, his jeans torn and muddy. He held a cloth to his forehead. Blood seeped through.

"Hey, buddy, what's your name?"

"Landon."

"Landon, I'm Caroline. I'm going to look at your leg first, and then we'll see what's going on with your head, okay?"

He nodded. She gently eased the stiff denim up. A shallow cut. No signs of debris.

"Are you going to stitch it?" His mother inched closer. "He's never had stitches before."

Caroline pulled on her gloves. "Let me clean it first."

Thoughts of another guy with a cut in his leg resurfaced. Jude. She pushed the pesky image aside. *Focus.*

She cleaned the wound. The boy winced.

"It's all right, buddy. I think you're going to be okay there. Mom, you all right if I put a bandage on this?"

"You don't want to give him stitches?"

"I really don't think it's necessary."

"Well, can you get Dr. Wallace in here and see what he thinks? Maybe a second opinion?"

Caroline clamped her mouth shut and looked at Wendy. "Can you see if Dr. Wallace can pop in, please?"

"Of course." Wendy stepped out of the room.

Caroline took her tablet and then turned to Landon.

"All right. Let me look at your eyes. There's something in there?"

Landon sniffed. "It hurts. Feels scratchy."

"Thanks for letting me know. I'll be careful." She pulled an ophthalmoscope from its base on the wall.

"It's the other eye," Landon's mother said. "I already told the nurse that."

Caroline drew in a calming breath. "I know, but I need something to compare it to. We always look at the normal one first. Then I can see what the differences are."

She gently examined both eyes. "You've got a piece of bark stuck to the inside of your eyelid." She grabbed sterile saline from the counter. "If you'll lie back all the way flat, I think I can rinse it out."

His mother inched closer. "Are you sure? What if you push it farther in?"

"Flushing out the eye is the best course of action. He'll be a lot more comfortable once we get that out." She tore open a piece of gauze and handed it to Landon. "Can you hold that, please? It'll catch the saline before it runs down into your ear."

He nodded. She flushed the eye gently. The fragment washed out.

"See? All gone." She held it up.

"Cool. Can we save it? I want to show my dad."

"Absolutely. I'll put it right here." She placed it on the gauze pad at the end of the table.

"All right. Let me take a look at your forehead, buddy."

She assessed the wound. He had about a three-inch gash. Edges were not approximated, and although the bleeding had subsided, sending him home with a bandage wasn't ideal. "This is where you're going to earn your stitches."

"Wait. Won't that leave a scar? I'd really feel more comfortable if Dr. Wallace came in here and took a look. What if we need a plastic-surgery consult?"

Caroline stepped back.

Oh boy.

"Listen, I don't want to be rude," the woman added, "but I remember what happened at Camp Midnight Sun. And the whole situation with the kid and the splint. I was there. So thanks for your help, but I'd really feel more comfortable if Dr. Wallace took over."

Heat climbed Caroline's neck. "Of course."

She scooted away just as Dr. Wallace stepped in.

"Hi, Evelyn. Landon. Nice to see you both this morning."

He washed his hands, then turned to Caroline. "What do you think?"

"I removed a fragment from his eye and assessed the wound on his leg. Evelyn would like you to take it from here. My professional opinion—he needs stitches in his forehead."

Someone knocked. Connie popped her head in.

"Excuse me. Pardon the interruption. Caroline, we just got a call from your family's resort. A client you treated over the weekend collapsed again."

"Excuse me, please."

Her doubts and fears returned in full force as she rushed out of the exam room. Evelyn's words dogged her. *The whole situation with the kid and the splint.*

"Thanks so much for that unwelcome stroll down memory lane," Caroline grumbled, collecting her bag and her jacket from the other room. Where could she go in this building—or in this town—where someone wouldn't remind her of her failures and shortcomings?

Five

OH NO, NOT AGAIN. NOT NOW.

Jude's knees hit the ground first. Then he collapsed onto his back. The cool, damp earth seeped through the back of his T-shirt. He rubbed his hand against the tightness in his chest, as if he could somehow knead the pain away. His lungs felt like they were shrinking, squeezing every ounce of air out of him. He'd been jogging on the trail behind the resort, ignoring the familiar twinge in his chest as well as the pain in his leg. Why had he forgotten his inhaler?

Green leaves from the cottonwood trees danced overhead, blurring in a dizzying swirl as he fought to stay conscious.

Footsteps thumped against the ground.

Help. Me.

His vision tunneled. He willed himself to stay conscious.

"Hey, Jude. Jude, can you hear me?"

He forced himself to focus. Caroline sank to her knees beside him, her wide eyes scanning his face.

"Jude?" she said, her voice rising with alarm. She unzipped

a pocket on her jacket with quick, jerky movements. "What's wrong? What happened?"

Jude shook his head side to side, trying to force out the words. "Can't—"

He wrestled against the vise grip on his lungs, clawing at the fabric on his chest. Why couldn't he get any air? Adrenaline zipped through his veins.

C'mon, man. Breathe.

She glanced over her shoulder. "Mom! I need my rescue pack. Hurry!"

"Jude, do you have a food allergy?" Caroline turned back to him, kneeling now.

He managed another weak shake of his head. His tongue felt thick, like it was swelling in his throat, and his lips tingled with pins and needles. "No," he croaked. He raised his hands to his throat, trying to signal the words he couldn't say.

"You're choking? On what?"

Two splotches of pink clung to her cheekbones. She looked even more beautiful when flustered. He felt a ridiculous urge to tell her so, but no air would come.

Her mother appeared, hovering over her shoulder. "Do you have asthma?"

Jude nodded, trying to curl onto his side. His leg throbbed, but it was nothing compared to the fire in his chest and the desperate, futile heaving of his lungs.

"Caroline, his lips are blue."

"I know!" Caroline's voice cracked as she unzipped the bag and dug through it. A triumphant cry escaped her as she held up a thick yellow pen. "Do you carry an EpiPen?"

He wanted to answer. He really did. He thought he might have nodded, but the world was starting to tilt. Did he have one? Yes. No. He'd left his inhaler on his dresser in the apartment he hardly ever lived in. His vision blurred into a kaleidoscope of colors and shapes.

"Jude, no. Stay with me. Here."

Her voice sounded far away, like she was shouting at him through a long tunnel. She yanked the cap off the EpiPen, tossing it to the ground as she scooted around to his right leg.

"Mom, we've got to help him sit up."

Mrs. McGuire knelt on his other side. Together, they eased him upright.

"Here."

What was that sound? Oh. It was him. Air trying to squeeze through his airway. Squeaking. Wheezing. He felt like an instrument someone didn't know how to play.

"Stay with me, Jude. This will only hurt for a second."

Before he could protest, a sharp pain jabbed his right leg.

No. Arching his back, he tried to grab her arm.

"Easy, there." Mrs. McGuire clasped his hand in hers. The warmth of her fingers against his soothed him somehow.

"Breathe, Jude." Caroline got in his face. "Do you hear me? Breathe."

He drew in one long, ragged pull, then another. Air seeped into his lungs, slow and glorious. The tight vise around his chest began to loosen. Finally. Finally, he could breathe again.

"That's it. Keep breathing." Relief flooded Caroline's features. "You've got this."

"Don't think so," he rasped, his voice thin and raw. "My chest. Tight."

Caroline glanced at her mother.

"Do I need to call an ambulance?" she asked, her brows pinching together.

"No." He shook his head weakly, forcing out the word. "Just . . . give me two minutes."

Caroline pressed her lips into a thin line. "I don't know that we can afford to wait."

He dipped his head back, closing his eyes. "I thought I could handle this."

"But you didn't handle it."

Her sharp reply made him open his eyes again. She hovered beside him, her face flushed with emotion.

"Sounds to me like you collapsed." She looked around. "What are you doing out here?"

"Working out," he said, his voice weak but defensive. "Like I'm supposed to."

She barked out a laugh, shaking her head. "Unbelievable."

Mrs. McGuire gave him a stern look. "Can you walk?"

"Hope so." Jude tried to push to his feet, but the effort made the world tilt again. "Help me up."

Caroline and her mother each took an arm, steadying him as he straightened. He winced, his leg throbbing anew.

Caroline glanced down, her eyes narrowing. "You tore a stitch. You're bleeding through your bandage."

"It's not a big deal."

"Jude."

First, the stick in his leg. Now, a random asthma attack. He shook his head. What a nightmare.

"An injection with an EpiPen requires an automatic emergency room visit. You—"

"What?" He stopped walking. "Why?"

"Because the epinephrine can impact your heart rhythm," she said.

"And not in a good way, I'm guessing?"

She shook her head.

They took it slow on the trail back toward the resort, Caroline and her mother sticking to him like glue. By the time they made it into the clearing behind the cabins, Jude's pride was in tatters. Caroline turned to face him, arms crossed.

"Why didn't you bring your inhaler?"

He refused to answer, staring at the ground.

"Jude."

"I didn't think I'd need it," he admitted, his voice soft. "I thought I was just going to take it easy. It's at my apartment back in New Hampshire."

"That was not a good choice."

"Thanks," he said sarcastically. "I see that now." Of course she was right. She was always right. But hearing her say it didn't hurt any less.

"Come on. I'll take you by the clinic. Let Dr. Wallace check you out," Caroline said, her tone of voice leaving no room for negotiation.

"For what?" Jude asked, his shoulders slumping.

"I want to make sure you're okay, all right? You've had two episodes in three days."

"Episodes?" he scoffed weakly. "What am I, a hundred ninety-seven?"

"Jude, as the owner of the resort, I think we would all feel better if you got checked out," Mrs. McGuire said firmly. "Do you want me to call ahead?"

"No." Caroline cut in before Jude could answer. "I'll take him. I'm supposed to be at work anyway."

She helped him into the truck, her hands steady and sure, though her expression and her body language telegraphed her irritation. She didn't say much on the drive, and her silence wasn't cold exactly. It felt more like she was tightly wound, a rubber band stretched to its breaking point.

Jude rode in the passenger seat, blood seeping through his bandage, his chest still sore from the asthma attack. Worse than the physical pain, though, was the gnawing ache of his shame. Rain had started again, light and misty, fogging up the windshield. Caroline kept one hand clenched on the steering wheel while the other nervously worried at her thumbnail.

"How long have you had exercise-induced asthma?" she finally asked, breaking the silence.

"Um, since forever," he said. "But I haven't had an attack in almost ten years."

"Really?" She glanced at him, her expression a mix of disbelief and irritation. "So then you know better than to leave home without your inhaler."

He didn't argue. He just turned his head to stare out the window, watching the droplets streak down the glass.

When they pulled into the gravel lot in front of the clinic, she cut the engine and turned to face him.

"Please be honest with Dr. Wallace," she said, her gaze pleading. "He's a good man, and he's seen it all. If you try to fake your way through this or act too proud to admit what's wrong, you'll regret it."

"Noted," Jude said, his tone dry. "Sheesh."

He opened the door just as she rounded the truck to meet him on the passenger side. She offered him her hand, but he waved her off. "I got it. Both of my legs still work."

"Barely," she muttered under her breath.

"Ha ha."

Inside, the waiting room was small and quiet, with six plastic chairs lined up against one wall. A TV mounted in the corner played an old Disney animated movie. A man and a woman sat with a young child, all three of them staring at the screen.

Caroline bypassed the front desk entirely, pushing through a side door with the air of someone who belonged there.

"Dr. Wallace?" she called, knocking lightly on a partially open door.

The door eased fully open, and an older man stepped out. He

was tall and wiry, his white hair standing at odd angles as if he'd just run his hands through it. He wore scrubs under a crisp white jacket, a half-eaten granola bar in one hand and reading glasses perched on top of his head.

"Hey there, kiddo," he said, a teasing smile tugging at his lips. Then his eyes shifted to Jude, assessing. "Ah, the biathlete. I was wondering when we were going to meet."

Caroline let out a long breath. "Yeah, well, today's your day. He tore his stitches and had an asthma attack on the trail behind the resort. And—of course—he wasn't carrying his inhaler. A true overachiever."

Dr. Wallace chuckled, but his eyes softened with concern as he set his granola bar down inside his office. "Come on. Let's pop into this exam room." He gestured for them to follow.

"Sorry to interrupt your lunch," Jude said as they entered.

"No worries. That's what I'm here for," Dr. Wallace said.

Caroline went in first, pulling a clean sheet of paper over the exam table. She tore off the edge, tossed the worn part into the trash, then washed her hands at the sink. When she was done, she stepped back to the table and patted the top. "Hop up here."

Jude obeyed, wincing as he sat back.

Caroline grabbed a bottle of saline and some sterile gauze, setting them on the counter. Then she stepped aside as Dr. Wallace washed his hands and pulled on a pair of gloves.

"All right, let's see," Dr. Wallace said, peeling back the bandage from Jude's thigh.

Jude looked away, staring at the far wall instead. After studying the wound about twenty times, he wasn't squeamish anymore. But he didn't need to see the mess he'd made of himself.

"Let's rinse that." Dr. Wallace glanced at Caroline. "What do you think?"

"Yep." Caroline quickly pulled on a pair of gloves, then squirted saline over the wound, her movements precise and efficient.

"I was going stir-crazy in that cabin," Jude said, filling the silence with excuses because that's what he did best. "I thought I could manage a short run. Guess I miscalculated."

"Perhaps," Dr. Wallace said. "Happens to the best of us."

Jude risked a glance at Caroline, who now stood beside the sink, arms crossed tightly over her chest. She was trying to look disapproving, but he caught the flicker of concern in her eyes.

"I'm glad the McGuires helped you out," Dr. Wallace said, his tone turning serious. "They're good like that. You ever have a full-blown attack in the woods without anyone around and no inhaler, the story might have a different ending."

Jude swallowed hard and nodded.

"Who did these stitches?" Dr. Wallace asked, inspecting Jude's leg.

"Um, whoever was on duty at the ER over the weekend, sir."

A muscle in the doctor's cheek twitched. "I bet Caroline could've done a better job."

Caroline's eyebrows sailed upward. "Wasn't officially employed yet, sir."

"Well, some guidelines are meant as suggestions, I suppose. But I'm glad you obeyed. Let me just add a few. A little garnish, if you will. Caroline, can you hand me the suture kit? Top drawer."

"Yes, right away."

"She's one of the good ones, you know," Dr. Wallace said, tilting his head toward Caroline. "Stubborn as all get-out, but good."

Caroline shook her head, a faint blush creeping up her neck. "Thanks so much."

"Oh, you're welcome. I seem to recall you pushed your limits around here once too. Worked yourself into a migraine so bad you passed out."

Jude blinked, his lips twitching into a crooked grin. "Really? Passed out, huh? Should we get you an inhaler?"

"Could we not?" Caroline shot him a glare, but the corner of her mouth lifted despite herself.

Dr. Wallace chuckled, unwrapping the suture kit with practiced ease. "She wasn't any good at asking for help back then. Still isn't, I'd bet."

"What? What is this?" Caroline shot Dr. Wallace a confused look. "Are you finished telling him all my past mistakes?"

Dr. Wallace gave her a look somewhere between pride and amusement. "No, probably not. But I'll give you a breather." He turned his attention back to Jude, patting his leg lightly. "Stitches are repaired. Keep them clean this time, and no more mountain climbing until we've given you clearance."

"Yes, sir," Jude replied, his voice laced with mock obedience.

Dr. Wallace adjusted his reading glasses, pulled out his stethoscope, and gestured for Jude to sit up straighter. "Let me listen to your heart and lungs real quick."

Jude did as instructed, sitting up as Dr. Wallace pressed the cold stethoscope against his chest and back. "Deep breath in. And out. Again."

The doctor stepped back, removing the stethoscope and nodding with approval. "You sound great to me. Just use sound judgment, okay?"

"Absolutely. Thanks again."

"Wait." Caroline stepped closer. "Since he didn't have an inhaler, I injected him with epinephrine. Doesn't that require a follow-up EKG? Observation?"

Dr. Wallace peeled off his gloves and discarded them in the bin. "Not always. That was quick thinking on your part though. Well done."

"Then how about a prescription for a new inhaler?"

"Sounds reasonable. I'll send it over to the pharmacy. Should be ready tomorrow." He patted Caroline on the back, then turned to leave. "Good to meet you, Jude," he called over his shoulder. "Take care."

Silence settled over the room, broken only by the faint hum of a fluorescent light overhead. Caroline busied herself cleaning up the empty wrappers and disposing of the used supplies in the proper bins. Jude watched her with quiet interest, noting how her fingers trembled just the tiniest bit.

"You all right?" he asked softly.

She froze for half a second before turning to him, her face carefully neutral. "Yeah. Just tired of people around here bringing up my past mistakes."

He nodded. "I get that."

Their eyes met, and for a moment, the room felt smaller, quieter. The weight of unspoken words hung between them.

"You don't have to prove anything to anyone around here."

He didn't crack a joke or deflect or try to hide behind his usual bravado. Instead, he held her gaze, letting the honesty of her words settle over him. "Maybe I'm trying to prove something to myself."

Her expression softened, the tension in her shoulders easing. "Relatable." She let out a small, humorless laugh. "You scared me, Jude."

"Ah, but you saved me." He offered a smile. "Again."

"That may be true," she said, her voice trembling slightly, "but please don't make a habit of this."

"First thing tomorrow, I'll stop by the pharmacy and pick up my new inhaler."

A small smile ghosted across her lips, and the warmth in her eyes returned. "Good plan."

She turned away and finished cleaning up the exam room. Jude sat quietly, watching her, the weight of the day settling into his bones. His leg ached, his chest felt tender, and his pride—well, that was another story entirely. But for the first time in days, he felt . . . grounded.

Caroline washed and dried her hands at the sink. "All right, let's get you out of here."

"Can't argue with that," Jude said, sliding off the table with a wince.

"Good. I'm exhausted." She reached out a hand to steady him, and this time, he didn't wave her off.

They walked out together, Caroline keeping a steadying hand on his arm as they made their way back to the truck. The rain had stopped, leaving the air crisp and clean.

As they climbed into the truck, Caroline shot him a sidelong glance. "You know, you're lucky my mom was there. She doesn't mess around in a crisis."

"Yeah, I noticed," Jude said, leaning back against the seat with a tired smile. "Remind me to thank her."

Caroline didn't reply right away. She started the engine and pulled onto the road, her fingers tapping lightly against the steering wheel.

"Jude," she said finally, her tone softer now, almost hesitant.

"Yeah?"

"You're not a burden, you know. Or some sort of . . . pariah. We genuinely want to help you." She glanced over at him, her gaze steady despite the vulnerability in her words. "So you don't have to feel guilty for needing us."

Her words hit him harder than he expected, cutting through the layers of guilt and pride he'd been carrying for days. He opened his mouth to respond, but the truth wouldn't come. Because he couldn't risk being vulnerable.

Instead, he amped up the charm. Let a slow grin spread across his face. "Why, Caroline McGuire, are you giving me a pep talk?"

Any goodwill he might've banked spontaneously combusted. The kindness in her eyes vanished. Her mouth formed an angry slant. "Um, I'm trying, but if you're going to deflect and pretend everything's fine, then I guess I won't waste my time."

Oh boy. He let out a slow breath and looked away. Embarrassment burned hot. Yeah, okay, so maybe she'd seen right through his pitiful attempts to avoid being real. She was right. He'd rather deflect than deal with his emotions.

Because letting her see past his carefully constructed walls scared him more than any injury or asthma attack ever had.

Why? Why did she feel the need to keep rescuing him? Especially when he tried to make jokes or use his charm to avoid authentic connection.

A question Caroline had wrestled with and struggled to answer since she'd brought Jude to the clinic after his asthma attack.

She still hadn't come up with an answer.

The fact that it was part of her job offered little comfort. Especially since he'd had the audacity to flash her that smile that made her heart turn backflips in the truck on the way back to the resort.

Warmth heated her cheeks as she scrolled through her schedule for Thursday-afternoon patients. Her first appointment after lunch had been canceled. Now she had eighteen extra minutes to update her electronic charts and do a quick internet search on how to treat altitude sickness.

Because that would probably be the next obstacle Jude had to conquer.

She stood tucked into her makeshift cubby at the end of the hall, past the exam rooms and diagonal from Dr. Wallace's office.

She'd overheard Dr. Monroe on the phone venting about her lack of dedicated office space, and Caroline couldn't entirely disagree. After all, this building hadn't changed in probably forty years, and it showed. Sure, Connie had tried to make the space a little more welcoming with a padded mat under Caroline's chair and a vase of daisies and forget-me-nots tucked in the corner on her laminate counter. But it still wasn't a real office. If she needed privacy, she had to slip into a vacant exam room to make a confidential call. It wasn't exactly the slick setup she'd seen during her interview at that healthcare practice in Richmond.

Then again, they hadn't offered her the job, so it didn't really matter, did it?

Caroline sighed, leaning back in her chair. This wasn't her dream job. Not even close. But she'd signed a one-year contract. Day four was not the time to start daydreaming about greener pastures. She tapped her pen against the desk, debating whether to dive into charts or search for quick and easy lunch recipes she could prep ahead of time, when Connie's voice broke through her thoughts.

"You got a minute, hon? Someone here to see you."

Caroline turned toward the hallway, her stomach tightening. Uh-oh. She logged out of the web browser and walked toward the reception area. As she rounded the corner, her gaze landed on a tall man standing on the other side of Connie's desk. Athletic build, late fifties, with a sun-weathered face and a faded flannel shirt layered over a T-shirt. Beside him stood a younger woman, her dark hair pulled into a no-nonsense ponytail, clutching a plastic folder to her chest.

"Hi there," the man said, his voice booming through the small reception area. "You're the new PA, right?"

Caroline smiled hesitantly and hovered in the doorway. "I am. And you are?"

"David Sutter," he replied, extending a hand. "I'm on the town council. And this here is Rhonda, my new assistant. We're promoting the Redemption Ridge Race."

"The what?" Caroline asked, her brow furrowing as she glanced at Connie. The name sounded vaguely familiar—maybe she'd seen something about it on the town's social-media page—but she couldn't recall the details.

David chuckled. "You're not from around here, are you?"

"I grew up here," Caroline said, crossing her arms over her chest. Her tone came out sharper than intended, so she softened it with a shrug. "It's been a while though."

"Well, we haven't done this race in a while, so it makes sense that you're confused," David said with a grin. "But we're bringing it back this year. It's really quite a thing—part road race, part mountain climb, part obstacle course. Folks are already registering and coming from all over to compete. It's not for the faint of heart though," he added, glancing at Rhonda.

"Facts," Rhonda said, nodding firmly. "It's intense."

"Yeah, sounds that way." Caroline shifted her weight from one foot to the other and snuck a glance at the clock mounted on the waiting-room wall. Her next patient should be checking in shortly.

"But it's also a huge community event," Rhonda chimed in, her expression brightening. "You can volunteer, cheer, compete. We're hoping everyone gets involved. You and Dr. Wallace could help out, you know, with first aid stations or medical support."

Caroline's stomach gave an uneasy twist. She forced a polite smile. "Makes sense that you'd need those."

"So, are you in?" David asked, his brown eyes gleaming. "Or maybe you want to enter the race yourself?"

"Oh, me?" Caroline let out a nervous laugh. "I don't know."

"Why not?" David leaned casually against the counter. "You look like you could handle it. It's a great way to meet people, get your name out there. Folks around here respect someone who isn't afraid to get involved."

Caroline hesitated, glancing at Connie and Rhonda, who were both eyeing her with interest. She hadn't competed in public in years—not since high school. She'd had some success on the track team. But that was years ago. What if she failed? Came in last? That would be so humiliating.

"I'm not exactly in race shape," she said.

David waved a hand dismissively. "You've got time to train. It's not until the third week in June. The festival coincides with the summer solstice. Besides, it's not about winning. We just want you to show up, push yourself, have fun."

You're overthinking it, Care Bear. Tate's voice echoed in her head, teasing and confident. *Just say yes.*

But doubt crept in, unrelenting. What did Dr. Wallace expect her to do?

"Well, we're going to set up the first aid stations either way," Rhonda said. "We'll staff them with volunteers from the community. But if you don't want to run, we could really use your expertise on the medical team. That'd be a huge help."

The safer option. The logical choice. Caroline's stomach twisted again. But what if she didn't want to do what everyone expected her to? Maybe David was right. Maybe this was her chance to show her hometown—and herself—that she was more than the shadow of Dr. Wallace.

"I'll think about it," she said finally. "When would you like me to decide?"

"Oh, registration's open, but we'll close it at the end of May," David said. "We need plenty of time to prep."

Caroline nodded. "I understand. Connie and I will speak to Dr. Wallace and let you know about the medical stations, all right?"

"Good." David smiled wide. "And if we put up a flyer on the bulletin board?" He gestured toward the wall just inside the front door.

"Wherever you can find space," Connie said, already spinning back to her computer. "Wow, I didn't think you'd want to run another race after what happened at that track meet back in the day."

Really? Caroline's pulse sped. Connie had to go there? Now?

Connie glanced up. "Was that your sophomore or junior year?"

"Sophomore." Caroline tipped her chin up, then strode toward the door that led back to the safety of her cubby and her laptop. "Let me know when my patient's ready."

Sheesh. It had been one dropped baton. One mistake. Why couldn't people just let it go?

Six

A MEAL WITH THE MCGUIRES. WAS CAROLINE included?

Jude pulled back a chair at the McGuire family dining table tucked behind the kitchen at the resort. The space was small but warm, with the scent of chicken soup or something clinging to the air. A vintage clock ticked steadily on the wall, and Mrs. McGuire hummed an old familiar hymn as she pulled a casserole dish from the oven. Jude sat down at the end of the table, the polished wood cool against his forearms. Liam McGuire claimed the spot to his left, the head of the table clearly his domain.

"Thanks for the invite," Jude said, glancing around. "I didn't know you fed guests with your family."

"Chicken pot pie tonight," Mrs. McGuire said, her voice cheerful. She placed a steaming dish in the center of the table, the savory aroma of roasted chicken, flaky pastry, and fresh vegetables wafting toward him. Jude's stomach growled audibly, and he chuckled, patting his middle.

"Go on, dig in, Jude. I made plenty," Mrs. McGuire said, settling into her seat across from him.

"Starving, obviously," Jude said, grinning. "Thank you, Mrs. McGuire. This already smells better than anything I could make for myself."

"Please, call me Cassie," she said with a warm smile, folding her hands on the table. "And you're welcome. It's nice to have a fresh face at the table. We don't get—"

"Oh, hey." Caroline breezed into the room, her voice light and casual but laced with a note of surprise when her gaze landed on Jude. She stopped short, her hand still on the doorway. "What's going on?"

His pulse sped at the sound of her voice. He feigned indifference, though, and offered a polite, "Hey." He hadn't seen her since she'd given him a ride back to the resort from the clinic. And after his botched attempt to lighten the conversation by teasing her about giving him a pep talk, he wouldn't be at all surprised if she didn't want to share a meal with him.

"I invited Jude to join us," Cassie said, gesturing to the empty chair beside her. "Get your drink, then come sit down."

"Okay." Caroline shrugged out of her jacket, her scrubs slightly wrinkled after what had clearly been a long day. Jude couldn't help but notice how the soft green fabric brought out the shades of aqua rimming her irises. She crossed to the counter, filled a glass with ice water, and returned to the table, sliding into the chair beside her mother.

"As I was saying," Cassie continued, "it's nice to have a fresh face at the table. Visitors don't usually get to join us for dinner."

"Mainly because we don't want them to," Liam said with a wink at Jude. "Not the case with you, of course."

"We have family dinners all the time," Caroline said, spreading her napkin across her lap. "It's no big deal."

"Well, family dinners aren't the same as having a guest." Cassie handed her husband the serving spoon. "Let's pray, shall we?"

"Oh, sure." Jude took Liam's outstretched hand and then reached across to take Caroline's. Her fingers were cool and smooth, and as they grasped his, warmth zinged up his arm. His mind drifted back to when he'd grasped the lapels on her jacket and gently tugged her to him, leaning in close, her breath warm against his cheek.

A throat cleared.

"Jude?" Caroline's voice snapped him back to the present. She let go of his hand.

"Sorry, my mind wandered," he said, his voice low.

Liam chuckled. "I can relate. Happens to me all the time."

"How are things at the clinic?" Liam asked, reaching for Caroline's plate. She passed it to him, and he served up a hearty portion for her.

"Okay, I guess. Kind of stressful." Caroline sighed. "I forgot how much people in this town love Dr. Wallace."

"It's hard following on the heels of an icon," Jude said, meeting her gaze.

"Yeah, no kidding." Her tone was sharp, but she didn't glare at him. He appreciated that she at least tried to be respectful, even if she didn't love the idea of him being here.

"Someone stopped by today. Sutter? Sutton?"

"David Sutter?" Cassie asked, passing her plate to Liam.

"Yes, that's him," Caroline said. "And his sidekick, Rhonda. They came into the clinic to promote a race."

"Ah, yes. The Redemption Ridge Race," Liam said, his brow furrowing. "It's been a while since we've had that event."

"Not a fan?" Jude asked, grateful for the generous portion of pot pie Liam scooped onto his plate.

"Oh, I think it'll pull in plenty of entrants." Caroline reached for her fork. "You should enter, Jude."

"Hmm." Jude raised an eyebrow. "What all's involved? Biking? Swimming? Road race? Hike?"

"No biking or swimming," Cassie said, spearing a piece of carrot with her fork. "Just a road race plus kind of an obstacle course. Straight up the side of a mountain."

"Doesn't that sound fun?" Liam said with a grin.

"Hmm, maybe." Jude glanced at Caroline. "Is it fun?"

"I don't know," she said, shrugging. "But I'm half tempted to enter."

"Ooh, honey, no," Cassie said, frowning. "Really? I thought you'd be medical tent supervisor."

"Mr. Sutter did ask, but I didn't get a chance to talk to Dr. Wallace about it. We had a hectic afternoon."

"Huh." Jude leaned back in his chair. "Well, I'm game if you are."

Her fork paused midair, and her brows lifted.

Jude grinned, leaning forward slightly. "Do you think I can't handle it?"

"It's not that." She set her fork down. "It's just . . . the rough terrain, the weather changes. If you're not used to—"

"Caroline," Liam interrupted, setting his glass down. "The boy's an Olympic athlete."

"Olympic *hopeful*," Jude corrected, holding up a hand. "Don't get ahead of yourself."

"Well, I'm sure you'll be fine," Cassie said, her tone light but teasing. "Lesser athletes have competed and even won."

Before he could respond, Caroline cut in. "I'm just concerned that with your injury, you're not going to have time to train."

There it is. Her concern was couched in practicality, but Jude could feel the underlying edge of doubt. "Your concern is oddly endearing," he said, resting his elbow on the table and his chin on his hand. "I love that you're worried about me."

"I'm worried about having to rescue you if something goes wrong." She didn't miss a beat, her fork slicing cleanly through her piece of chicken pot pie. Steam curled into the air as she raised the bite to her lips without looking at him.

"Ouch." Jude pressed a hand dramatically over his heart. "That stings."

Caroline rolled her eyes. "I'm serious. That race is dangerous if you're not prepared."

"You hear this, Cassie?" Jude said, turning to Caroline's mother with mock hurt. "Your daughter thinks I'm reckless."

Cassie laughed softly, patting Caroline's shoulder. "Well, to be fair, you have given us reason to wonder lately."

"See?" Caroline shrugged. "Excellent judgment."

Jude held up his hands in surrender, his grin widening. "Okay, I get it. I promise, if I enter the race, I'll be careful. And tomorrow when we scout for the commercial too. Your brothers won't have to cart me back down the mountain on a gurney."

Caroline didn't look convinced. Her lips pressed into a thin line, and the faintest crease formed between her brows. It didn't seem like worry exactly—it was something deeper, something he couldn't quite put his finger on. She didn't say anything, though, letting the conversation shift as Liam brought up the ongoing repairs from the tidal wave.

Jude chimed in here and there, but his attention kept drifting back to Caroline. She stayed quiet for the most part, only offering the occasional witty comment or dry observation. There was something brewing beneath the surface—something vulnerable—but she kept it tightly guarded, and it only made him more curious.

When dinner was over, Caroline stood, folding her napkin neatly and placing it on the table. "Thanks again, Mom. I should get going."

"You're not staying for dessert?" Cassie frowned, already halfway out of her chair. "I made your favorite—carrot cake with cream cheese frosting."

"Not tonight." Caroline grabbed her purse and coat, slinging them over her arm. "Save me a slice for tomorrow."

She paused by the doorway, glancing back at Jude. Her expression softened, just for a moment, and her voice dropped slightly. "Please be careful tomorrow. These mountains are no joke, even in May."

Her tone caught him off guard. It wasn't teasing or exasperated. Maybe genuine concern? Jude met her gaze, and something about the way her eyes held his kept him from making the snarky comment that had been on the tip of his tongue. "I will," he said simply. "Thanks."

She gave him a small nod and disappeared, her footsteps soft against the hardwood floor. Jude leaned back in his chair, staring at the empty doorway for a beat longer than he probably should have.

"She's right, you know," Liam said, breaking the silence as he refilled his glass of iced tea. "The terrain can be unforgiving. Don't let her scare you off though. She likes to worry."

"Yeah, I noticed," Jude said, picking up his fork and finishing off the last bite of his chicken pot pie. But Caroline's words lingered in his mind, undermining his usual confidence. *She likes to worry, sure. But maybe there's more to it than that.*

Frankly, his workouts hadn't been going as well as he wanted. His leg hurt. A dull reminder of how far he had to go to get back to peak form. And the asthma attack a few days ago didn't exactly inspire confidence. Signing up for a race that involved scaling a mountain might be a little reckless. *Maybe she's right. Maybe I'm not ready.*

He hated admitting that, even to himself. The thought made his chest tighten—whether from frustration or something else, he wasn't sure. But one thing was clear: Caroline's concern wasn't just about the race. There was something personal in it, something that made him feel like he wasn't just some guy passing through town.

And that realization? More terrifying than falling down a mountain.

Friday morning. One full week of work nearly complete. Time to celebrate. Caroline grabbed her bag, stepped out of her apartment, locked the door, then hurried down the stairs. When she pushed through the door at the bottom, rain greeted her. She tugged her hood up over her head, looked both ways, and crossed the street to the coffee shop.

When she opened the front door, the warm, sweet aroma of cinnamon rolls and espresso wrapped around her. She paused and let herself breathe it in. Wow, it was early, barely past six, but the place already buzzed. A few fishermen huddled near the counter, a couple of tourists clutched to-go cups, and a guy at a tall two-top slid his headphones on, then opened his tablet.

She joined the line snaking back from the register. When it was her turn, she offered a tired smile to her little sister, Megan.

"Here you go," Megan said, sliding a large to-go cup across the counter with a smiley face drawn on the side. She followed it up with something that smelled delicious, wrapped in paper. "A bacon, egg, and cheese bagel plus a mocha. No whip."

"Aww, thanks, Meg. You're a lifesaver."

Megan raised a brow. "You look like you slept about four hours and wrestled an angry moose in your dreams."

Caroline blew out a tired laugh. "Close. Sub in an ornery, charming biathlete who invaded my dreams, and you'd be spot on." She wasn't about to tell her sister the whole truth though.

She reached for her wallet, but a familiar voice cut through the chatter.

"Morning, girls."

Megan smiled. "Hey, Dad. Want your usual?"

"Please."

Caroline turned, surprised to see her dad sitting behind her in his wheelchair, rain dripping from his gray anorak. His cheeks were flushed. "Do you usually start out this early?"

"I'm meeting my men's group here at seven. Luke gave me a ride over."

She tapped her card on the reader to pay, then tucked a few bucks in the tip jar. "Good for you for getting an early start."

He gestured to an empty table nearby that accommodated his chair. "Can we talk?"

She hesitated. "Now?"

"I think that would be best."

She shot Megan a puzzled look. Her sister shrugged and turned to take the next customer's order.

Caroline followed her dad to the table. She slid her coffee and sandwich onto the reclaimed wood's surface, then sat down. He maneuvered his chair into the wide, empty space opposite her. She expected small talk—the weather, plans for the resort, maybe her mom's weird obsession with true-crime podcasts.

Instead, his piercing gaze met hers. "So, about dinner last night . . ."

"What about it?" She unwrapped her sandwich and took a bite. The toasted bagel, savory bacon, fluffy egg, and sharp cheddar practically melted in her mouth. Man, that hit the spot.

"There was a lot of chemistry snapping between you and Jude."

Heat climbed her neck. She swallowed. "Um, okay."

"I know you like to help people. It's what makes you great at your job, but, sweetheart, guys like Jude are sometimes . . . unreliable."

She bristled. "Dad, he tripped on our property and got a trail marker stuck in his leg. Then he had an asthma attack—again, on our property. Stands to reason we'd better step up and provide quality attention, don't you think?"

Her dad's shoulders stiffened. "Are you implying he's going to sue us?"

"I'm not implying anything. But he was in trouble. I was called to assist. I couldn't just leave him on the trail."

"I'm not saying you should have."

Megan appeared and set a black coffee and a blueberry muffin on the table. "Here you go." She leaned over and pressed a kiss to his forehead. "Enjoy."

"Thanks, pumpkin."

When Megan walked away, Caroline stared at him, her heart thudding. "You think I'm getting too involved."

"Aren't you?"

She opened her mouth, closed it again, and reached for her coffee. What could she say? He wasn't wrong. Not completely.

She tried to stay detached. Professional. But Jude had found a way to get under her skin with his infuriating confidence and that reckless charm. She kind of hated that those qualities appealed to her. And yes, the kiss. It had been months ago, but she still wasn't over it. And now he was back, wreaking havoc in her world.

"I don't really know what's going on, to be honest," she said, taking another bite of her sandwich.

Her dad leaned forward. "I know you want to believe people can change. But change doesn't come from claiming a spot on a podium or filming a cool commercial. I did some research, and he's dealing with quite the scandal."

"Based on mistakes he's made or false accusations?"

Doubt flashed across her father's face. "You'd have to ask him. But I know what heartache looks like, and I know you. You give people the benefit of the doubt and then beat yourself up when they let you down. I don't want that for you again."

Again. She looked away. He hadn't said it, but he didn't have to. They were both thinking it: her last boyfriend, the one who had promised the world and then fled when things got hard.

"I'm not naive," she said softly, picking at the cardboard liner on her coffee cup.

"I didn't say you were. I said you're good, and that makes you vulnerable. And as your father, I can't ignore the warning flags, then sit back and watch you get hurt."

She polished off the last of her sandwich. "Maybe he's here to prove he can change."

Dad's gaze narrowed. "Let him prove it to someone else."

But that was the thing. Part of her wanted him to prove he'd changed . . . for *her.*

"I'd better get to work," she said, crumpling her empty wrapper.

He put a hand on her arm. "Just promise me you'll be careful."

She gave a tight nod. "I will." But doubt bloomed in her chest because Jude blew right past all of her caution flags. No matter how many times she tried to tell herself he was flawed and impossible, she couldn't quite forget that flash of vulnerability in his eyes when she'd pressed the EpiPen to his leg. The way he'd stared up at her like she was the only person in the world who saw him hurting and didn't walk away.

"You're ridiculous," she whispered, waving to her sister as she tossed her trash in the container by the door. She stepped out onto the sidewalk, the rain a steady drizzle now. Usually, she'd walk to the clinic, but the conversation with her father had vanquished her motivation to exercise. She headed for the parking lot where she'd left the family's borrowed car.

Except Jude rounded the corner of the building and nearly bumped into her.

"Hey. Good morning." He wore running shorts and a red T-shirt that hugged his well-defined chest and muscular biceps. His rain-slicked hair was pushed back, and a waterproof bandage was visible on his quad.

"Hey." She pointed to his leg. "Are you cleared to run?"

He glanced down. "Not yet."

"But you look like you've been running."

"Nah, just a little jog. Not an all-out sprint. I'm headed over to the high school to see if I can run a few laps on the track."

"Do you have your inhaler?"

"Not yet. Pharmacy's working on it though." He winked. "Do I get stars on my crown?"

"Absolutely not." She frowned. "Didn't you tear your stitches a few days ago?"

"I'm healing."

"You're stubborn."

His mouth twitched. "Let's go with determined."

"You're going to hurt yourself."

His smile faded. "Maybe. But that's my risk to take."

Her heart fluttered. Oy, this man. "So my dad just warned me about how you're going to break my heart."

Jude's eyes widened. "Wow. That's blunt."

She held his gaze. "He's not wrong. I can't get near you because of what you did last time."

Jude raked his hand through his damp hair. "Caroline, I'm sorry. I didn't mean to ghost you. That was a lousy decision. Honestly, I thought I was doing you a favor."

"A favor? How?"

"My life was—is—hectic. I'm not the kind of guy who stays in one place for very long. I didn't want you to get hurt since our photo was posted on social media."

She sucked in a breath. Seriously? "So instead you kissed me and then vanished? Told people I meant nothing to you? That's the quickest way to hurt someone. Just FYI."

"I know." His face flushed. "And again, I'm sorry. I thought I was protecting you."

She studied him. Was he genuinely contrite? Sort of looked that way. Still, she wasn't sure she could trust him.

They stared at each other, the air between them heavy with unspoken words. Jude gestured toward the flyer posted inside the window of Redemption Outfitters. "Did you sign up for the race?"

She pulled out her phone and scanned the QR code. "You know what? I'm signing up right now."

"Yeah, same." His grin tugged at her resolve. "Since you're so worried about me, why don't you be my training partner?"

Caroline hesitated, her thumb hovering over the screen. Every instinct screamed *no*. But then she thought about her father's words, about Jude's vulnerability on the trail, about the way he was looking at her now. Equal parts hopeful and determined.

She hit submit. Then she met his gaze, her voice quiet but firm. "Okay. Fine. Let's do this."

Seven

HE STILL COULDN'T BELIEVE SHE'D SAID YES.

Let's do this.

Caroline's words echoed in his head as the persistent hum of the rotors sliced through the air, carrying him on a chopper into the Chugach Mountains. Caroline McGuire had agreed not only to enter the Redemption Ridge Race but to train with him too. No coercion. No begging. Just *yes.*

He leaned toward the window in the helicopter, his elbows resting on his knees. Grinning, he scanned the snow-covered ground below.

Luke glanced over his shoulder from the copilot seat. "You look happy today," he said, his voice crackling through the headset. "Saw you running this morning. Good workout?"

Jude shrugged. "It was all right. Taking it easy still." He patted his leg.

"Right." Luke nodded. "I heard about that. Here's to a quick recovery."

Next to him, Ethan flipped a switch on the console. "Did I hear that you persuaded our sister Caroline to enter the Redemption Ridge Race?"

"Yep," Jude said, not even trying to conceal his enthusiasm. "Just asked her this morning."

"Huh." Luke adjusted his headset. "I thought for sure she'd be chairing the committee that handles first aid."

"I think she was asked to do so, but she wants to participate in the race instead."

"Interesting," Ethan chimed in.

Will, the scout from the athletic apparel company sitting beside Jude, set down his phone and joined the conversation. "Is this the same woman you're with in that picture going around?"

"What picture?" Ethan shot Jude a steely glance.

Jude shifted in his seat. "For the record, I didn't post it."

Luke glanced back at him, frowning. "What kind of post?"

"Relax." Jude held up both palms. "It's just the two of us talking in the church parking lot. All sweet and innocent. I'd posted a selfie with some teenage boys inside, but someone must've taken more pictures after I left."

"Oh, right. That makes sense." Will nodded. "Well, she's got this whole thing going on. Authentic. That's gold for our brand. If you two decide to train together, we'll probably want some more footage."

Jude's stomach clenched. "Yeah, I don't know that Caroline's into that. Pressure from sponsors. Social-media comments from strangers. That doesn't seem like her thing."

"No, it does not," Ethan said. "You better run this by her before you decide you're going to be putting her in your influencer campaigns."

"Wow." Luke playfully punched his brother in the shoulder. "Influencer, huh? Didn't know you were so social-media savvy."

"I know things, little brother," Ethan said, and they all chuckled. Then he cleared his throat. "We're about five minutes out. The clearing is just ahead. I'm going to set us down near that ridge by the lake. You might have to hike a little."

"Roger that," Luke said.

The helicopter began its slow descent. A few bushes poked up from the remaining clumps of snow, their leaves blowing sideways in the rotor wash. Jude glanced out the window, his adrenaline kicking into gear as the terrain leveled out. This looked like the kind of place that could chew you up and spit you out.

As soon as the skids hit the ground, Ethan cut the engine and popped the door. Cool air rushed in, fresh and clean. They climbed out one by one, ducking to clear the rotors.

Jude slung his backpack over his shoulder. Luke pulled out a drone case from a storage compartment.

"I'll send this up. Maybe we can get some aerials that'll help you out."

"Sweet," Will said. "Thanks."

Will walked beside Jude as they followed Luke toward a rocky outcropping.

"This'll look amazing on camera." Will turned in a slow circle. "This ridge and this view are unbelievable."

"You're not wrong," Jude said, surveying their surroundings. The whole area was ringed by snowcapped mountains, with ridges, valleys, and hills spilling down into Redemption in the distance, lush and green. The lake beside the helicopter was a deep alpine blue—and looked incredibly cold.

Jagged terrain, unpredictable weather, high altitude.

He'd looked forward to this. But Caroline's warnings spooled through his head.

Are you cleared to run? Be careful.

Ethan picked his way across a moss-covered bed of rocks and came to a sudden stop. He raised a hand. "Luke, check this out."

Luke set the drone carefully on the ground and straightened. "What is it?"

Ethan crouched near the base of a crumbling ledge, then pulled a walking stick from his pack, extended it, and prodded at something partially buried beneath a layer of muddy snow and dirt.

"Bring a phone or a camera or something to take pictures, would you?"

"Gotcha." Luke glanced at Jude and Will. "Be right back. What'd you find?" he called out as he approached.

Ethan didn't answer. He reached down and used his stick to carefully lift a torn piece of fabric—a shredded sweatshirt sleeve, frayed and soggy.

"Whoa," Luke murmured.

Ethan held the fabric suspended on the end of his stick while Luke took pictures.

Then Ethan walked slowly back toward Will and Jude, his expression unreadable. "A local pilot, Trevor, went missing about ten months ago in a plane crash. Long story short, after the tidal wave, evidence of his plane appeared not too far from here."

"So what's this?" Will asked. "You think it's connected?"

Ethan's brow furrowed. "Trevor always wore a navy hoodie—at least in most of the recent pictures I've seen. I just wonder if this might be his. It's kind of a long shot, but . . ." He trailed off. "It's worth looking into. We're close to where his rescue beacon last pinged. I didn't think we'd find anything out here, but this . . ."

Luke gestured to the scrap of fabric. "This is something. Let me get a plastic bag from the chopper. Be right back."

The air shifted. Jude studied Ethan. "Do you think he's still alive?"

Ethan exhaled hard. "I don't know what to think anymore. Every time I start to let it go, the idea of finding him reels me back in."

Will shoved his hands into the pockets of his jacket. "If you don't mind me asking, was he a friend of yours?"

A muscle in Ethan's jaw ticked. "He was my childhood best

friend's brother. His brother died in a father-son boating accident when I was a teenager. It tears me up inside that their mom has lost her husband and now both of her sons."

"That's awful," Will said. "Is there anything we can do to help you search?"

"Well, I'm going to take down the GPS coordinates," Ethan said. "I'll call the police department when we're back in Redemption."

Luke handed Ethan the bag, and they carefully wrapped the remnants of the fabric. Then Luke launched the drone while Jude and Will walked around, scanning the underbrush for anything—boots, a backpack, a shred of tarp, metal.

But there was nothing.

Eventually, Ethan stood and pointed to the sky. "That doesn't look good." Black and purple clouds boiled in the distance. "Weather's not going to be on our side here shortly."

"Got it." Will took out his phone and snapped several more pictures. "Jude, I think we could work with what's up here. My vision is: we'll have a tent pitched. You'll get out wearing products from our apparel line—fleece, pants, shoes, the whole nine yards. Then maybe light a fire. We'll get shots of you fixing a healthy breakfast and then cut away to you working out."

"Wow," Jude said. "That's great. I'm in."

"Good," Will said. "Might need to scout a few more sites. I'll put some notes together and send them to my project manager, then I'll let you know. As soon as the details are squared away, Ben and Rachel will fly in and handle the rest."

Jude bumped Will's outstretched fist, then followed him back to the chopper.

As he settled into his seat, his phone buzzed. A text from Braxton lit the screen.

Braxton

Hey, we need to talk. Something's come up.

His stomach dropped. The last time he'd heard those words, it had cost him everything.

Wow, Emma did not mess around with her workouts.

Caroline tugged her hoodie on, then carefully pulled up her joggers over legs that felt like they'd turned to Jell-O. She grabbed her bag and slung it over her shoulder, wincing as her sore muscles complained. The faint scent of chlorine clung to her as she strode down the hallway and pushed through the double doors that led into the courtyard outside the high school.

The sky above Redemption was dotted with puffy clouds, and the morning air carried the sounds of birds chirping. A few robins flitted down onto the lush green lawn. Daisies swayed from a narrow strip of grass dividing the sidewalk from the parking lot. Nearby, a group of women lingered near their cars, chatting as if they had all the time in the world.

"Water aerobics was way more fun than I expected," Caroline said, stretching her arms over her head with a groan. "But what a tough way to start my Saturday."

Emma grinned, looking adorable in flip-flops, leggings, and an oversized T-shirt. Her red curls were clipped up in a casual twist that somehow made her look effortlessly stylish. "Well, are you secretly training for the Olympics too? Because you were really pushing hard in there."

Caroline laughed, shaking her head. "Please. I was just trying not to drown during that last round of..." She trailed off, searching for the name of the workout. "What was it called again? 'Death by Flutter Kicks'? Hope I can get out of bed tomorrow."

Emma snorted. "We call those leg lifts of doom. They're brutal."

"Well, you definitely looked like you were having a good time," Lainey said, bumping her shoulder lightly. Her short blonde hair stuck up in damp spikes, and her gym bag hung casually over one shoulder.

"That's because I was standing next to you," Caroline said, grinning. "Your witty comments kept me laughing."

"Guilty." Lainey shrugged. "If I have to suffer, I'm taking the rest of you down with me."

Abbie, the last to join the group, slid her oversized sunglasses into place and pulled out her phone. "Okay, post-workout selfie time. Let's make it look like we crushed it in there and weren't just chatting in the shallow end."

"Speak for yourself," Emma said, rolling her eyes as they all moved to stand in front of the high school sign. She glanced up at the building and sighed. "Whoa, this brings back memories."

Abbie held up her phone, angling it just right. She snapped the photo, then analyzed with a satisfied nod. "Perfect. I'll text it to you guys in a minute."

Anyone else would've been tempted to scroll through filters and hashtags, but not Abbie. She was efficient, always moving on to the next thing. "Anyone feel like being extra productive today? The community center has painting supplies, and Chloe would love it if we could knock out a few rooms before dinner."

"A few rooms?" Caroline repeated, her eyebrows shooting up. "Wait, that's a lot."

"Oh, come on. You'll love it," Emma said. "Besides, afterward we can reward ourselves with dinner at Dockside Pizza."

"Works for me if it works for you," Abbie said, checking her phone. "My hubby took the kids to see his parents, and my mother-in-law is making them dinner."

"What a gift," Lainey said with a dramatic sigh. "Meanwhile, Caroline, you're in training mode, right? You're going to need to load up on carbs."

"Don't start," Caroline said, a warning tone in her voice. But she knew exactly where this was heading.

"Here we go," Abbie said, grinning.

Emma's eyes sparkled with amusement. "Let's talk about the real reason Redemption's rumor mill is on fire."

"No," Caroline said quickly, holding up a hand. "Don't even."

"Too late," Emma said, her face alight with mock innocence. "I'm just glad they're talking about somebody else for a change." She angled her head, pretending to think. "Do you two know that a lady at the grocery store asked me if you and Jude were an item? I didn't even know how to answer."

"An item?" Caroline pressed her palm to her forehead. "That's a word I haven't heard in *eons*. Why would anyone think we're an item? We're training partners. And sworn enemies. That's it."

"Uh-huh," Lainey said, digging her keys out of her tote bag. "That's how all the great love stories start. Training partners."

"Oh, I don't know," Abbie said. "I hear enemies-to-lovers romances are the best kind."

Caroline groaned, tipping her head back. "Please. He asked me yesterday morning if I was going to enter the Redemption race, and I said yes. Then he asked if we could train together. That's literally all it is."

Emma pinned her with a knowing look. "Uh-huh. Training with an elite athlete you've rescued twice? Maybe people are seeing you together and assuming you're headed for at least your second date."

"We're not dating." Caroline headed for her car. "Not now. Not ever. He just told me his life is too hectic."

"Oh, I don't believe that for a second," Emma said. "How about you, Abs?"

Abbie traded her phone for her car keys. "I can't wait to pull up my lawn chair, eat some popcorn, and invest in this romance."

Caroline opened her car door and tossed her bag inside, shaking her head. "You are *terrible* people."

"We are *delightful* people," Lainey corrected, flashing a grin.

"And we'll be even more delightful after we do some community service and share pizza."

"What time should we meet at the community center?" Caroline asked, her voice tinged with resignation.

"Give me twenty minutes to go change," Emma said. "See you there?"

Caroline nodded, though her heart was still doing a little fluttery dance in her chest. She had meant what she said—she and Jude were just training partners. Low pressure. Totally platonic.

Right?

She climbed into her car and shut the door, but the doubt lingered, slinking around her like a prowling feline. No matter how many times she repeated it to herself, she couldn't quite convince her heart that it was true.

An hour later, Caroline dipped her roller into a tray of pale-yellow paint and stretched to reach the upper corner of the community center's entryway. Emma and Lainey worked the opposite wall while Abbie edged around the windows. Lainey had pulled up a '90s country playlist and streamed it through a portable speaker perched on the windowsill. With the doors propped open, briny air drifted in from the harbor, cutting the sharp tang of paint fumes.

"So," Emma said, lowering the volume on the music, "tell us more about how training with Jude is going to go. Like, is he going to text you motivational quotes every morning? Because if he writes out a workout plan, I want to see it."

Caroline hesitated, then carefully rolled the paint onto the wall. "Of course I welcome your input. But no, I don't think he's the 'daily affirmation' type."

Abbie swiped her brush along the window frame. "Are you excited? Nervous? Secretly hoping he trips over a log so you can carry him down the mountain like a wilderness superhero?"

Caroline laughed. "A little nervous. Sort of excited? It's been years since I trained for anything seriously. And let's be honest—Jude's kind of a big deal."

Lainey arched a brow. "That's an understatement. Did you know he has almost a *million* followers on Instagram?"

"I hate to admit it," Caroline said, focusing on a stubborn streak of primer, "but yes. I'm aware. And for the record, I do *not* plan on being featured on his socials."

A beat of silence.

"Too late," Lainey said.

Caroline froze. "What do you mean?"

Lainey held up her phone. "I wasn't snooping. The photo popped up on my explore page."

Caroline crossed the room, roller abandoned, and took the phone. Her stomach dropped.

The photo showed her hovering over Jude lying on the trail, her palm splayed against his chest. She remembered the scenario. It had been stressful. Intense. She'd debated about how to handle his obstructed airway. But whoever had taken the photo had captured a much different image. Frankly, nothing about her expression screamed medical emergency. Instead, the way she stared at him was almost . . . reverent.

"Oh no." She swallowed hard. "That is *not* how that moment played out."

Emma peered over Lainey's shoulder. "Camera says otherwise."

"Maybe don't read the comments," Abbie said, then gently squeezed her arm. "People are nasty sometimes."

Caroline turned away, cheeks burning, and reached for her roller. Before she could finish her stroke, her phone buzzed in her back pocket. She pulled it out.

Jude

Hey. Want to talk about this?

Attached was a screenshot of the same photo.

Jude

Are you free later tonight?

Her heart thumped. She read the message twice.

"I take it he's aware of the post," Emma said.

Caroline sighed. "Yeah. He wants to talk."

"Well, we were already planning to hit Dockside for pizza tonight," Abbie said. "Tell him that's where you'll be. If he wants to talk, he knows where to find you."

Caroline hesitated. "I don't want to make this a *thing*."

Lainey grinned. "Sweetheart, it's already a thing."

Eight

THE AROMA HIT HIM BEFORE HE EVEN STEPPED inside the restaurant—wood-fired crust, melted cheese, garlic, marinara. Stomach rumbling, Jude paused outside Dockside Pizza, one hand on the door handle.

Through the window, he spotted her.

Caroline.

Mid-laugh, her head tipped back, golden hair catching the light. Her friends were scattered around a big corner table, half-empty glasses and bread baskets between them. She looked happy. Uninhibited, even.

Maybe this was a bad idea.

But he opened the door anyway. They had to talk about that social media post.

A few heads turned as he stepped in. That familiar, almost theatrical hush fell over the room. Jude wasn't above admitting that he kind of liked the attention. It lasted all of three seconds before someone waved him down.

"Hey, Jude!"

He blinked, squinting at the contrast between the bright evening light outside and the dim, ambient glow inside.

Lainey, he remembered. The sassiest of the group.

"Nice Beatles reference," he said with a grin.

She winked. "Takes effort not to say it every time. Come on, pull up a chair."

Jude hesitated. Caroline stared down at her soda, jabbing ice in the tall red plastic cup with her straw. If her friends noticed the tension radiating off her, they didn't show it.

"Unless you have cooler friends to hang out with," she teased.

He waved her off. "Pfft. Of course not."

"Perfect," Abbie said, sliding a laminated menu toward the open seat across the table. "We were just talking about how someone's famous now."

She sang out the last words and tipped her head toward Caroline.

"Well, that would be me," Jude said, pressing his hand to his chest with mock pretension. He couldn't resist tossing a grin Caroline's way as he claimed the empty seat between her and Abbie. "But I'll share the spotlight tonight."

Caroline didn't smile. She gave him a dry, level look. "Who posted that photo?"

Oof. Jude grimaced.

"Let's look on the bright side. You were doing your job. And the lighting was great. I'm a sucker for good lighting—aren't you all?"

"Mm-hmm. Absolutely. It's essential," the ladies chimed in with dramatic nods.

"You could've warned me," Caroline said. Her expression didn't soften. "My phone exploded today. I had to turn off all notifications."

"I didn't take the picture, nor am I responsible for posting it," Jude said. "If you want, I can have my people try to get it taken down. Based on the account's handle, I'm assuming it's a guest who is no longer at the resort."

Sighing, she looked away. "Let me think about it. I don't want to cause a ruckus."

Lainey pushed a basket of garlic knots his way. "We need a guy's opinion. Abbie thinks that now that Caroline's internet famous, she should demand a collab. Maybe branded athletic wear? Crop tops? Spandex leggings for your next training session. Thoughts?"

Heat flared up his neck. Jude nearly choked on his water.

He coughed. "I think I'm staying out of this."

"Coward," Emma said.

He grinned, wiping his mouth with a napkin. "More like smart."

He stole a glance at Caroline. The crease between her brows was still there, but the tension in her shoulders had eased—maybe a little. She tucked a loose strand of hair behind her ear. His fingers itched to reach over and thumb away a fleck of paint from her cheek.

Man, she's stunning.

Thankfully, the server came by, and he banished all thoughts of Caroline as he placed his order.

The table broke into easy chatter. They swapped stories, starting with the worst painting disasters they'd survived. Lainey's hilariously questionable dating history. Emma's cringe-worthy moment with a Boston client. Jude shared a story about getting chased by an aggressive goose during a training session in Oregon.

"Geese are vicious," he said, leaning in. "I swear they remember your face. They're like feathered mob bosses."

Even Caroline laughed at that, a soft, surprised sound that made something in his chest pull tight.

That's when he felt it.

A thread tugging taut between them. Not just the rush of a good hike or the calm camaraderie of a shared goal. No, this was different.

He couldn't ignore the way her eyes lingered on him when she didn't mean them to. The soft flush on her cheeks when he caught her looking and she looked away too quickly.

This is bad. Really bad.

Because for the first time in a long time, he wasn't thinking about pace splits or training schedules. He was thinking about her. Her laugh. Her fierce loyalty to her friends. The way she looked at him like she maybe wanted to believe he was worth trusting—but didn't know if she could.

The conversation shifted into smaller threads. Emma and Abbie debated the best pizza toppings. Lainey pulled up reviews of a San Diego resort she wanted to visit.

Jude shifted slightly, lowering his voice. "You okay?"

Caroline nodded and reached for her drink. "This is just . . . a lot, Jude. I didn't expect to be the flavor of the month on your socials."

Ouch. That one cut deep.

"I get it," he said quietly. "It's not like that. But for what it's worth, you're handling it like a pro. Half those comments? People are jealous."

"Of what?"

"Of you. That you get to live here. Train here. Work out with me." He offered a crooked smile. "Clearly, you have excellent taste in workout partners."

She rolled her eyes and lightly punched his shoulder. "Stop."

"Never."

But then her smile faded. "We weren't working out though. So why let people believe something that's not entirely accurate?"

He hesitated, the air around them tightening. "People are going to believe what they want to believe. To me, it's better to just let it ride. Trust me, this will be old news by tomorrow." He leaned in. "Besides, I like the way you look at me when you think no one's watching."

Her lips parted. "Jude. I . . ."

Uh-oh. His pulse sped. Maybe that had been a bridge too far. He grabbed his glass and tipped it against hers. "We're just friends, right? Two people who want to win the Redemption Ridge Race."

Doubt flickered across her face. "Right."

But their eyes stayed locked. Long enough for the sound around them to blur.

This is dangerous. Evasive maneuvers. Now.

Warnings clanged in his head. Because he wasn't supposed to get attached. Redemption was temporary. He was here to rehab his image, train, and shoot one commercial. Then leave. That was the plan.

Except . . .

Caroline made him want to stay.

Before he could say something stupid—or worse, honest—his phone buzzed. He glanced at it.

A message from Braxton.

Braxton

Huge opportunity. National brand wants a multiweek shoot in Finland. Getting you out of the country is our smartest move yet. Need to know ASAP.

Jude stared at the screen, pulse ticking faster.

Exactly what he wanted. Lucrative deals. New opportunities. Getting away from the scandal.

He looked up. Caroline was chatting with Abbie, smiling again, unaware that the ground beneath him had just shifted.

He slid his phone back into his pocket without replying.

That now-familiar tug pulled tighter.

Yep. He was definitely in trouble.

Nine patients tomorrow and no backup? Caroline leaned

forward at her workstation, resting her forearms on the cool laminate counter. She touched the computer screen and scrolled down. Recounted the appointments—again. Nine patients. Her stomach sank further with each name on the list.

Why was she the only provider?

From the reception area, the muffled twang of a country-music station drifted down the short hallway, and the faint smell of the cleaner Wendy used to spray down the exam tables lingered in the air.

Caroline exhaled through her nose, her fingers hovering over the keyboard. She had just finished with her last patient for the day, and this was supposed to be her time to catch up on charts, order any prescriptions from the pharmacy, and reset her mind before heading to the gym. Instead, the thought of handling the clinic solo tomorrow—without her mentor—made her palms clammy.

"Nothing to worry about," she whispered, trying to talk herself into believing it.

The sound of footsteps pulled her from her thoughts. Dr. Wallace strolled out of his office, humming a familiar tune she couldn't quite place. He draped his white coat over his arm, then paused. "I can tell by the look on your face that you're already freaking out. No need. You've got this, Caroline."

She frowned. "Are you sure? Nine patients by myself is a lot."

"Welcome to my world." Dr. Wallace chuckled as he turned back to his office door, shutting it with a soft click before locking it. "My family's surprising me with a full-day halibut fishing charter. Early Father's Day gift. The weather looks perfect tomorrow, so off I go." He slipped the key into his pocket.

"Of course. I wouldn't want you to miss that."

"Exactly," he said, patting her shoulder as he walked past. "You'll be fine. See you later."

And then he was gone, the back door closing behind him with a firm click that echoed down the hallway.

Caroline stared at the now-empty doorway, trying to summon the confidence he seemed to think she had.

Nine patients. Alone.

"Everything okay?" Connie's voice broke the silence. Caroline turned to see the receptionist peeking her head around the corner, her penciled-in brows sailing upward.

Caroline rubbed her temples with her fingertips, trying to ease the tension that had settled there. "Yeah, I think so. Tomorrow's just . . . gonna be a lot. Running this place solo wasn't something I expected this soon."

Connie stepped fully into the hallway, offering her a reassuring smile. "You'll do fine. I'll be here, and we've got this."

"Right. Thanks for that." Caroline glanced at her smartwatch. "I've got to go work out. I need to clear my head."

"Are you working out with Jude?"

Caroline blinked at the question, a faint flush rising to her cheeks. "Um, yeah. Why?"

Connie's lips twitched as if she was holding back a grin. "Just wondered. I'm sure he'll keep you nice and distracted."

"Probably so." Caroline tucked her laptop into her bag and slung it over her shoulder. The idea of working out with Jude made her heart race for reasons she wasn't entirely comfortable with.

She gave Connie a quick wave, heading for the door.

Distraction. Connie was right. That's what she needed.

A few minutes later, Caroline parked at the resort, changed her clothes, then headed out to the shed. She stepped inside, expecting to find Jude waiting, but the place was empty.

Caroline dribbled the basketball against the polished floor, the rhythmic thud echoing through the empty gym. She pulled up and launched an easy jump shot from the top of the key. The ball clanked against the back of the rim, ricocheted off, hit the floor, and rolled away into the corner.

She propped her hands on her hips and glared at the ball. "Seriously?"

Jogging over, she scooped it up and returned to the crooked zigzag of orange cones she'd set up earlier. This was supposed to be a productive workout. Useful. Instead, she felt clumsy and ill-equipped, like a rookie trying out for a team she had no business being on.

But if she was going to run that race, she had to step up her training regimen. There was no room for mistakes.

She bounced the ball twice and started weaving through the cones. Right, left, crossover—too fast. The ball bounced off her sneaker and spun across the court again.

"Oy," she muttered, swiping a palm across her sweaty forehead.

She'd grown up in this gym. Why couldn't she do this? Her brother Ethan had practically lived here during junior high and high school. Mom and Dad had built the place so all five of their kids could burn off steam. Especially on those long, dark winter days.

But today, everything felt off. Sluggish legs. Sloppy timing. And her brain wouldn't stop obsessing over Jude's comment.

I like the way you look at me when you think no one's watching.

The deep voice, that stupidly handsome face. How could he be so charming and devastating at the same time?

She'd tried to play it cool during their last training session, but later, alone in her apartment above the sporting-goods store, she'd tossed and turned, unable to forget the way his gaze had lingered on hers. The way he'd made her feel like the only person in the room.

She hadn't come here for that. She didn't *do* that.

Focus, Caroline.

She retrieved the basketball, setting it back on the rack where Ethan would want it. Then she turned to the next obstacle: a makeshift hurdle she'd created by balancing a broomstick between two folding chairs. Nothing fancy, but it would do.

Backing up, she quickly stretched her quads, drew a deep breath, and took a running start. Her sneakers squeaked on the rubber all-purpose floor as she launched herself into the air.

Except her foot caught the edge of the stick and it clattered to the floor.

And down she went.

The impact jarred her hands and knees, the shock zipping up her arms to her shoulders. Wincing, she stayed on all fours, breathing hard. Her knees stung and her hands ached, but it was her pride that had taken the biggest hit.

Fine. So finesse and coordination weren't her strong points today.

Pushing to her feet, Caroline crossed to the end of the court. The overhead lights hummed, glinting off the polished floor. She glanced at her smartwatch and started a timer.

She used to run a wind sprint—down and back in seventeen seconds. Probably wasn't happening tonight, but she had to start somewhere.

Bolting to the far end of the court, she forced herself to touch her sneaker to the end line. Then back again. And again. Over and over.

Her breath turned ragged, a sharp stitch forming in her side. What was she doing? Why was she letting him get to her like this?

She'd been so sure she could handle being around Jude. Helping him. She'd agreed to the training sessions because she thought it would be no big deal. But then he'd gone and looked at her like *that.* Flirted. Said something *real.* Made her feel like maybe she wasn't just a short-term thing or an ego boost.

And that scared her more than anything.

"If this is how you usually work out, I feel deeply betrayed."

Caroline squealed, her heart hammering, and whirled around.

Jude stood just inside the open double doors of the shed, arms crossed over his chest, a smile tugging at the corners of his mouth. He looked ridiculously good in gray athletic shorts, a red vintage Boulder, Colorado T-shirt, and his hair ruffled as if he'd just rolled out of bed.

"How long have you been standing there?" she demanded, her breathing still uneven.

"Long enough to witness your highly questionable hurdle technique."

She winced. That had been, what, three minutes ago? "What are you, a creep?"

"No." His smile widened. "But I *would* pay good money to watch you tackle four-hundred-meter hurdles again. So what are you doing, working out without me?"

"You were late."

He glanced at his watch. "Twenty minutes. I had to grab some protein bars and hydrate. Do you want this peanut butter kind or the mystery flavor?" He held out an individually wrapped bar.

"Neither," she said, wrinkling her nose. "Those are full of junk."

"I think not." He tore the wrapper off the peanut butter bar and took a bite. "I'm a professional athlete. Pretty sure I know the difference between junk and quality energy-replacement snacks."

She studied him. "Tastes like cardboard, doesn't it?"

"Uh, yeah. A little." He chewed, then shrugged. "I'm going to choke it down though."

She tipped her head toward the cooler and the disposable cups. "There's water over there."

"Yeah, thanks. Having a rough day?"

She shrugged, the weight of it all pressing heavily on her chest. "I thought this would be easier."

"It's not easy working out, is it? Especially if you abuse the sports equipment."

"Ha ha."

He was quiet for a beat, then softer as he crumpled the empty wrapper in his hand. "You want to talk about it?"

"No. Yes. Maybe." She tipped her head back and stared at the rafters. "Last night kind of got to me."

He grew still. "The garlic knots? Because I'm pretty sure Lainey warned you they were addictive."

She heaved a sigh and met his gaze. "No. You."

"What? I was on my absolute best behavior."

"You said something, and I haven't been able to stop thinking about it."

"Ah." He grinned. "When I said I like how you look at me when you think no one's watching?"

Her pulse sped. "Don't say it like that."

"Say it like what?"

He moved closer. She took a step back.

"This isn't part of the plan, Jude. We're supposed to be training buddies. Friendly. Professional. Not . . ." She waved her hand between them. "Not whatever this is."

His gaze held hers, steady and probing. "Whatever this is, Caroline, it's not one-sided. So if you're confused, join the club. I didn't come here expecting *this* either."

She looked away, her chest tightening. "You don't get it. My family's here. I just started this job. I can't afford to get caught up in something that's got an expiration date."

He didn't say a word. When she dragged her gaze back to meet his, a muscle in his jaw twitched.

Uh-oh. She hadn't meant to hurt him. Not really.

"You think I'm a flight risk?"

"Um, I'm pretty sure you have a plane ticket out of here the minute that race is over."

He rubbed his fingers along his stubbly five o'clock shadow. "Maybe I do, but that doesn't mean I don't care. And it sure doesn't mean this—you—doesn't matter."

Her throat tightened. "I don't want to get hurt again."

He flinched. "I deserve that."

The look on his face nearly unraveled her. He wasn't teasing. Wasn't hiding behind his charm or his wit. He was here, real and honest, in a way that made her scalp prickle.

He reached down and picked up the plyometrics ladder she'd spread out earlier but hadn't had the courage to use. "Want me to show you how to use this thing?"

"Maybe. If you go easy on me."

He grinned. "Deal. But if I face-plant, you can't tell anyone."

"That's fair."

As he spread out the bright orange ladder, things felt easier. Not simple. Not safe. But if they focused on timing and footwork—and kept their hearts out of it—maybe, just maybe, she could handle this.

Nine

HE DID NOT HAVE POST-WORKOUT BONFIRE ON his bingo card.

Evidently, they'd stepped out of the shed and into a party.

Jude let out a low whistle. "Whoa. What's going on here?"

Flames in the firepit flickered, kicking sparks up. Guests scattered across the lawn, sitting on blankets and squishing together at the picnic tables.

"Fully loaded s'mores bar," Caroline said. "A Cassie McGuire specialty."

She grinned and handed him a bottle of water from the galvanized steel horse trough turned ice bucket.

"Thanks." He took it and eyed the rows of graham crackers, marshmallows, and chocolate squares arranged on a table decorated with a red, white, and blue plastic cover.

Cassie wore a red-and-white polka-dot apron tied over her T-shirt and denim shorts, smiling as she handed out skewers.

"You're probably the reigning marshmallow-roasting champ in three counties, aren't you?" Caroline said, nudging his arm.

He couldn't help but smile. "I'll defend my title later. How'd you know?"

She shrugged. "You just strike me as somebody who likes to be the best at everything."

"Huh, that's cute, says the girl who's probably about to hyperventilate because those stacks of graham crackers are about to tip over."

Gasping, she whirled around and faced the table. "No way. Where?"

He laughed.

She fired a glare over her shoulder. "That's not funny."

They claimed a spot outside the main circle, settling onto an insulated blanket. Someone handed Caroline two sticks, and she popped a pillow of white sugar on the end, then held it toward the fire. He stretched out beside her, one knee bent, rested his elbow on his leg, and stared at the flames. Laughter rippled through the evening air. Overhead, sun bled into the mountains, and it looked like somebody had spilled a can of orange paint across the pale-blue sky.

She slowly turned the skewer. "Can I ask you something?"

He studied her. "Sure."

"Do you remember the moment you knew you wanted to be a competitive athlete?"

He almost tossed out a canned answer, something about winning a first-place ribbon at field day in second grade. But for once, he let his mask slip away. He shifted, the warmth of the fire heating his skin.

"Yeah," he said, "I do."

She waited.

"I was eight, competing in a sledding race back home in New Hampshire. I wiped out on a downhill curve and broke my arm. So I'm bawling, because it hurts, but also because I couldn't breathe too well. My dad made it halfway down the hill before I even got up. He didn't even look at my arm. He just stood there and yelled at me in front of everyone, told me to toughen up, said crying didn't win medals."

Her heart lurched. She pressed her fingertips to her mouth.

"That was the day I learned my emotions were a real liability." His voice sounded flat even to him, like he was reporting someone else's sad saga. "If you wanted to win, you had to be tough. So I got tough. Fast. Learned to block everything else out and just perform."

He paused, his brow furrowing as he stared into the fire. "But I think it was later that same year, during my first swim meet, that I fell in love with competing. I remember standing on the starting block, nerves eating me alive, and then the gun went off. For a minute or two, everything else disappeared—the pressure, the fear, my dad. Just me and the water. I won that race, and for the first time, I felt . . . free. And I've been chasing that freedom ever since."

Caroline didn't say anything, but the tenderness in her gaze made him want to get up and run. He raked a hand through his hair.

"Anyway." He forced a shrug. "Guess it worked. World championships, endorsement deals. Spare bedroom full of equipment and a closet full of . . . athleisurewear."

"Yeah," she said softly. "You've accomplished a lot. But at what cost?"

He looked away, staring into the orange and yellow flames licking at the dry logs. "I wasn't aware that my s'more came with a side of psychoanalysis."

"I'm not analyzing you, Jude. I'm just curious is all. Maybe you're here to remember that you're more than the last race you won."

Ouch.

Someone across the lawn let out a cheer as a beanbag landed square in the hole. Caroline's sister, Megan, thrust both fists in the air, then offered a dramatic bow.

"You know," Caroline added, "I didn't ask because I wanted to dig up your trauma. I just wanted to know what made you fall in love with sports. With competing."

He pushed to his feet.

"Jude. Where are you going? You haven't even had a s'more yet."

"Uh, too much sugar," he said, brushing his hands off on his shorts. "And my legs are tight. I need to stretch."

"Now?"

He grabbed his bottled water off the blanket. "Yes, now. Stretching matters, Caroline. I'm surprised you don't know that."

He turned away. She didn't try to stop him. Her voice followed him though.

"You don't have to hide here, Jude. Not from me."

His steps faltered, but he didn't answer. He couldn't. He strode across the lawn, moving away from the fire, away from the people, away from her.

When he reached his cabin, he found his phone and then went back out on the porch and dropped down on the Adirondack chair. The scent of pine mixed with campfire smoke enveloped him. A mosquito buzzed in his ear, and he swatted it away, then opened Braxton's recent message he still hadn't answered.

Braxton

Confirmed spot. Finland awaits.
Name your start date. You in?

His fingers hovered over the keyboard. This was supposed to feel like freedom. A clean escape. But instead, it weighed on him like a boat anchor.

I'm pretty sure you have a plane ticket out of here the minute that race is over.

Caroline's words echoed in his head. She wasn't wrong. But that didn't mean he had to let her be right either.

He closed his eyes. The mountains. The fresh alpine air. Perfect snow. An ideal course. That would set the tone for the next phase of his competitive career. And he couldn't bring himself to reply.

The smart move would be to accept. To go. He'd told himself for weeks that Redemption was just a stopover, a breather. Not a place to put down roots. And not a place to fall for a girl he'd shared one incredible kiss with and whose eyes saw straight through him.

"This isn't part of the plan," she'd said.

Yeah, well, he couldn't agree more. But if he had come here to fall in love with someone, she'd be it.

He leaned forward and braced his elbows on his knees. A sliver of moon in the evening sky and a sprinkle of stars drew his gaze upward. Everything about this place—the town, the resort, *her*—seeped into his bones. It felt like home. He'd forgotten what it was like to have family around, to belong.

Oh, come on. Pull yourself together.

If he told Caroline about his options, it would probably just confirm every fear she had—that he was, in fact, just passing through. But if he didn't tell her, was it lying to keep it to himself? Or just choosing to embrace the moment?

He dropped his phone face down in his lap without answering.

Three patients down, six more to go. So far, flying solo at the clinic wasn't as hard as she thought. Maybe she could do this.

Caroline glanced up from the monitor on her laptop as Valerie poked her head around the corner. The same tall, willowy nurse who had assisted in the ER the night Jude had that stick impaled in his leg. Funny thing—today she wore the same tense expression, lips pinched in a line, thin brows slanted in concern.

"Caroline, the guy in exam room two is . . . Well, he's kind of a handful. Insists he needs to see Dr. Wallace. Says it's urgent."

"Does he have an appointment?" Caroline clicked out of the

patient chart she'd been reviewing and stood, checking the pocket of her white coat for her stethoscope.

"Yes. Gary Sheridan."

"Oh." Caroline smiled. "I've known his stepdaughter, Lainey, for ages. No problem."

"Yeah, well, when I told him Dr. Wallace is unavailable, he was not thrilled."

Caroline sighed. "Thanks. I'll take it from here."

She took the tablet off the docking station, then approached exam room two. At the door, she paused, hand on the knob. *Breathe. Pray.*

Patience, Lord. Please grant me patience and confidence. With Dr. Wallace out, this is my chance to show people that I know what I'm doing.

She pasted on her brightest, most reassuring smile and stepped into the room.

Gary Sheridan sat slouched on the edge of the exam table, his battered Seahawks cap pulled low over his brow, salt-and-pepper hair greasy at the nape of his neck. A portable oxygen tank stood beside him like a loyal but weary companion. He looked up as Caroline entered, eyes bloodshot and heavy-lidded, and scratched at the scraggly beard on his jaw.

"Hey, Mr. Sheridan," Caroline said, easing the wheeled stool closer to him. "Heard you're having a rough day."

He huffed, a sound like gravel spinning in a blender. "I told the other gal, I'm not here for no nurse. I need Dr. Wallace. This is important."

She kept her voice even, steady. The tablet sat face down on her lap. "Dr. Wallace is out fishing. I'm the provider on duty today, but I promise I'll make sure you get the care you need."

He squinted at her. "Last time I saw you, you was just a kid. You got an MD behind your name now or what?"

"I'm a physician assistant." She smiled. "And yes, Lainey and I have been friends a long time. I think I saw you at Thanksgiving a few years back."

He grumbled, but the tension in his face eased slightly. "Yeah, you brought some kind of weird green-bean casserole thing with onions."

She laughed. "Green-bean casserole. Classic recipe. Not your kind of dish, huh?"

He adjusted his nasal cannula with a grunt. "Look, I need Wallace. He understands my pain. He knows what I've been through."

"I'm sure he does." She opened his chart and scrolled through it. "I see it's been a long road for you. How's your breathing been this week?"

He shifted, the paper beneath him crinkling. "Same as always. Hurts to breathe, hurts to move, can't sleep. My back's killing me. They gave me this new inhaler, but the darn thing just makes my throat dry."

She typed the notes. "And your chest pain—on a scale of one to ten?"

"The usual. Five. Worse at night."

He glanced toward the window, jaw tightening. "Look, I need something for this pain. The oxy Wallace gave me last time helped. But I'm almost out."

He pulled an orange bottle from his shirt pocket and shook it. Caroline glanced at it. Maybe three pills rattled inside.

"Have you been taking it as prescribed?"

He bristled and shoved the bottle out of sight. "I ain't no addict, if that's what you're asking. I know what people say about me. I'm just in pain all the time. You ever work sixteen-hour shifts scrubbing sludge off rocks?"

She held his gaze, letting the silence speak first. "No, I haven't."

"Didn't think so." He coughed, his oxygen tube rattling. "I tried stretching, like that one therapist said. It hurts too much. And that salad Lainey tries to get me to eat tastes like lawn clippings. I am *not* made for kale, honey."

She couldn't hold back a laugh. "Mr. Sheridan, I want to help you. But it's also my job to keep you safe and give you the best medical advice I have. According to your chart, you're on a lot of medications, and with your breathing, I'm concerned about adding more opioids in addition to what's already been prescribed. Are you still smoking?"

His gaze dropped to his lap. "I'm trying to cut back. It's hard stuck in the house all day though. And I don't got much else to do. Lainey says I'm collecting too much junk."

"I get it. I can't comment on the collector's items," she said. "But the cigarettes are likely making your lungs worse. And pain pills can impact your breathing. How can we work together on this?"

He picked at the hem of his shirt. "You're not going to help me, are you?"

"I can give you something for the pain, but I'd like to see you back next week. And I want to try a different approach—maybe a lower dose and a referral to the pain clinic in Anchorage. There are some new treatments available: nerve blocks, more physical therapy, even acupuncture, if you're open to it."

He made a face. "Needles? No thanks."

"You survived cleaning up a massive oil spill, Mr. Sheridan. I bet you could handle a few tiny needles. But only if you want to. I'm not here to make you miserable. I want you to feel better."

"You talk a good game." His eyes sparkled. "You sure you're not related to Wallace?"

"No relation. But I've admired him most of my life. He inspired me to do what I'm doing."

Wincing, he scratched at his beard. "Well, all right. Whatever you can do for me. And if you'll tell Lainey what to do, I'll try that clinic thing in Anchorage. But you *cannot* tell her about the cigarettes or I won't go."

She patted his arm. "I can't talk to Lainey about what we discussed today. That's confidential. But I'll let her know you're open to the referral and would like her help with it. Fair?"

"Suppose so."

"All right. I'll have Valerie bring in more information about the referral, and I'll get that script to the pharmacy. Any other questions? Concerns?"

"No. You did *almost* as good as Wallace. But don't let it go to your head."

She smiled. "I'll try not to. I'll see you soon, okay?"

She stepped out. Valerie met her, but before she could speak, Caroline's phone vibrated in her pocket.

"He needs a referral to the pain clinic in Anchorage," Caroline said quickly. "Updates on acupuncture options, and I'm going to write him a script. I'd really like for him to come back next week or the week after."

"Got it. Nice work. I actually heard you laughing."

"Yeah. He's complicated, but not so bad if you just listen to him."

Her phone vibrated again. She ducked into the break room, thumbed the screen. "Hello, this is Caroline."

"Caroline, I need you in the OR. Complications." Dr. Monroe's voice was strained. Breathless. "This baby's in distress and labor's not progressing. Please. I can't manage this alone, and Wallace isn't here to save me."

Caroline's stomach dropped. "But I'm the only provider at the clinic—"

"Caroline, I don't have time to argue. If you don't give me backup, we might have a loss of life on our hands."

Chills shot down her arms and legs. "Be there in five."

There were two kids with fevers, a pregnant woman due for a checkup, and a child with asthma who needed an inhaler refill. She found Connie at her desk.

"Hey, I'm so sorry," she said, lowering her voice so the waiting patients wouldn't hear. "Dr. Monroe's having a crisis in the OR. I've got to go."

Connie's eyes widened. "What about the patients?"

"Tell them I'm sorry. If any emergencies come up, call 911 or send them straight over to the ER. I don't know that I'll be back anytime soon."

She hurried down the hall, grabbed her purse, then raced to the hospital. Her heart hammered against her ribs. Guilt gnawed at her—leaving behind patients who'd waited for care they desperately needed. But she couldn't let Dr. Monroe struggle either.

Adrenaline surged as she hurried into the labor-and-delivery space.

Chaos erupted. Alarms, voices, flashing lights. Caroline scrubbed in with shaking hands, then joined Dr. Monroe at the bedside. A young mother writhed on the bed, her face streaked with sweat and tears. The fetal monitor screamed a shrill alarm.

A nurse barked updates. "Heart rate's dropping. Baby's still breech. No progress dilating."

"We've got to call the medevac," Dr. Monroe said, frantic. "Unless you have any bright ideas. This baby's breech."

"Oh my goodness . . ." Caroline's voice caught in her throat.

The father stood at the mother's head, tears running down his face. "Please . . . please, you have to save them."

Dr. Monroe stepped forward, but Caroline raised her hand. "Let me try something."

A muscle in Dr. Monroe's jaw twitched. "If it's an ECV, you're out of your mind. Way too risky."

"Riskier than not trying at all?"

Anger flashed in Dr. Monroe's eyes. "Caroline—"

"I've done this in training," she insisted. "If we don't move now, that baby won't make it."

She turned to the mother. "Ma'am, I'm going to try to help turn your baby from the outside. It might not work, but it's our best chance right now, okay?"

The woman nodded through clenched teeth, too exhausted to speak.

"What if it doesn't work?" her husband asked, his face flushed red and his hands shaking.

"Then we call the chopper and you're on your way to Anchorage." Caroline placed her hands on the swollen curve of the woman's belly, gently but firmly pressing. Her mind raced through the steps—palpate the head, locate the spine, rotate slowly . . . The baby shifted slightly, but not enough. The mother groaned. The baby's heart rate dipped again.

Caroline gritted her teeth. "Come on, come on . . ." She adjusted her grip, tried again—more pressure this time. The room held its breath.

But the baby wouldn't budge.

The monitor let out a sharp alarm. The heart rate was crashing.

"We're out of time," she said hoarsely, looking Dr. Monroe in the eye. "Call the medevac. Now."

Dr. Monroe tipped her chin up, a solid I-told-you-so expression flickering across her face, then she turned to the nurse and gave the order.

Caroline stepped back, her whole body trembling. She'd tried. She'd done everything she could. And it hadn't been enough.

The medevac team burst through the double doors. Within minutes, they had the woman prepped, then rushed her out. Caroline trailed the husband out onto the helicopter pad. He climbed in, then Caroline stood watching as the chopper rose into the gray sky. Rain freckled her skin.

Dr. Monroe paced in a slow circle, hands on her head, chest heaving. "That was horrible!"

"We got them on the chopper," Caroline said, her throat raw. "That's what matters."

"I don't think that baby's going to make it. Or the mom." Dr. Monroe pressed her palms to her face.

Caroline stood frozen, rain dripping from her hair. Her hands braced on her hips, shoulders hunched. Her scrubs clung to her skin, and her heart felt soaked too.

She'd left her patients behind. Hadn't offered Dr. Monroe an ounce of backup until it was nearly too late. And now—

"We did what we had to do," she whispered, barely able to get the words out.

Tears stung her eyes. She thought of Mr. Sheridan. Of the muttered doubts she'd overheard. The comments. The way patients asked for Dr. Wallace, not her.

Maybe they were right. Maybe she wasn't cut out for this.

The weight of it all settled like a mountain on her chest.

She felt so completely overwhelmed.

Ten

A HEALTHY MEAL, FRESH AIR, AND A GREAT night's sleep—then he'd be all set. Ready and willing to nail that commercial in the morning.

Jude balanced his takeout container in one hand and a bottle of sparkling water in the other as he stepped off the sidewalk outside of Homeport onto the gravel path that wound around Redemption's small boat harbor.

A couple of kids were tossing stones into the water at the edge of the sandy beach. A young couple sat at a nearby picnic table, heads bent close together, their soft laughter carrying on the breeze. The scent of grilled fish, marinara, and garlic mingled in the cool evening air, drifting from the restaurant's patio.

Jude claimed one of the picnic tables farthest from the couple, closest to the sidewalk, with a decent view of the boats bobbing in their slips. Overhead, seagulls cawed, dipping and gathering on a railing nearby. The pale-blue sky, streaked with wispy clouds, provided a breathtaking backdrop for the sun slowly cruising toward the horizon beyond the jagged mountains that rimmed the bay.

He could've taken his food back to his cabin or eaten in the common area at the resort, but he needed quiet. Focus.

Because tomorrow he flew into the mountains to start filming.

It had ended up being a logistic nightmare, but thanks to Braxton and his team, hopefully all the kinks had been ironed out. Still, Jude couldn't shake the tight feeling in his chest. It was good exposure. Maybe a way to polish his tarnished image.

That's what Braxton kept telling him, anyway.

He fished out a napkin, a packet of salad dressing, and a plastic-wrapped set of utensils from the bag. His phone buzzed, but he shoved it back into the pocket of his hoodie without checking it. Now would be a great time to film some B-roll, maybe snap a picture of the view—post a few things to keep his fan base engaged. But honestly? He kind of enjoyed lying low. Taking time off.

At least this way he couldn't see the hateful comments.

And oh, how the haters loved to hate.

His stomach growled. He unlatched the top of the to-go container. Grilled salmon, wild rice, kale salad with blueberries. Fuel. Nothing more.

He planned to get up early and take a run on the trails behind the resort before lifting off in the helicopter with Luke or Ethan.

He took a bite and forced himself to chew slowly. The salmon had been grilled on a cedar plank, glazed with something sweet—maple syrup, maybe. Not bad. The breeze kicked up and the branches on the spruce trees nearby bounced. The crisp air, the golden sunlight—even at nearly seven—made for perfect ambiance.

Then—footsteps behind him. Fast, crunching on the gravel.

He turned.

Caroline.

She walked quickly, head down, hair windblown and messy. Something stirred inside him—an instinct, a protective urge. Her scrubs were light blue, wrinkled, with smudges near the knees. Her shoulders were stiff, her arms crossed like she was holding herself together. Barely.

Jude stood. "Caroline?"

She stopped and turned. Her eyes lifted to his. Had she been crying?

"Hey." She turned to keep going.

"Wait." He put the bottle of water on top of the container to keep it from blowing away. "Are you all right?"

She looked away, pressing a trembling hand to her mouth.

"Caroline." He took another careful step toward her and gently placed a hand on her arm.

"Talk to me. What's going on?"

"I can't," she whispered, her voice cracking.

"Okay. Well, don't say anything then, but why don't you come sit down? I don't want to leave you by yourself."

She blew out a shaky breath and turned toward the harbor. A tear tracked down her flushed cheek. Jude stayed still, hands in the pockets of his hoodie, though his fingers itched to reach out and pull her close.

"We had to medevac a baby and her mom," she said quietly. "It was bad."

His chest tightened. "I'm sorry to hear that."

"I tried to turn the baby even though Dr. Monroe said I shouldn't. But I thought I could. I thought it would buy us some time, you know? But I wonder if we should have made a different call. Maybe we should have just delivered."

"No." He kept his voice low but firm. "You did everything you could."

She shook her head. "You don't know that. You weren't there."

"I know you," he said softly, stepping in front of her. "I've seen how you fight for people. How you give it everything you've got."

"It wasn't enough." Her arms wrapped around her middle. "We might've lost them both."

"Sometimes even your best efforts won't get the results you'd hoped for," he said. "That's not failure though. That's being human."

She looked at him then. Her eyes shimmered with pain, defiance, shame. It wrecked him. Not just because she was hurting, but because she wouldn't let herself lean on anyone. Not even now.

"Come on. Sit down," he said. "You don't have to talk. I won't force-feed you my salmon. Just . . . sit."

After a long pause, she relented and joined him at the picnic table. He sat beside her, careful to leave just enough space to keep their shoulders from touching. His heart beat faster anyway.

She rubbed a hand over her face. "I was doing okay here. I mean, okay, some self-doubt to work through, but I really thought, all things considered, I was settling in quickly, making good decisions, and maybe, just maybe, everybody could forget about my past mistakes and acknowledge that I'm well trained. And then a day like today happens, and I feel like I'm back to being little Caroline McGuire who did something dumb at camp."

Jude frowned, then leaned forward. "What happened at camp?"

She stared at a spot on the ground. Was she debating about whether to tell him?

"I was nineteen, volunteering at a local camp. It's part sports, part outreach, part summer childcare for local kids. People come from all over Alaska. Anyway, I wanted to shadow Dr. Wallace and help out wherever I could. I was probably a little confident—too confident. So sure I could help people. And he said he was happy to have me along."

She paused. "Then a camper fell during a hike, twisted her ankle—or at least that's what I thought happened. But when I tried to help her, I realized it was so much worse. She had an open fracture. Bone showing and everything."

Jude winced.

"I freaked out. Didn't call an adult first, just ran to grab the emergency kit. Then I pulled out this vacuum splint because it looked like the right thing to use. I had no idea you weren't supposed to use that kind of splint on an open fracture. I just thought I was helping."

She blew out a shaky breath.

"What happened?"

"I made it worse. The splint compressed the wound, and by the time Dr. Wallace got there, the poor girl was in so much pain. And the camp owners were furious—terrified they'd lose their insurance coverage because I was a minor and not properly supervised. They yelled at Dr. Wallace about it. Said I had no business trying to help. And they made a valid point."

She looked up at Jude, hurt swimming in her eyes. "After that, word spread. Everyone in town knew what had happened. I was the girl who thought she was a doctor and almost made someone lose their leg. That's all anyone remembers."

"I doubt she would've lost her leg," Jude said softly. "And you were only a volunteer."

"Well, it didn't matter. And it doesn't matter now because no one here forgets anything, Jude." She gave a small laugh, bitter and tired. "Thanks for listening though."

"I really am trying to help." He twisted the cap off his water and handed it to her. "You're not a machine. Nobody expects you to be one."

She took the water. "Thanks."

A moment passed in silence. He opened the container, and she glanced at his food. "Wow. That's quite the meal you've got there. I'm impressed."

"I want to be well-fed and well-rested since I've got that commercial tomorrow. One of your brothers is flying me out at nine."

"That's right." She studied him. "Are you excited?"

"I don't know." He shrugged. "At first I was. But I'd rather be training instead of filming a commercial. And I really want to be reinstated. I want my suspension lifted, you know? I didn't do anything wrong."

"You're human. Everybody makes mistakes." She parroted his earlier words.

He took his fork and stabbed at the salad. "I didn't say you made a mistake."

"I know." She took a long sip of the water and then handed it back. "Thanks. I should get going."

"You don't have to go. Relax. Hang out."

She shook her head. "Thank you for stopping me. I really didn't want my family to see me like this."

"Why not?"

"Because I just don't want to hear it."

"That tracks," he said. "But surely they wouldn't tease you about a hard day at work. Besides, none of them have probably ever delivered a baby. Well, Ethan, maybe."

"I just don't want them to think I'm weak," she added quietly, picking at some chipped polish on her fingernail.

"Nobody sees weakness," Jude said. "I think the fact that you care so much that it hurts says a lot about your character."

"Does it?" Her voice cracked. "Caring so much that it hurts seems to get me in a lot of trouble."

Indeed.

Something shifted between them. Electric. Snappy. Like the crackle before a summer storm.

He didn't reach for her hand, though he wanted to. He wouldn't push. He'd hurt her once, and now he was afraid that if he reached for her, she'd just pull away.

He was a grown man. He made his own choices. Jude had lived thirty-some years without her input.

So why did she care so much?

Caroline paced the windows inside the resort's great room. Rain pelted the glass, and a thick blanket of fog clung to the hillside. She crossed her arms over her V-neck T-shirt, and her ballet flats skimmed across the carpeted floor.

She stopped and faced her brothers Luke and Ethan. "Why didn't they take overnight gear?"

Luke sat on the stone hearth, scrolling through his phone, calm as ever.

How can he be so calm?

"They figured they wouldn't need it," he said without looking up. "Supposed to be in and out. A few shots, drone footage. Camera operator was confident he could get everything he needed in a couple of takes."

"Didn't you guys check the forecast?" Caroline pulled her phone from the back pocket of her jeans. No texts. Not a single word from Jude since they'd sat at the picnic table by the harbor last night. She'd been inches away from falling apart and crying on his shoulder. You'd think maybe he'd reach out and let her know if he was safe. But whatever.

Ethan, lounging on the leather sofa, tracked her movement. "We did. Filed a flight plan as well."

"Then why did you drop him off?" Her voice rose, frustration bubbling just beneath the surface.

Irritation flickered in Ethan's eyes. "We had plenty of clearance, but as is often the case here in Alaska, visibility dropped quickly. We didn't plan on leaving them overnight. Our plan all along has been to go back. There's also no point in pushing our limits."

"Except there's people involved."

"They'll be fine," Ethan said. "No worries."

Yeah, well, tell that to her churning stomach.

"They'll be soggy and probably a little cold," Luke added, glancing up. "But their lives are not in danger."

Caroline sank onto the arm of the couch across the coffee table from Ethan, her knees bouncing. She dug her fingernails into her palms until the sting distracted her from the rising tide in her chest.

"But he could be sick. You said Jude looked sick."

Ethan and Luke exchanged a look.

"I said he *might* have food poisoning," Ethan clarified. He reached for his can of soda. "He looked pale when we dropped him off, and he mentioned his stomach felt off. But he hiked away with the others. They were all laughing, making jokes."

She wanted to believe him. Really, she did. Ethan and Luke had never steered her wrong before. Still, her mind conjured image after image—Jude sitting alone on a wet mountain slope, doubled over, shivering. Vomiting. Trying to act like everything was fine until he physically couldn't anymore.

Oh, why had she let herself care again?

"But what if it's not food poisoning?" she whispered.

"I don't know for sure what he's dealing with." Ethan's tone softened. "But I know he's strong and he's smart."

"Smart, huh?" Her gaze narrowed. "Except this is the same guy who doesn't always admit when he's hurting. He bottles things up, tries to act like everything's fine until—wham." She clapped her hands together. "He crashes and burns."

A thick and awkward silence blanketed the room. Luke cleared his throat.

Ugh. She'd said too much. Again.

"Caroline," Luke said slowly, "I get that you're worried. The truth is—we *can't* fly right now. The cloud cover, the wind . . . This storm is unpredictable. I'm not going to risk my life or Ethan's or yours or anyone's. Jude and the people he's with are gonna be okay." Luke crossed the room and gently set his hands on her shoulders. "He has a sat phone. If something is truly wrong, they'll reach out. And as soon as we have even the tiniest sliver of visibility, we'll go."

Her throat tightened. That was probably the right call. The safe call. Still, her body didn't seem to get the message. She stood again, resuming her pacing. Her arms wrapped tighter around herself as if she could squeeze the anxiety out.

"I'm not asking anyone to risk your lives," she said. "I'm just . . ." She pressed her fingers to her cheeks, cold and clammy. "I hate this."

"We all do," Ethan said. "But this is life in Alaska. You make your best plans. You double-check the forecast. But then a pressure system rolls in and says, 'Try again next time, pal.'"

She turned back to the window. The mountains had completely disappeared into the fog, erased as if they never existed. They should have waited. He should have waited. It was too fast.

"We had clearance this morning," Luke reminded her. "None of us saw this coming."

"But what if this is worse than food poisoning?" she asked, spinning around to face them both again. "What if he's stuck up there and they don't have supplies? What if they get hypothermia? What if he's dehydrated?"

She gritted her teeth and looked away. Oh, she hated how much this hurt. Hated that the mere idea of Jude being sick had unraveled her. All those carefully tied knots of detachment? Useless now. She'd been doing fine. Guarded. Controlled. Not letting anything in. But now?

Now she couldn't stop imagining the worst.

"Did he eat something bad? What did he have last night?"

Luke looked to Ethan. "Not sure. Thought he said something about salmon and wild rice from Homeport?"

She snapped her fingers. "That's right. I spoke to him. He was sitting out at the picnic table, and he had a to-go container with the food."

"If there's an issue with food poisoning, there will likely be additional cases," Luke said. "Want to check in with any of your coworkers?"

"Not yet," she said. "I don't want to start rumors."

"A restaurant causing foodborne illnesses?" Ethan made a face. "That won't stay a secret for long."

Her stomach clenched. "What is wrong with me? I know how to keep calm in emergencies. So why do I feel like I'm coming unglued?"

"Because you care about him," Luke said, wrapping his arm around her and pulling her into a sideways hug.

"Yeah, well . . . that's becoming a problem."

He chuckled. "Maybe. But it's also what makes you *you*."

"It doesn't make you weak because you care," Ethan added.

She exhaled sharply, trying to calm the roaring in her ears. "Hmm. You sound like Jude."

Ethan shrugged. "I told you he was a smart guy."

The wind howled around the building, and a low moan echoed from the eaves.

"We'll keep watching the radar," Ethan said, pulling out his phone. "If there's a break, we'll be the first in the air."

She nodded, but the gesture was hollow. His words couldn't quiet the ache in her chest. Couldn't stop the looping reel of worst-case scenarios.

Luke and Ethan drifted out of the room, murmuring something to each other. But she stayed by the window. Watching. Waiting.

Praying.

Eleven

WHY HAD HE AGREED TO FILM AN OUTDOOR-APparel commercial on a mountainside in Alaska?

Oh, right. Because he'd lost the rest of his endorsement deals.

The rain drummed on the tarp they'd rigged between two green bushes. A curtain of thick fog hung low, blocking his view of the valley below. A blanket of spongy moss, jagged rocks, and a few spindly shrubs surrounded him. Jude slumped against a mossy boulder, his shirt stuck to his skin from where the rain had seeped through his windbreaker. Or maybe it was the sweat. Man, he'd been sweating so much. His face tingled and his pulse kept jumping all over the place. Mosquitoes whined around his ears, relentless, like tiny airborne demons. He'd stopped swatting hours ago. Too tired. Too sick. Too miserable.

"I'd rather have two sticks impaled in my legs than throw up one more time," he mumbled.

"Pretty sure you said that already," Ben, the camera operator, said without looking up from the corner of their makeshift camp.

Jude blew out a ragged breath. "Because it's true."

Rain dripped from the edges of the tarp and pooled in the mud at their feet. Rachel, Ben's assistant, sat huddled under a thermal blanket. Her teeth chattered as she glanced at Jude. His head rolled back for a minute, and he just stared out at the gray sky, thick with more fog and billowy gray clouds. His stomach lurched. There was nothing left though. Only a hollow ache and the occasional humiliating retch. He rested his forehead against his knees, willing his body to stay still. The slightest motion made everything spin. And his face—ugh, his face was just so hot.

"These thermal blankets," Rachel said. "Saving our butts right now. I'm still freezing though."

Ben shifted, his nylon pants swishing together as he stretched his legs out in front of him. "We are officially not paid enough for this."

"Jude is definitely not paid enough." Rachel patted his shoulder. "You okay?"

"Define *okay*." Jude forced his eyes open. "I can tell you with some confidence that I am not dead."

"Yet," Ben added.

Jude groaned. "Do you two have a mute button? Maybe some duct tape in that fanny pack of yours?"

"Ouch. Grumpy," Rachel said.

"You're supposed to be the hero, remember?" Ben's tone was flat. "Rugged outdoorsman who makes everyone want to buy thermal socks, waterproof jackets, and high-end backpacks."

Jude groaned. "Rugged is so overrated."

Thankfully, they lapsed into silence. All Jude heard was the rain and the soft hiss of water on wet foliage. Occasionally, the wind picked up and rattled across the basin they sat in between two towering mountains. Well, he thought there were mountains there. He hadn't seen them since the billows of fog rolled in, smothering the peaks. Somewhere out there, the helicopter that should've picked them up hours ago probably sat grounded by the same miserable weather.

He pressed his forehead to his knees. What time was it? He hadn't seen the sun for several hours. Maybe it was 3:00 p.m.? Maybe 3:00 a.m.?

And that salmon. Ugh, that horrid salmon. Why had he eaten that? He'd been trying so hard to eat healthy. Lean protein? Grains? Fiber? That was a stupid mistake. He should've gone with a cheeseburger. They probably cooked those properly.

Caroline would have something to say about this. She always did. With that sharp-witted edge in her voice and that look in her eye when he pushed himself too far. When he was invincible and acted like nothing could touch him.

You're not invincible, you know.

Her words played on repeat in his head.

Facts. Far from it. Evidently.

The wind picked up, and a branch tumbled by. Rachel yanked her blanket tighter around her shoulders and Ben groaned.

"Wait." Rachel peeked her head out. "Do you hear that?"

"Hear what?" Jude grumbled.

"Listen."

She crawled out onto the wet ground, moss squishing under her knees, then pushed to her feet.

"Hey!" She waved at nothing.

Although maybe it wasn't nothing. Or maybe he was delirious.

No, there it was. Faint, but moving closer. A dull, rhythmic *wump-wump-wump.* Like someone beating a giant drum.

His stomach tightened again. But thankfully, he did not throw up.

"Helicopter!"

Ben scrambled out from under the tarp, stood up, and waved both arms. Jude sat up too fast. The world tilted. Wildly. Then the sound got louder, more distinct. Slicing through the fog.

Hope with rotors.

"Oh, thank You, Lord," he whispered. "Tell me I'm not hallucinating."

"You're not," Rachel said. "They found us."

Tears pricked behind his eyes. He blamed dehydration and exhaustion. Or that stupid salmon. Or maybe it was the fact that he had spent part of the night thinking he could actually die on this mountain. Less than thirty minutes from the nearest warm bed.

The red chopper broke through the clouds and settled nearby, on the flattest section of the mountainside, kicking up loose debris and pine needles. Jude shielded his face with his arm, blinking against the wind and the grit.

The door slid open and Luke jumped out, followed closely by—his heart hiccuped—Caroline.

She wore a yellow water-resistant parka. Her hair twisted into a bun underneath a navy-blue Redemption Resort ball cap. Her eyes found his, wide and searching.

He tried to wave, but his hand just flopped in the air.

"Jude!"

"I'm good," he called back, then doubled over, groaning. "Okay, I lied."

Ethan kneeled beside Ben. "You guys okay?"

"Yes, just please get us out of here," Ben said, lugging his camera bag onto his back. Rachel followed behind, hauling a duffel bag.

Caroline crouched in front of Jude. "You're a mess," she said.

"Appreciate the diagnosis."

"Can you walk?"

He pushed himself upright, grunting. "If you mean stagger like an elderly man with a new hip, then maybe?"

Luke joined his sister. "Wow, you look terrible."

"Sheesh, thanks so much."

Luke gave him a tight smile. "I mean that in the most compassionate way possible."

Jude reached out, not thinking. His filter completely evaporated. He just needed her. His fingers tangled with hers. Clumsy, cold.

Her eyes widened.

"I missed you," he whispered, then leaned forward and pressed a tender kiss between her knuckles.

Her cheeks flushed. "Jude—"

"I'm fine," he said again. "Just a little sick."

"A little?"

"Come on, man. Let's get you out of here." Luke scooped his arm under Jude. "Easy does it."

Together, Luke and Caroline pulled Jude to his feet. He swayed hard to the left and Caroline caught him before he could fall.

"Careful," she said.

"I need electrolytes." He could barely get the word out. "And dry socks. Maybe I could lie down for like a month?"

"Okay, champ, come on."

They made their way back to the chopper, Jude half limping, half dragged between Caroline and Luke. Ben and Rachel sat inside, wrapped in blankets and clutching insulated mugs. Somehow, Luke and Caroline got Jude situated in the middle seat. He let his head fall back against the cushion.

The warmth inside the chopper was almost too much. A fresh wave of nausea washed over him, bringing on a level of shaking he couldn't stop.

Caroline tucked a blanket around his shoulders. Her fingers brushed his temple. "You are burning up."

"Maybe it's love."

She rolled her eyes. "Maybe it's food poisoning and dehydration."

"Details." He shrugged.

Her hand lingered on his cheek for a second longer than necessary. He leaned into it, eyes fluttering shut.

"I was scared," she said.

He cracked one eye open. "Me too."

The helicopter lifted off, and he let the vibrations lull him. His stomach hurt and his head throbbed. But he was off the mountain and Caroline was here.

He let his head rest against her shoulder, and she did not protest.

Maybe this hadn't been such a terrible thing after all. Even if he never wanted to see salmon again.

"Sorry I'm late."

Caroline squeezed into the empty seat between her mother and Tisha at the table in the McGuires' kitchen. Steam rose from a plate of teriyaki chicken thighs—her mom's specialty. Bowls of broccoli, white rice, and fresh pineapple greeted her. She spread her napkin across her lap as Tate passed the sesame seeds down the table.

Luke fumbled the bowl, managing to catch it at the last second when Sadie knocked over her plastic cup of milk.

"Oh, honey," Tisha groaned, reaching behind her and grabbing a discarded dish towel from the counter.

"It's okay," Ethan said. "Just an accident."

"It slipped," Sadie protested, her lower lip trembling.

"It's no big deal." Brody shrugged. "I spill stuff all the time."

Ethan reached over and ruffled his son's hair. "That was nice of you, bud. We all make mistakes, don't we?"

"You can have mine." Brody passed Sadie his cup.

"Oh, sweetie, thank you, but I'll just pour some more," Tisha said.

"So glad you all made it off the mountain," Liam said, glancing at Caroline. "How's the patient?"

"He's all right." Caroline scooted her chair in. "Hopefully sleeping."

Grinning, Luke shook his head. "That was wild."

"Tell us." Mom nudged her gently with her elbow. "What really happened?"

Caroline took the bowl of rice and served herself. "Jude got takeout from Homeport the other night. Last time he tries to make a healthy lifestyle choice."

Laughter echoed around the table.

"They're usually so good about their food," Dad said, his brow furrowed. "I'm surprised. You think this was food poisoning?"

"He was a wreck," Luke said. "Whatever it was, poor guy. Pale, sweaty, and barely conscious."

Ethan nodded, his expression grim. "If there had been any more of a weather delay, things could've gone badly."

Caroline glanced at him. "And here you told me no worries. I guess I didn't know how bad it was."

Ethan held a plastic cup while Tisha filled it with milk. "You didn't admit him?"

"No, not yet. I think it's classic scombroid fish poisoning based on some research I did today." Caroline layered chicken on top of her rice. "No one else is reporting symptoms."

"What's that?" Brody wrinkled his nose. "Sounds disgusting."

"His body reacts like he's having an allergic reaction," Caroline said, reaching for her glass of iced tea, "except he's not allergic to fish. There's some kind of histamine buildup in the fish that's affecting Jude's whole system."

"Histamine?" Brody sounded out the word. "What is that?"

"It's complicated, but—"

Ethan added a scoop of rice to Brody's plate. "After you've eaten, I'll explain it to you."

"So not the salmon itself?" Dad sprinkled sesame seeds on his chicken. "More like the way it was handled?"

Caroline nodded. "I think so. He had almost all the symptoms: flushed face, headache, heart palpitations, nausea. His system was overwhelmed."

"Poor guy," Emma said. "Luke says he was in rough shape when you got him into the chopper."

Caroline's cheeks heated. "Indeed. Saying stuff he shouldn't say."

Luke shot her a look and smirked.

"I gave him a combination of antihistamines that should knock the symptoms back, but I'm gonna have to go check on him in a few minutes."

"Please eat first," her mom said. "You have to take care of you."

"True."

"Is it fast-acting?" Ethan offered Sadie a slice of pineapple.

"Yes. Both medications work together to reduce the buildup of histamine. Not something I'd hand out casually, especially not to a high-performance athlete."

Ethan nodded. "Smart."

"I don't know." She sighed. "It was a tough call. I was concerned about getting his heart rate stable and stopping the vomiting."

Her dad gave her a proud smile. "You did the right thing."

"Thanks," Caroline said softly. "I hope so."

Tate passed the broccoli to Megan, sitting on his right. "Good thing you guys were available. Sounds like he's gonna be okay."

"But what if he wasn't . . ."

She trailed off and set her fork down. The noise at the table carried on, but her thoughts were already with Jude.

"You know what? I'd better go check on him."

"Oh, honey, wait," her mom said. "Tell him he's welcome to come in here and eat."

"I'm too nervous to finish my dinner. I'll be back." Caroline pushed back her chair.

"Tell him we'll save him some!" Megan called.

"Tell him we're not serving salmon," Luke added, earning laughter from around the table.

She grabbed the bag she'd packed earlier—crackers, electrolyte drink, and the small container of antihistamine—and headed out the back door.

Clouds had parted. Sunlight streamed across the lush green lawn. Evergreen branches glistened, raindrops still clinging to some of them. Guests had ventured out; someone was attempting to start a fire in the fire pit. Kids were playing tag in front of the cabins. The drone of a prop plane flying low overhead caught her attention.

She crossed toward the cabin where they'd tucked Jude in after they'd brought him back. She knocked once. No answer.

She pushed open the door. His frame filled the bed. "Jude?"

His hair was damp, cheeks flushed. He opened his eyes.

"Hey," she said, setting the bag on the nightstand. She crouched beside him and pressed her palm to his forehead. "I brought something for you."

The corner of his mouth hitched up. "Did you now? You're a vision."

"And you're delirious."

"Maybe," he croaked, voice hoarse, "but you're still beautiful."

She sat beside him on the edge of the bed, then opened the bottle of Gatorade and held it out. "Sip slowly."

He pushed up on one elbow, wincing. "This tastes awful."

"Sorry. Would you rather dry heave?"

He winced. "No."

She took out the pill bottles. "These are what I gave you earlier. I need you to take another dose of both."

"Okay." He popped the pills into his mouth and took another small sip of the drink. He slowly lowered himself back onto the pillow and closed his eyes. "You saved me."

"You would've been fine. Ben and Rachel wouldn't have let you die out there."

"I don't know," he said. "But I knew you'd come."

Her pulse sped. "Of course."

His fingers reached for hers. "Thank you for checking on me."

She didn't answer right away, savoring the warmth of his hand clutching hers. She gave a gentle squeeze and slowly pulled away. "Try to rest, okay?"

He nodded, his breath beginning to even out. She was tempted to take his temperature but decided against it. She stood to leave.

"Caroline?"

She turned. "Yeah?"

His eyes were barely open, his voice a whisper.

"You make everything feel less awful."

Her pulse tripped over itself. She smiled, even though he couldn't see her, and stepped back toward the bed. She reached over and gently brushed his damp hair off his forehead.

"Same," she whispered.

Twelve

HE ALMOST FELT HUMAN AGAIN.

Jude stepped out onto the porch in front of his cabin and blinked against the bright light that greeted him. Late-morning air enveloped him, cool and clean, carrying the now-familiar scent of evergreen trees. He moved slowly. His stomach was still tender and his limbs weak and jiggly. But maybe he should be thankful he wasn't doubled over anymore.

He lowered himself onto the Adirondack chair. The plastic, cool under his palms, grounded him. He leaned back, breathed in deep, let the distant sound of music streaming from a speaker wash over him, and watched the magpies and swallows flitting between the lawn and the trees.

He reached for the bottle of water he'd brought with him. His mouth felt dry as chalk. He took a slow sip and grimaced as the cool liquid hit his hollow stomach. Days without proper food had made him weak—groggy, even—but he wasn't ready to delve back into eating a full meal.

His phone buzzed. He fished it from the pocket of his joggers. Braxton's name filled the screen.

Oh, he wasn't ready. But he couldn't ignore him.

He swiped to answer.

"Hey, Jude. Finally. I was starting to think they'd abandoned you out in the wild."

"Not quite." Jude stifled a yawn. "It was close. I got sick. Bad salmon or something, and then the weather trapped us for several hours. We didn't get home until yesterday."

Home. He lingered on that word. Redemption wasn't home. That could never be. Could it?

"That sounds awful." Braxton's voice pulled him back. "How are you feeling today?"

"I'm getting better. Weak, but I'm sitting up. Haven't puked in several hours, so that's progress."

"Wow. Glad to hear that. Listen, I've got two voicemails and an email from that product sponsor. Are you going to finish the shoot? What's the status?"

Jude massaged his forehead, trying to think clearly. "We're not done. We lost two days. Camera op and producer are supposed to still be at the hotel in town. Last text I read said they're waiting on me to give them the green light. I should be ready in another day. I have to be able to keep food and water down."

And I'm not sure I can get back on that chopper. But he kept that part to himself.

"That's all I need to hear. Thanks. I'll let him know."

Braxton paused.

Jude felt the vibe shift. Uh-oh.

"There's one more thing."

Jude's chest tightened. "What is it?"

"So, I've heard from the committee. About Myles."

"Yes." He braced himself.

"And also you."

"Me?" He raked his hand through his messy hair. "What now?"

"Myles's team has denied your accusations and fired right back. He's claiming *you* cheat. Says doping."

Jude sat bolt upright. His chair creaked beneath him. "What?"

"Yep. Filed a formal complaint. Committee called me this morning. They want you to submit a blood test before you're allowed to be reinstated and compete again. Full panel. Independent lab. You know the drill."

Jude curled his hand into a fist. He stared out at the trees, but all he saw was red.

"You have *got* to be kidding me. That's garbage, Braxton."

"I know, but the optics. You—"

"The optics." Jude's voice rose, the words scraping against his raw throat. "*I'm* the one who called out the cheater. I've been clean my whole stinking career, but now I'm the villain because I caught Myles cheating?"

"Jude. Easy there."

"Don't tell me to take it easy! Where was this committee when I won nationals? Squeaky clean. Where were they when Myles's numbers didn't add up? And I asked why he was communicating through an earpiece. Has anybody thought to look at some stills? Maybe some replays? Why are they taking a dig at *me*?"

A long silence filled the line.

His heart thudded. His dizziness returned—probably more from outrage than hunger. All those days. Waking up before dawn to train. The sacrifices, the aches, the injuries, the failed relationships. Every ounce of himself he'd poured into this sport. And he had never once cheated.

"Listen, I get it, Jude. I really do," Braxton said. "But if you don't do the blood test, it looks like you've got something to hide. And they *will* ban you. Maybe for good."

Jude growled low in his throat. "I'm so sick of this. I'm out here busting my tail. Sick as a dog. And all they care about is covering their tracks."

"I know, but you're clean, right?"

Jude winced. "You have to ask?"

"It's not about what I think. We've got to shut this down before it gets legs. Get the blood work done. When it comes back clean, I'm sure they'll reinstate you. And you can move forward with your name clear."

Jude gritted his teeth and stared at his hand—calloused, scarred, shaking. "Myles is a liar. He's been cheating for years. No one listens to me though. Now *I'm* the one on trial."

"It's not a trial," Braxton said. "We are going to do everything the committee asked us to do. Dot all of our i's, cross all of our t's. But I need your word that you'll follow through."

He wanted to scream. Throw his phone into the trees. Mostly, he just wanted someone—anyone—to believe in him. To commend him for how hard he'd worked. For not cutting corners.

"Fine," he said at last. "I'll do the stupid test. I've got nothing to hide."

"Great. Glad to hear it. I'll set it up. Surely there's a lab nearby?"

He thought of Caroline. "I know someone who can help me."

"Good." Braxton exhaled, clearly relieved. "Thank you for your cooperation, Jude. It means a lot. Hang in there, man. You'll get through this."

"Yeah. Braxton?"

"Yeah?"

"I'm not perfect. But I don't cheat. I never did."

"I believe you," Braxton said. "Talk soon."

Jude ended the call and sat back in his chair, dropping the phone into his lap. The powder-blue sky stretched overhead, sunlight streaming through the trees, fresh air brushing against his skin.

He closed his eyes and soaked in the peace and quiet.

Yeah, he'd do the test. Then he'd prove them all wrong. And when he did, he'd make sure no one forgot that Myles was the real cheater here.

Because he had *nothing* to hide.

This was just a house call. Totally professional.

Caroline shifted the bag of groceries to her hip, grabbed her medical bag, then headed down the path toward the resort's cabins. This visit had nothing to do with the way Jude had looked at her the last time she checked on him. Like maybe she was the only person he trusted. Or the way her stomach flipped when he said her name in that rough, tired voice and told her she made everything less awful.

She spotted him sitting on the porch, slouched in the chair, his head tipped back.

"Wow, you look like someone who lost a fight with a salmon."

His mouth twitched as he sat up. "It wasn't exactly a fair fight."

She stopped in front of him. "How are you feeling?"

"My stomach's still staging a protest." He raked his hands through his hair, and she couldn't help but notice the way flecks of gold mixed in with the dark hair in the scruff on his jawline. "I'm upright—sort of—so, small victory?"

"Absolutely. I brought you some chicken noodle soup and fresh bread. Some applesauce."

"Wow, thanks." He squinted as he glanced up at her. "And more Gatorade? You didn't have to do that."

"Well, somebody's got to look after you, right?"

"I suppose so."

She set the groceries down near his feet. "Is it okay if I check your vitals?"

"I wouldn't complain," he said, voice low, teasing.

And there went her heart, skittering like a precocious little puppy. *Stop it.* This was not a date. This was healthcare.

"Let me see your wrist." She pressed her fingers to the pulse point. Faint. Thready, a little. But improving. "You've got a heartbeat."

His lips twitched. "Is that your official medical opinion? Patient has pulse?"

"Yep. I'm a professional." She put her stethoscope in her ears. "Lean forward, please."

"Yes, ma'am."

She pressed the disc against his back, hyperaware of the way his T-shirt clung to his back and the warmth of his skin seeping through the thin fabric into her palm. "Deep breaths."

He obeyed, straightening his torso, then exhaling. "You know, this isn't a bad way to spend a day," he said. "Great view, fresh air, and a beautiful woman putting her hands on me."

She took off her stethoscope and stepped back, arching a brow. "Hmm. If you think you're going to get around-the-clock care . . ."

"I mean, I wouldn't complain." He held up both palms. "Is that an offer?"

She rolled her eyes but couldn't stop the laugh that bubbled up. "You're a mess."

"A hot mess?"

She reached out and pressed her palm to his forehead. "I thought maybe you were feverish."

"All that nonsense coming out of my mouth?" He grinned. His eyes drifted to her lips, and her breath hitched.

Oh, have mercy.

She jerked her gaze away and pretended to rummage in her bag. "You do look better. Pale though. How's your blood sugar?"

She handed him a Gatorade, but he pointed to the bottle he'd parked under his chair. "Thanks for the spare. I gotta take small sips, right?"

"Of course. The soup is bland, but chicken noodle has salt in it, so that'll . . ."

"Sodium will help me get my electrolytes back," he finished for her.

"Exactly."

"Cool. Thanks. Nothing like a little comfort food. Have a seat," he said, gesturing to the chair beside his.

"I'm not staying."

"So this is a house call? I didn't know you did that."

"It's not advertised. Part of the job though."

"Dr. Wallace do house calls?"

"Oh, absolutely."

He unwrapped one of the saltine crackers and took a bite. "You don't have to do this, you know," he said through a mouthful. "Supplies, groceries, lecturing me to take fluids . . ."

She brushed a strand of hair behind her ear. "You looked pitiful the last time I was here."

"There it is. Stellar bedside manner, Miss McGuire."

"Just eat your crackers, Mercer."

He took another bite. "Delicious. Or maybe they just taste better because you're here."

The words caught her off guard. Sincere and casual. Did he realize the weight they carried?

She felt like she was standing on the edge of a dock when a wake from a boat washed in—wobbly, unstable. *Focus.*

"Have you figured out what you're going to do next? Are you rescheduling your shoot?"

He nodded and reached for his drink. "Yeah, Braxton's working that all out."

"I figured. Any other news?"

He hesitated, then dragged his hand down his face. "Just . . . biathlon politics." He shrugged. "I don't want to talk about it."

"Okay."

"Thanks for asking."

"You're welcome."

Silence fell between them. She tried not to fidget, tried not to stare at his profile or the way the bicep muscles curved beneath the sleeve of his jade-green T-shirt.

Snap out of it, Caroline.

His phone buzzed. He glanced at it, frowned.

"Everything okay?"

"Yeah. Just Braxton giving me a couple updates." He shoved the phone back in his pocket. "If I needed repeat blood work, is there a lab here that can do that?"

"Yeah. Your physician can send the orders electronically. Then you just show up."

"Just show up and let them stab me?"

"Pretty much."

"Cool. So . . . what's new? You getting ready for the race?"

"Ugh." She groaned. "Not nearly as ready as I want to be. I'm going to do a longer run tomorrow."

"Wish I could join you, but I don't think I'm up for any kind of running."

"No, probably not. Another day or two, maybe." She reached for her bag. "You could rest, hydrate, call your mom."

"My mom? Why?"

"I don't know." She shrugged. "Don't moms want to hear from their kids?"

He grew still. Something she couldn't quite decipher flickered in his eyes. "I suppose."

"Don't you have a family group chat? Or does she just keep up with you by your socials?"

"Oy." He grimaced. "Hope not."

She hesitated. What had happened? They'd been bantering. And it had felt . . . comfortable. Familiar. But now a tense feeling swirled in the air. She didn't like it.

He leaned forward, elbows on his knees. His gaze found hers, intense and unflinching.

"I want to ask you something."

"Yeah? What is it?"

"So, when I'm not half dead and you're not swamped at that clinic . . . would you go to dinner with me?"

Her pulse skyrocketed. It had been a long time since anyone had asked her out. And he—he'd kind of wrecked her when he kissed her and then disappeared.

But he made her laugh. Made her think. And the way he was staring at her now, she felt like he saw her. Really saw her.

Say yes, her heart whispered.

But her logical brain was louder. He was suspended, hiding out, tangled in drama and scandal and so many things she didn't want to get mixed up with.

"If you weren't half dead, I might consider it."

"Might," he echoed.

"I said *might*. That's not *definitely*."

He grinned. "I'll take it. How about tomorrow?"

"Um, no." She jumped to her feet. "I'm off tomorrow, but after I take that long run, I have things I need to do."

"What kind of things?"

"Just . . . things."

She tried not to stumble as she backed away. She needed air. Distance. Space. Better excuses, apparently.

"All right." He leaned back again. "I'm a patient man. I'll wait."

"You are *not* patient at all, Jude Mercer."

He grinned. That same smile that threatened to undo her every single time.

"Fine." She blew out a shaky breath. "I'll text you after my run."

"I'll be waiting."

Thirteen

JUDE RAN A HAND OVER HIS FRESHLY SHAVED jaw, rubbed in the aftershave, then checked his reflection in the small mirror over the cabin's bathroom sink. Not bad for a guy who'd been dehydrated and battling food poisoning less than forty-eight hours ago.

He buttoned the last button on his pale-blue shirt—clean, ironed, and ready to go. He stepped back, gave himself another once-over. Khaki shorts. Actual shoes. Wallet. Keys. Subtle—not trying too hard—but he wanted to step up his game a little from joggers and athletic shorts.

Except he hadn't heard from Caroline.

He checked his phone again, just in case the text had come in while he'd been in the shower and he'd somehow missed it. Still nothing.

"How much of a run is she taking?"

He'd sent a text earlier reminding her to let him know when she was back. He'd added: *Please give me an excuse to see you again tonight. Now would be good.*

But he'd come to his senses and erased it before pressing Send.

Wait. He had erased it. Right? Adrenaline surged through his veins as he scrolled back to make sure the more candid message hadn't gone out.

Jude

Hope you had a great run. Let me know when you're back.

Relief bloomed in his chest. Not the candid version.

Maybe she was avoiding him. Maybe when she'd said *might*, what she really meant was *You don't stand a chance, buddy*. But no—she said she'd text when her run was finished, and Caroline didn't seem like the type to leave somebody hanging.

He winced. Then again, he kind of deserved to be stood up. After what had happened in Colorado . . . but if she was still holding a grudge, why had she let him flirt with her? Why had she been so kind?

Unease curled up his spine as he slid his phone into his pocket and headed out.

Late-afternoon sun cast golden beams across the path. The air held a crisp edge, tinged with salt and spruce. He swatted at a mosquito and picked up his pace.

He ducked into the resort lobby, where country music played softly from a speaker and the scent of fresh-baked cookies lingered in the air. Mrs. McGuire stood at the front desk, straightening a basket of brochures.

"Hi," he said.

She smiled. "You clean up nice, Jude."

"Thanks." He leaned his elbows against the counter. "Have you seen Caroline? She said she'd text me after her run, but I haven't heard from her."

Her smile faded. "She did come by earlier and mentioned she wanted to take the Dock Point Trail. Needed to clear her head." She tapped her smartwatch. "That must've been around two."

"How long would you say that loop is?"

"Hmm. Not sure exactly, but I can't think of a time recently when Caroline has gone on a three-hour run. I mean, we don't talk about her exercise routine, and she did just move back . . . but that seems out of the ordinary. Unless she decided to walk it instead."

His stomach twisted. "Did she say she was coming back after?"

"No."

Just then, the door flew open and a boy around eight burst inside. "Guess what! Guess what! We were fishing down at the dock and there's a bear!"

"Really?" Mrs. McGuire's expression shifted into mom-mode skepticism. "Jackson, have you ever seen a bear before?"

"Nope. It was big too!"

Mrs. McGuire's brow furrowed. "Is everybody okay?"

"Yep. Somebody told me that he eats the trash out of the dumpsters. So gross," Jackson said, wrinkling his nose. "Why would a bear eat trash? I thought they liked honey and fish."

"Yeah, sometimes they do eat garbage. Along with fish and berries and whatever else they can find." Mrs. McGuire craned her neck to see out the window. "Are your folks with you, Jackson?"

Jude straightened. "If I go down to the harbor, will I see the entrance to the trail?"

"Absolutely. Here." She pulled her keys from her pocket. "Take my car. It's the same one I drove to church. Crossover SUV, silver, parked out back."

"Thanks. I'll keep you posted. You'll text me—or have her text me—if you see her first?"

"Of course."

Jude jogged out to the car, climbed inside, and started the engine. Once he left the resort, he had to squint. His surroundings glinted with light reflecting off the water. Tapping the brakes, he slowed as he got stuck behind a slow-moving RV with an out-of-state license plate.

"Come on, come on . . ." He resisted the urge to honk. At the four-way stop, the RV turned left and he went right, cutting around toward the harbor.

He parked across from Dockside Pizza Company. His mind raced with possible scenarios. She stopped for a break? Forgot her phone? Got lost in thought? Ran into an emergency?

Or maybe she saw that bear.

He didn't like that idea at all.

A sign marked the entrance to Dock Point Trail: Beware of tidal zones.

He glanced at the shoreline. Mudflats stretched wide to the left—bare, slick, and scattered with tide pools. Was the tide going in or out? He hesitated, then shook it off. He'd find Caroline before that mattered.

A family with two young kids approached. "Hey," he said, "did you by any chance see a woman jogging?"

They shook their heads. "No, but . . . we're headed in because we heard there was a bear."

"Yeah, I heard the same. Did you see it?"

The man shook his head, herding his kids forward. "Didn't want to take our chances though."

"Understood. Have a good night."

Jude picked up the pace. His canvas shoes and lack of socks were terrible for running. "Caroline!" he called.

A twig snapped. A bald eagle lifted off from a tree, its massive wingspan whooshing through the air.

"Caroline!" he yelled again. The trail split. He veered right toward the water. It was less steep, more scenic. He scanned the trees, listening for any movement, rubbing at the tightness in his chest.

"Caroline!"

He rounded a bend. A narrow rivulet cut across the trail. He leapt it, landing with a grunt and wincing at the hot spot forming on his heel. A blister was a small price to pay.

"Caroline?"

Then he saw her.

Slumped on the ground. One knee bent as she hugged her leg to her chest. Scrapes marred one side of her face. Dirt streaked her arms. Her water bottle lay a few feet away.

"Caroline!" He dropped to his knees beside her, heart slamming against his ribs.

Her eyes fluttered open. "Jude?"

"You're okay," he said, his voice shaky. "What happened?"

"I tripped. Rolled my ankle really hard. I tried to get up, but it hurt too much."

"Did you hit your head?" He scanned her leg. Her lower left calf was already turning bluish-purple and swelling fast.

"I don't know. Maybe. It doesn't hurt. I'm not dizzy." She tried to sit up, then winced.

"Hey." She reached for him, her fingers brushing his shirt, rubbing the fabric between her thumb and finger. "You got dressed up."

"Trying to impress you." He managed a grin.

She smiled. "It worked. Super impressed."

He glanced behind them. The water had crept farther up the shore, swallowing the mudflats. "Tide's coming in."

Caroline paled. "We're cut off from the trailhead, aren't we?"

"Yeah." He stood, scanning the woods. "I'll carry you if I have to—"

A low rustle. Then the unmistakable chuff of something heavy moving through the underbrush.

Caroline's eyes widened. "Jude."

He turned. Through the trees, a dark shape moved. Lumbering. Broad. Low to the ground. A grizzly.

His blood turned cold.

"Okay. No sudden movements." His voice dropped to a whisper. "Don't panic."

She clawed at his arm with her hand. "What do we do?"

"I saw something back there. Looked like . . . maybe an old yurt or shelter. Can you put your arm around my shoulders?"

She nodded, her breath hitching. "This used to be a campground. Let's try the yurt."

They moved slowly, her weight leaning into him. Every few steps, she gasped in pain. Jude kept glancing back, heart pounding.

The bear didn't follow. Yet.

They reached a clearing. A faded, sun-bleached yurt stood half hidden by wild rosebushes. He stumbled, struggling to keep Caroline upright. Sweat soaked the back of his shirt. "Almost there," he grunted.

When he got to the two rustic plywood steps, he helped Caroline hobble up, then he shoved the door open.

Empty. Musty. But intact.

A shaft of light pierced a tear in the canvas overhead. Two forgotten paperbacks and an olive-green blanket sat on the basic wooden shelves pushed against one of the curved walls. In the center of the dimly lit room sat an old stove, its pipe jutting up and out through the ceiling.

He eased her inside and shut the door, dragging a rickety wooden bench across the plywood floor and wedging the door closed.

Caroline collapsed onto a dusty mattress. "We're safe? Maybe?"

"For now," he said, crouching beside her.

Outside, the wind kicked up. Salty air seeped inside, and the bear's heavy footfalls crunched somewhere nearby, circling but not approaching.

Inside the yurt, Caroline threaded her fingers through his, her breath coming in short gasps. His heart pounded, thrashing against his ribs. What would he do if that bear came through the canvas wall?

Oh, she so did *not* want to spend the night in this yurt.

Her ankle throbbed, and the bear prowled around outside, huffing at the door. She lay curled on the thin mattress of the bottom bunk. Her fingers brushed a crusty, abandoned wool blanket—she pushed it aside with a grimace. Her teeth chattered, probably more from nerves than temperature. She tightened her fists and tucked them under her chin as the bear pawed at the yurt's flimsy door.

"Why won't it go away?" she whispered through gritted teeth.

Jude didn't answer. He sat on the old bench with his back against the door, a muscle in his jaw tightening, legs outstretched and arms crossed tightly over his broad chest. Light spilled through a narrow opening near the top of the yurt.

"Hungry, probably," he said.

The door wiggled.

Caroline stifled a scream, slapping her hand over her mouth. Her heart banged against her ribs like it was trying to break free.

Jude clutched a hiking stick they'd found leaning in the corner.

"Jude," she whispered.

He pressed his finger to his lips.

"I don't think it's going to get in. It's just sniffing around, curious. You probably smell delicious." His mouth twitched.

"That's not funny."

"Come on, it's a little funny."

"Well, I think he probably smells your aftershave. Spicy. Outdoorsy."

His eyebrows arched in mock innocence. "So you noticed, huh?"

Heat rose to her cheeks and she looked away. "This is not the time for you to flirt with me."

"It's the perfect time to flirt. Keeps you distracted. Please. Devote all of your attention to me."

She met his gaze again. "That's how you like it, isn't it?"

His expression softened, turned serious. "You have no idea."

Huh. For a guy who didn't like to be vulnerable, that was quite the intel.

"How's the pain?" he asked a few minutes later.

"It's there."

"On a scale of one to ten?"

"Don't." She held up her palm.

He chuckled, and it was a low, soothing sound in the middle of her panic. "Ah, so the physician assistant does not enjoy being a patient. Isn't that interesting?"

"I just don't think it matters what my pain level is since we're about to become bear food."

"Easy there," he said. "Where's your positive attitude?"

The crunching of sticks and the unsettling huffing had decreased. The quiet made her ears ring.

"I think he's moving on."

"Hope so," she said, though her fingers stayed clenched.

"I hate that you got hurt. I wish I'd gotten here sooner."

"At least you found me before it was too late. That's what matters."

"I really thought something terrible had happened," he said.

"Um, getting hurt and a bear almost eating me is already terrible."

"I didn't think a bear was going to eat you, but when I saw you lying there . . ." He trailed off, swallowing hard.

"Jude, this isn't your fault. You know that, right?"

He didn't answer right away.

"I made my own choice. I'm the one who decided to come out here and run without paying attention to the tide. We McGuires . . . we think we're pretty sharp, but we have a history of getting ourselves into unfortunate situations."

His brows scrunched together. "What are you talking about?"

"My dad is in that wheelchair because he tried to save the resort from burning down. A fire that was . . . kind of sort of his fault."

Jude winced. "That's terrible."

"I know. Damage to his spinal cord, broken ribs, smoke inhalation . . . A beam from the ceiling fell on him. Now he has these brace things he can wear on his lower legs, and between those plus some tremendous assistance from a walker or my mom beside him, he's able to take a few steps. But it's grueling. I think he prefers the wheelchair."

"I'm so sorry."

"Thanks. I was just a teenager. It was devastating because everything changed overnight. I was *not* a big fan of spending time with him before the accident. I was scared a lot."

Something flickered in Jude's eyes. "What do you mean? Scared in what way?"

"He had a temper. Yelled a lot. Known to throw things. But after the accident, that version of him just disappeared. I mean, he still has his moments of battling his pride like we all do, but . . . something broke. Poor choice of words, but you know what I mean. In a good way. He became softer, kinder, more generous. The pain cracked him wide open, and he let the Lord into his life, and now the good stuff just spills out."

"Wow. That's quite the story. Not usually the way people with anger-management issues are spoken of."

"I know. Which is why I kind of feel terrible saying it that way. It's like I'm rejoicing in his suffering, but . . . he *did* lose his ability to walk independently. And on the flip side, we all get to live with a better version of him."

"It's not terrible," Jude said. "It's honest."

"Do you ever feel like the broken parts of you are the parts that you end up connecting with people over?"

"Oh boy." He leaned his head back, blew out a slow breath, and stared at a point somewhere above her head. “More than I’d care to talk about.”

“I’m guessing your dad wasn’t the warm fuzzy type.”

“Nope. More like ‘Don’t cry unless you’re bleeding out because your arm fell off.’”

“Ooh, wow,” she said. “Way harsh.”

“Yeah.”

She studied him, her voice quieter now. “Is that why you, um . . . That explains a few things.”

He glanced at her again. “What do you mean?”

“Well . . . you kind of act like nothing bothers you. You mask your real emotions with a joke or a smirk.”

“That’s how I survive. I told you—it wasn’t safe to be sensitive when I was growing up. So I learned that if I act like I don’t care, I don’t get hurt as bad.”

He set the stick down and pushed to his feet. Tucked his hands into the pockets of his shorts. “But the thing is, you forget how to let people in . . . even when you want to.”

“Yeah,” she whispered. “I know the feeling.”

Their eyes locked across the tiny space. Outside, the breeze picked up. Branches rustled. Water lapped at the shore somewhere nearby.

“Do you ever think about Colorado?” he asked.

She sat up, swung her legs over the edge of the bunk, her ankle twinging as she moved.

“What do you mean?”

“That night, when we . . .”

She blinked at him. “Kissed?”

“Yeah.”

The memory rolled in like fog over the water—his mouth on hers, the snow falling around them, the laughter of the crowd fading. Fireworks from a local festival had popped and fizzed in the sky. She’d missed it all. But the kiss had been worth it.

"I really thought that kiss meant something," she said. "Guess not."

"No, Caroline." He closed the distance between them and sank down in front of her. He put his warm hand on her knee. "It *did* mean something. It still does."

She shook her head, though her heart swelled. "Then why didn't I ever hear from you again?"

"I was scared," he said. "Like we just talked about. Sometimes I push people away because it keeps me safe."

"I'm harmless, Jude. What are you scared of?"

"I'm scared of feeling too much." He reached up and tucked a strand of hair behind her ear. "Of wanting something real. You were light and funny and gracious and kind. I didn't deserve you. I still don't think I do."

She reached for him without thinking. Caught his hand gently in hers.

"Jude . . ."

"I'm still scared," he said, "but not of *you*."

He dragged the pad of his thumb across her knuckles. Warmth shot up her arm like a flare. "I'm not scared of you, but I *am* afraid of doing something stupid and hurting you. Again."

"Then don't do anything stupid."

Jude leaned closer. His eyes drifted to her lips.

She tipped her chin up. Her pulse quickened. A wild fluttering started in her chest.

"Tell me to stop, Caroline."

She didn't. She couldn't.

Instead, her lips parted. She tilted her head. And then he kissed her.

Slow. Searching. Incredibly tender.

His hand cupped the side of her face, and she leaned in, her whole body aching with the kind of longing she had tried so hard to bury.

The kiss deepened, and suddenly she was back in Colorado. Snowflakes in her hair. Her heart skidding sideways. But this time, she wasn't that same girl, and he wasn't that same man. She wasn't going to blindly walk into this and give away her heart. And even if he wasn't going to be stupid, the man wasn't staying in Redemption, and she couldn't be stupid either.

When they broke apart, her breathing was uneven. Her heart thrummed out a warning beat. "This was a mistake," she said, pressing her fingers to her lips.

Jude flinched. "What?"

"Jude, I'm so sorry." She pulled away and scooted back on the bunk. "I just . . . I thought . . . I *can't* let you break my heart again. I just can't."

He nodded, but the pain in his eyes made her regret the words.

Fourteen

MAN, HE COULDN'T GET OUT OF THAT YURT fast enough.

Jude stood outside on the steps, the damp air cool against his hot skin. He surveyed the surrounding woods, but there was no sign of the grizzly bear. Water in the tide pool still divided their tiny island of land from the Dock Point Trail. Light lingered in the sky even though it was after nine o'clock—an endless Alaskan evening that refused to give way to night.

In the distance, a cruise ship sailed out of port, probably headed for Seward or Whittier, or maybe farther south across the Gulf of Alaska. It was peaceful. Quiet. The perfect escape. If his insides weren't churning like Class 5 rapids. And if Caroline's panicked "This was a mistake" wasn't still echoing in his head.

He braced his hands on his hips, drew in a deep breath, and blew it out slowly. Same breathing technique he used at the start of every race. Although it didn't really help right now. He should go back inside and let her know that the bear had gone and the tide had probably crested.

But if he did, he might say something he couldn't take back.

Something honest. Something blunt like "I want to stay, but I can't."

And that would only hurt her. And that was the one thing he'd said he didn't want to do.

Voices broke through the quiet.

Jude squinted toward the forest. On the other side of the tide pool, three familiar figures emerged on the driftwood-strewn edge of the shore. They carried a bright red inflatable raft balanced on their shoulders. Ethan led, his plaid flannel unbuttoned and open over a white T-shirt. He wore cargo shorts and hiking boots. Behind him, Tate and Luke rounded out the trio.

They'd come. Relief swept through him.

Relief—and something sharper. The brothers would take over. Caroline didn't need him anymore. Not really.

He hopped off the steps and crossed to the edge of the tide pool.

"Hey," he said, raising a hand. "Thanks for coming."

"Not a problem. Thanks for letting our mom know where you were." Luke scanned left and right. "Bear's gone, I'm guessing?"

"As far as I know. When he didn't find food, I guess he took off."

"You good?" Ethan called out.

"Fine," Jude said.

Not really, but he wasn't going to get into the state of his heart.

"Caroline's not in great shape. Hurt her ankle when she fell. She's not going to be able to walk without help."

Luke's expression tightened. His gaze darted toward the yurt. "Broken?"

Jude shrugged. "I have no idea. Probably not. She's trying to downplay it, but there's no way she's going to put weight on that foot tonight."

Luke nodded, then jerked his thumb over his shoulder. "We've got the truck back at the trailhead. Obviously, you still have Mom's car. Ethan was dying to hover over with the chopper and lower the sling. But that seemed like it was a bit much."

"Oh, come on," Ethan said. "I had to at least try. Old habits die hard and all that."

"We have crutches, splints, vacuum splints, and a first aid kit." Tate held up both bags. "Dry socks, blankets, water, and energy bars in my backpack. Did I forget anything?"

Luke grinned. "Marshmallows? Chocolate bars? A little smoked salmon for the bear?"

Jude couldn't help but laugh. "No, I think you've covered it. Thanks."

He glanced at the raft as Ethan clung to the edge and held it while Luke climbed in. It wasn't big, but it was stable enough. Three people could fit in. They could easily load Caroline in and shuttle it back and forth until they were all on the opposite side of the tide pool. Simple. Safe. Efficient.

And yet, he rubbed at the ache in his chest.

Ethan and Tate gave the raft a shove. Luke plucked an oar off the bottom and paddled his way across. Ethan held onto the rope just in case. Probably to keep him from getting swept up in a current and scuttled out to the bay.

"You got it, Luke?" Tate moved closer to the shore.

"This is not as easy as it looks," Luke grunted, jabbing his paddle into the dark, coarse sand.

Jude kind of hated that Luke had arrived already. He really didn't want to go back in there and see the way she wouldn't meet his eyes. Didn't want to watch while her brothers rescued her and she got to lock herself back behind that wall of hers.

It had been beautiful watching her let her guard down. He'd relished the freedom in letting her see the real him. Getting lost in her kiss. But the heroic thing to do now? Put her needs first. Shelve his own.

"Ready?" Jude grabbed the rope Luke tossed him. "Or I can send this raft back over and get more help."

"No, I think we got it."

They tied off the rope to a heavy piece of driftwood. Luke made sure the oar was secure inside the raft, and they headed up to the yurt. Pushed inside.

"Look who I found," Jude said, forcing a lightness into his voice that he did not at all feel.

Caroline looked up from where she sat on the bottom bunk. Shadows crossed her face in the dim light.

"Hey." Her mouth formed a tired smile. "You're here."

Luke, still in motion, crouched beside her. "You didn't think we'd leave you out here all night, stranded, did you?"

A small, strained laugh slipped from her mouth. "Well, we kind of deserved it. I shouldn't have gone running out here alone."

"I don't know about that." Luke squeezed her shoulder. "Let us help you into the raft."

Caroline's expression sobered. "I'm really okay to walk."

"You are absolutely not," Jude said. "That is not up for debate."

She frowned. Instantly, he hated the sharpness in his tone. But he couldn't soften it either. He couldn't fake it.

Luke's curious gaze pinged between the two of them. "So . . . I've got a splint here, if you'll allow me."

"No, no, no." She waved him off with her hand. "That is not necessary."

"But it is. I can't believe you're trying to get out of wearing one of these cool splints."

"You are not going to put that vacuum splint on me, Luke McGuire."

"Wow." Luke shook his head. "You are so bossy. How about the Aircast?" He held up the two stirrup-shaped pieces of plastic with the air-filled padding and Velcro. "Easy peasy. Won't feel a thing."

She huffed out an exasperated breath. "All right, fine." She nodded, her fingers twisted in the fabric of her T-shirt.

"This might hurt a little." Jude crouched down and gently loosened her shoe.

"I can handle it."

Right.

He worked in silence, gingerly pulling the shoe off while Luke braced the ankle with the splint and secured the Velcro. She wrinkled her nose but didn't make a sound.

Then they straightened. Luke shouldered the splint bag and then they lifted her from the bed.

Caroline dipped her chin and stared at the floor. Oh, how he wished she'd lean into him, even now. Even after calling what they had shared a mistake.

But she did loop her arm around his waist, though she leaned mostly into Luke as they managed to guide her while she hopped on her uninjured leg toward the door.

Jude hesitated. "Any parting words for the yurt?"

"Talk to you never," she said.

Jude and Luke laughed.

"All right. Let's do this," Caroline said. "Close the door."

They made their way across the gravel down the embankment. Ethan and Tate cheered and clapped from the other side. It wasn't easy, and the raft wiggled and swayed as they settled her in. Luke stayed at the bow with a steadying hand.

"You good?"

"Yeah." Jude climbed in. "I think we can all fit."

Luke handed him the oar and untied the rope, gave the raft a hefty shove. It splashed through the water.

"Luke, you're going to get soaked," Caroline said.

"It's all right. Beats having to ferry people back and forth across."

"Let's go," Jude said.

Luke waded in, the water sloshing around his legs, then he climbed in and guided the raft slowly. When they got close, Jude threw the other oar to Ethan, and he and Tate worked to tow them the rest of the way in. The smell of mud and salt tinged his nostrils.

When they reached the shore, they all worked together to

maneuver Caroline out of the raft. Jude stayed in. He was the last one out, his chest twisting every time she winced or gritted her teeth.

She probably didn't want to show her brothers how much it hurt. Because that's who she was—brave, stubborn, refusing to be a burden even when she clearly needed someone. Maybe especially when she needed someone.

Ethan and Tate sprang into action, hauling the raft up onto the shore. Jude stepped back while Luke kept his arm around Caroline.

He shouldn't care that she wasn't really looking at him. Shouldn't let the ache of her hasty retreat unravel him. But the hurt was there, gnawing at the edges of everything.

"Jude," Tate said, clapping him on the shoulder. "Thanks for getting this rescue started."

He nodded. "No problem. Glad you guys got here when you did."

Ethan gave him a long look. "We'll get her to the truck. You good to follow in Mom's car?"

"Yeah," Jude said, pulling the car keys from his pocket. Caroline still didn't look at him. "See you back at the resort."

As the brothers helped her get to the trailhead, Jude followed behind them.

He didn't regret that kiss. Didn't regret the way he'd held her or the way her lips had trembled against his. But man, he could not stand that she'd panicked. Pushed him away.

He let out a slow, ragged breath.

Whatever it took, he'd make sure she got better. That was what mattered. He could deal with the wreckage inside himself later.

Why did she have to be the one to get injured? She should have just done something safer, smarter, quicker—gone for a walk or hopped on a treadmill. But no. She had to go for a complicated trail run, and now she was injured. She wouldn't be able to do her job and . . .

Ugh, that kiss.

She shifted in her seat in the back of the Suburban as Tate pulled into the gravel lot behind the resort and parked near the back door. Her ankle throbbed worse than before—the swelling had probably increased. Every bump in the road had made her wince. Exhausted, cold, and still fighting the sting of tears she refused to let fall, she hugged her arms around herself.

Ethan hopped out of the passenger seat, turned, and opened her door.

"I can walk," she said.

"Not unless you've developed some magical healing powers in the last ten minutes," Ethan replied, looping an arm under hers. "Let us help you."

"There's an elevator in my building, you know," Caroline said. "I don't need to stay here, and you guys don't need to babysit me."

Luke carried the bag of splints around the Suburban toward the shed. He paused mid-step.

"Sure. And who's going to bring you food? Or help you get to the bathroom at three in the morning when your ankle feels like it's on fire?"

"I can crawl."

Tate grinned. "That's the spirit."

"You're not staying alone," Ethan said. His tone left no room for argument. "We have an empty guest room on the first floor. You'll have a comfortable bed, access to food, and I'm not sure who's going to help you with the bathroom part, but your overly annoying and attentive brothers will be here first thing tomorrow."

"Not me. After work," Tate added.

"Well, Luke and I will check on you then."

Caroline opened her mouth to protest, but her attention shifted as she noticed Jude sitting in her mom's SUV in a nearby spot. He'd cut the engine, but he hadn't gotten out. He just sat in the driver's seat.

What was he doing? Texting? Taking a call? Giving himself a pep talk? Thinking about that kiss?

Her stomach sank. She turned away and let Ethan and Tate help her toward the back door while Luke jogged ahead to open it. Everything in her body protested, but she couldn't decide what hurt worse—her swollen ankle or the memory of Jude's face. Steady, calm, totally present. Exactly what she wanted, hoped for.

Until she kissed him. Until she panicked.

The kiss was epic—he was right—but it had been a mistake, right? She had a job to do, a professional reputation to maintain. There were so many doubts and fears swamping her. She couldn't let a romantic relationship cloud her judgment. Because she'd been worried about her job all along.

Her brothers helped her into the resort and down the short hallway. Inside the guest room, Ethan helped her ease down onto the edge of the bed, then fluffed her pillows.

"You good for a few minutes? I'll go get you some water. Need a snack?"

"Sure," she murmured. "Whatever you can find."

"I'll get some crutches. Need anything from your place? Toothbrush? Face wash? Jammies?" Tate asked.

"You don't have to do all that, Tate."

"I don't have to, but I want to." He nodded toward Luke. "Luke will stay here with you."

Luke gave a little shrug and moved to stand near the window. After Tate and Ethan headed out, the room got quiet. Too quiet. Caroline shivered.

Luke didn't move. He just stood there, watching her.

"So, you and Jude. What's going on there?"

"Nothing."

He raised a brow. "There's enough tension between you two to snap a fishing line."

She turned and punched a pillow.

He opened the closet door, grabbed a couple more pillows, and crossed the room. "Here. Let's elevate that ankle." He gently propped them under her foot.

It wasn't judgmental, just observant.

"Did he say something to you that he shouldn't have?"

"What?" She winced, then scooted back and leaned her head against the pillows. "Oh, this is heaven. No, he didn't say anything he shouldn't."

Luke tilted his head. "Are you sure? Because if he did, I'd be glad to have a word."

"He didn't." She closed her eyes. "It wasn't him."

"Then what happened?"

Silence stretched between them. She opened her eyes, wishing the feathery-soft bed would swallow her up. Luke just stood there, patiently waiting.

That was the problem with her brothers—when they wanted answers, they would wait you out.

She finally exhaled. "I kissed him."

"You kissed him?"

"Mm-hmm."

"And he didn't handle that well?"

Heat climbed her neck. "He handled it quite well, actually. It was me. I'm the problem. I kissed him . . ." She looked away. "And then I freaked out. Told him it was a mistake."

"Ouch." Luke crossed his arms. "That's not cool."

"No kidding." She scrubbed a hand down her face. "I didn't mean to—I mean, I meant to kiss him. I just didn't mean to hurt him."

Luke bent down so he was at eye level. His expression softened.

"I know you don't like to mess up, Care Bear. You take it super personally. But relationships are messy, and sometimes—"

"Don't." She looked away.

"I'm serious. You're really hard on yourself. So sometimes you're hard on others too." He paused. "Just let it happen."

"No. It's not that easy."

"You're right. It's not. But I don't think Jude's the flaky performer that he wants us all to think he is."

"How do you know?"

"I don't. It's just a hunch. But he did hike out into the woods without a second thought because he thought something could've happened to you. He sat with you. He helped make sure you got home safely."

Tears pricked the corners of her eyes again. "I don't want to need him."

"I know. Maybe you need each other. But you're both just really good at hiding it."

She blew out a shaky breath and swiped at the moisture on her cheeks. "He's probably furious."

"Furious? I don't know. Hurt? Yeah, probably." Luke reached out and squeezed her arm. "You're just scared. Scared to mess up. Scared to let people down. Those are normal feelings, but . . ."

"What if he's exactly what I need?" Her voice caught in her throat. "Or what if he's . . . the wrong thing? Wrong place, wrong time, wrong guy, wrong everything?"

Luke's gaze held hers. "Hmm. I have my doubts."

"Why do you always have to be the one to give me the tough love?"

"Because Ethan and Tate are too nice and Mom's asleep," he said, winking. He tugged on her hair.

She tried to swat him, but he dodged her hand. "I don't like it when you're right."

"Yeah. What else is new?" He walked toward the door and

glanced back. "Get some rest, and tomorrow maybe work up the courage to talk to him. He's less than a football field away at the cabin."

"Yeah, don't remind me." She tugged the blanket up to her chin, still in her workout clothes. If Tate got back with her pajamas, she'd change.

Her ankle hurt, but her pride hurt more.

What if Luke was right? What if something precious had already slipped through her fingers?

Fifteen

DEW CLINGING TO THE GRASS DAMPENED HIS sneakers as he crossed the lawn toward the resort. Finally, a gorgeous day. No imminent threats of storms, not a cloud in the pale-blue sky. Ethan had texted him and told him to meet at the resort's front desk at 8:00 a.m. sharp. They'd pick up Ben and Rachel and be on their way to finish filming the commercial. Not a bad way to spend a Saturday.

He opened the back door, and the smell of fresh coffee and maple syrup greeted him. His stomach growled. Mrs. McGuire came out of the kitchen, spatula in hand.

"Good morning, Jude." She tipped her head to the side. "Why don't you join us? I have plenty of breakfast."

He hesitated, clutching the strap on his backpack. "I thought breakfast was included in my stay on Sundays only?"

She smiled warmly. "You rescued my girl last night, so I feel like pancakes are the least I can do to thank you."

"It was nothing."

"Oh, I think it was something. Come on in. Sadie and Brody

have already made a dent in the first batch, but I've got plenty more."

He followed the buttery scent into the kitchen. Morning sunlight streamed through the wide windows, catching the glass jars of wildflowers lined up along the sill. Sadie and Brody sat on one side of the table, debating who had eaten the biggest pancake. Mrs. McGuire flipped another pancake from the griddle on top of the oven.

"Would you like some coffee?"

"Please."

"Kids, you've met Jude, right?"

They nodded eagerly. "Good morning!"

"Morning," he said with a small smile.

The cozy, lived-in atmosphere of the family kitchen enveloped him, soothing the tightness in his chest. Between the kids chatting and Mrs. McGuire making breakfast, it kind of reminded him of how things used to feel with his own family before life got complicated.

"Thanks again for letting me crash breakfast," he said.

She waved him off. "You are most welcome."

He crossed to the pot on the counter and filled a mug. Steam curled up, warm and inviting.

"There's plenty of creamer in the fridge."

"I'll drink it black, thanks."

Brody shoveled a forkful of pancake into his mouth. "Did you help rescue somebody last night?"

"It was Aunt Caroline," Sadie said quickly. "I heard my mom talking about it."

"He was a real hero, rescuing our girl from a grizzly." Mrs. McGuire brought a bowl of blueberries to the table.

Jude pulled out a chair, sat down, then set his coffee on the table with a soft clink. He rubbed the back of his neck, feeling heat creep up the sides of his face.

"I don't know about that. I think she would have managed."

"My dad said her ankle's broken." Brody reached for his glass of milk. "Is it?"

"I'm not sure. She'll probably need an X-ray," Jude said.

Mrs. McGuire brought over a plate and some silverware wrapped in a napkin, along with butter and syrup.

"Next stack of pancakes coming right up. Super important question: chocolate chips or no chocolate chips?"

"Chocolate chips!" Brody and Sadie chimed in together.

Mrs. McGuire gave them a playful frown. "Let our guest choose, please."

Jude chuckled. "Chocolate chips, please. Sounds like that's the popular choice."

She patted his shoulder. "Caroline doesn't like to make mistakes. She thinks she has to be perfect. Her inner critic is likely quite brutal."

Jude shook his head. "Maybe that's why she doesn't want anyone seeing that she's hurting. Even last night she kept trying to convince her brother she could walk it off. Did not want to admit she needed help."

"I've heard her say bad words a couple times, but she doesn't cry," Brody said, solemnly.

Mrs. McGuire ruffled Brody's hair. "Sounds about right."

Jude leaned back in his chair and reached for his coffee again, cradling it in his hands.

"Honestly, I feel like she's used to doing everything herself, and maybe she doesn't know how to let people help. And she's worried about what people here think of her. She doesn't want to admit it to anyone, but she's super stressed about replacing Dr. Wallace."

The words hadn't come out harsh. At least, he hadn't meant them to. Really, he admired her. She had a lot of courage coming back to her hometown. More than he'd had when things fell apart for him. He sure didn't get a lot of second chances in his hometown. Nobody would even let him coach or teach. At least, not now.

A small noise at the doorway made him turn. Crutches thudded against the wood floor.

Caroline.

Her hair was shoved into a messy ponytail, and she wore a pair of soft shorts and a hoodie. Her skin was pale and her eyes rimmed with exhaustion. Or was that anger?

"Wow, that's a nice conversation to walk into," she said, glaring. "Do you always talk about me like this behind my back?"

Jude glanced at Mrs. McGuire, who looked stricken. Empathy flashed in her eyes. He started to rise, but Caroline's glare froze him in place.

"Caroline, don't—"

She swung forward on her crutches, moving closer. Her face pinched in pain, but her frigid gaze kept him seated. "You don't get to sit here and talk about how broken I am."

His gut twisted. He raised a hand slightly in defense. "That is not what I said. We're worried that your fear of making mistakes is stressing you out."

"That's because when I mess up, people get hurt. And they never forget it and seem to enjoy reminding me of my shortcomings."

Mrs. McGuire put her hand gently on Caroline's arm. "Honey, Jude wasn't saying—"

"No, you're not going to defend him." Caroline shrugged her off. "Thanks for playing hero, but I'll take it from here."

Brody and Sadie both stared, forks suspended midair. The air felt thick enough to choke on.

Jude gritted his teeth. Something sharp clawed at his insides, but he forced himself to stay calm. Yeah, okay. She was hurting and more than a little angry. No matter how badly he wished he could fix this, lashing out would only make it worse.

He nodded stiffly. "Got it."

Mrs. McGuire sighed before returning to the stove. She picked up the platter and busied herself flipping more pancakes. Jude sat there, heart pounding, watching Caroline hover awkwardly at the doorway.

She faltered, nearly stumbling. Instinct shoved him halfway out of his chair to go to her, but she righted herself before he reached her. She threw him a warning glare over her shoulder, then disappeared around the corner.

For a long moment, the only sound was the kids' forks scraping against their plates.

Sadie finally whispered, "Oh, she is big mad."

Jude scrubbed his hand down his face, then reclaimed his seat. He'd survived worse. He could take her anger. What he couldn't take was the way it cracked open something deeper inside him. He really wanted to be the person she let in.

Mrs. McGuire brought him more pancakes and a side of three slices of bacon.

"Give her time," she said. "When she is being particularly hard on herself, she gets extra sensitive."

He nodded, swallowing the hard lump in his throat. "Yeah," he said. "I noticed." Not that he had much hope he'd be able to help. She wasn't real receptive to his input.

He tucked into his breakfast, mechanically cutting into the pancakes. He had to get ready to film this commercial. Had to focus, give her all the space she clearly wanted. He forced a grin for Sadie and Brody's sake, laughing at something Brody said about wanting to build a pancake tower taller than Sadie.

Caroline might have called last night a mistake, and this morning's awkward interaction would probably only underscore that perspective, but one thing was for sure—he couldn't possibly forget that kiss.

Maybe it wasn't broken.

Maybe her ankle was just severely sprained. A girl could hope, right?

Caroline scooted back on the exam table, her injured foot throbbing in protest as she bumped it on the end of the table. The paper crinkled under her body, and the scent of antibacterial cleaning wipes enveloped her. How many times had she sat in this very clinic as a kid, clutching a sprained wrist or a deep cut or battling a virus and waiting for Dr. Wallace to patch her up or help her get well? Back then she'd felt invincible, but now she just felt exposed. And Jude's conversation with her mother had just added another layer of heartache.

She gnawed on her thumbnail and scanned the infographic taped to the back of the door. Domestic-violence hotline. How to tell if you are having an allergic reaction. Tips on dealing with insect bites.

The door opened and Dr. Wallace stepped in, wearing a gray polo shirt, black slacks, and a white lab coat. His warm smile did little to ease her anxiety.

"Well, well, if it isn't my favorite PA," he said, wheeling the stool closer before sitting down. "We've already had a good look. Waiting on the X-rays to confirm. How're you holding up?"

She moved her crutches out of the way and leaned them against the wall. "I feel foolish for tripping. And I can't believe I had to hide out in a yurt and wait for my brothers to rescue me."

She left out the part about Jude's orchestrating the rescue efforts. She didn't want to talk about it, didn't want to think about it, really. She offered a weak smile.

A knock sounded at the door, and Dr. Wallace turned. "Come on in."

JR, the X-ray tech, stepped inside, handing over the films, still warm from development. "Thanks, JR." Dr. Wallace took the X-rays.

"You're welcome." JR frowned. "Hey, Caroline. Sorry to hear about your injury."

"Thanks. Me too."

He closed the door quietly, and Dr. Wallace clipped the films into the lightboard. He glanced over at her. "Well, tell me what you see."

She scooted closer and scanned both images, comparing the left to the right. "Tib, fib. Both look normal and intact. That's good, right?"

"Yeah, nobody wants a fractured tibia or fibula. What else do you see?"

She surveyed all the tiny bones in her feet, zeroed in on the outside of her right foot—and groaned. Pressing her hands to her face, she slumped back.

He clicked the light off and sat back down on the stool. "Yeah, you saw it then. I hate to confirm the bad news, kiddo. That's a Jones fracture, fifth metatarsal. Common, but as you know, a little stubborn when it comes to healing."

She blew out a long breath. "What's your recommended treatment plan?"

"Oh, you know, walking boot, crutches as needed. Six to eight weeks of healing time." His expression softened. "No running. And no Redemption Ridge race. I know you were training for that."

She nodded, biting the inside of her cheek. She would not cry, not here, not now.

"I know. Tough blow," he said. "But like I used to tell you back in high school—you're more than your race times, Caroline. You're strong-willed and smart and capable. You'll heal. And maybe you'll find another race to run. There will be future opportunities, but . . ."

It was a good speech, a kind one. She forced a wobbly smile. "Thank you, Dr. Wallace."

"Of course. And if you need to take some time off, don't push."

"I'll be back after lunch," she said. "I need to work." It wasn't what she should have said, but she needed to feel useful. Especially since her heart felt like it was stitched together with dental floss.

"Just half a day," he said. "But if you overdo it, I will pull you off the schedule myself. Understood?"

"Understood."

"Valerie will be in with a walking boot in just a minute."

"No."

"I know," he said, sliding the X-rays into an envelope. "But an Aircast won't do the trick. You need to protect those bones so they can heal."

"I know. You're right."

He left the room. Moments later, Valerie came in, a big smile on her face. She held up two boots. "Gray or black?"

"Um, you don't have a pink one?" Caroline asked, half joking.

Valerie chuckled. "I'm afraid not, sweetie."

"Gray, I guess."

"All right, you know the drill." She slid Caroline's foot into the walking boot and dragged the Velcro into place, the scratchy noise harsh in the quiet room.

"This is not going to go well with my sundresses."

"Well, it'll look cute with leggings. Got any skinny jeans in your closet?"

"Yeah, probably."

"All right, this visit's on the house."

"Thanks."

"Are you working this afternoon, or . . . ?"

Caroline nodded and reached for her crutches. "Yep. I'll be back after lunch. Just need to go home, put on something a little more professional, and get something to eat."

"All right. See you soon. Sorry this happened to you. You'll be boot-free in no time, I know it."

"Eh, hope so."

Valerie left the door open. Caroline worked her way into the hall and then through the doors into the waiting room. She just wanted to get out, get in the car, breathe for a second, and pull herself together.

The low murmur of conversation trailed after her as she crutched toward the door. A voice, she didn't know whose, rose above the rest.

"Oh, poor thing, not even back a month and already falling apart."

Laughter, muffled but unmistakable, followed.

"Always a go-getter, that one. Maybe this will get us in to see Dr. Wallace faster if she's sidelined."

Her face burned hot and hotter. She opened her mouth to protest but stopped herself. Gritting her teeth, she kept her chin up and crutched toward the exit.

Outside, the sun felt too bright. She squinted.

Megan, her sister, gave her beat-up Jeep a gentle beep with the horn and eased closer to the door. Caroline made it down the ramp, her arms already tired from using the crutches. She balanced on her healthy leg, yanked the door open, collapsed into the passenger seat, and tossed her crutches into the back seat.

"Whoa, Care Bear," Megan said, concern flashing in her eyes. "Rough morning?"

She tried to answer but the words tangled in her tight throat. Then the tears came hot and fast.

"Oh no." Megan handed her a water bottle. "It's okay. You're allowed to have a meltdown."

Caroline shook her head, swiped at her cheeks with the back of her hand, and took the water. "I hate this. I'm such a failure. Everyone was right about me."

"What? Who's everyone? Gossipy old geezers at the diner?" Megan shook her head and dug through her purse until she came up with a tiny packet of Kleenex. "Forget what people say. You're doing fine."

"I'm not." Caroline took a small sip of the water. "I didn't want to come back here, Meg. I'm sure you heard. Jude's telling everybody. But this job was all I had and now I'm broken, literally."

Megan handed her the tissues. "I had heard that maybe this wasn't your first choice. And that's okay. You're not broken, sweetie. You're human. And mistakes are just part of the process. You've always had it together, even when the rest of us were falling apart. Maybe it's time to let yourself be messy for once."

Caroline barked out a laugh that sounded more like a sob. "Yeah, well, Redemption doesn't exactly roll out the welcome mat for messes."

"Not true," Megan said. "I've come home lots of times and you all have welcomed me."

"Yeah, true."

"You're allowed to be hurt," Megan said. "You're allowed to be mad. And none of us are offended if you hate that you feel stuck here. But don't let some idiot's comments or one broken bone tell you who you are."

Caroline dabbed at her face with the tissues, sniffling.

"And for the record," Megan said, "I think you're awesome. For coming back here and being willing to practice medicine and follow after Dr. Wallace. This is a tough, tough place to replace a hero."

"Yeah, no kidding."

They sat for a minute, then Megan shifted into gear and pulled away from the clinic. Caroline stared out the window as familiar parts of the small town she'd tried to outrun went past.

She didn't have much time. She glanced at the clock on Megan's dashboard. She'd have to get ready to see patients, somehow hobble around the clinic, and pretend she didn't care if half the town thought she was a walking disaster.

"You sure you don't want me to just drive you home and let you hide under a blanket for the rest of the day?"

She shook her head. "I need to work. I need to feel like I'm good at something."

"You're good at a lot of things," Megan said, clicking on her blinker. "Especially carrying the weight of the world on your shoulders. Why don't you give yourself a break?"

Caroline didn't answer, just watched as the café, the hardware store, and then the building where she lived came into view. Megan pulled up in front of Redemption Outfitters. Two guys in splattered clothes were coming through the propped-open doors.

Caroline hesitated. She did not want to crutch all the way up to her apartment. Mostly, she didn't want to be alone.

"Want me to help you get in the elevator?"

"No, I got it."

Some small stupid part of her hoped that maybe, just maybe, Jude would be waiting there, apologizing, telling her that he hadn't meant his words the way they'd sounded, that he hadn't meant to betray her confidence. Maybe he'd be standing there with that familiar smile on his face, holding a bouquet of wildflowers.

But the street was empty, except for a stray cat darting across the sidewalk.

Of course he wasn't here. He was off shooting his stupid commercial, living his big stupid life without her.

Caroline slid out of the Jeep, grabbed the crutches, every movement aching with more than just physical pain.

"See you later," Megan said.

Caroline nodded. "Yeah, thanks for the ride."

Megan gave a small wave and then pulled away.

Caroline turned and made her way toward the open door. The walking boot was heavy and sweaty and clumsy on her injured foot. She stepped inside the clothing store, the smell of paint greeting her. The elevator was tucked away in the back near the restrooms. She offered a tight smile to the painting crew and slowly crutched her way across the concrete floor. One step at a time, that was all she could do, even if her heart ached with every single one.

Sixteen

THE HELICOPTER BLADES WHIPPED THE DUST into a frenzy as Jude ducked and jogged away from the chopper. Ethan had brought him back to the resort and the landing pad after a ten-hour day of shooting the commercial. His sneakers hit the asphalt hard, the fatigue settling bone deep as the adrenaline wore off. It had gone better than he could have hoped. He'd climbed, sprinted, endured, pretended to sip about a bazillion cups of coffee around a fire holding a vintage mug. His muscles screamed, he was dead tired, but finally, they'd finished. He'd followed through, and Ben and Rachel had seemed super stoked about the footage. He tugged off his ball cap, compliments of the sponsor, and wiped his face with his hand.

While he waited for Rachel and Ben to get out of the chopper and Ethan to unload his stuff from the rack, he checked his phone. No texts. Two missed calls though—and a voicemail from Braxton. He took a few steps away from the chopper, pressed his phone to his ear, and played back the message.

"Hey, Jude, call me back as soon as you get this. It's about the reinstatement. It's tough, man. Call me as soon as you can."

The hair on the back of his neck prickled. He stabbed the button to call, but it went straight to voicemail.

"Hey, Braxton, it's me. Just got finished shooting a commercial. All good on my end. Call or text when you can."

He pulled the phone from his ear and glared at it. Another notification popped up—an email from the biathlon committee, forwarded from Braxton. His heart hammered.

> Your recent blood work has returned positive for banned substances (methadone). As a result, your suspension will remain in place indefinitely.

What? Spots peppered his vision, and the words blurred. Banned substances? Impossible. He hadn't touched a thing. Other than the antibiotics for his leg injury and that Tylenol. Wait. Fragments of a memory hit him—Caroline's hands steady as she jabbed the EpiPen into his uninjured thigh. Her face tightened with worry. The tablets she'd given him after his reaction to the salmon. What were they?

Dread spread through him. Surely she wouldn't have given him something illegal. Not on purpose, anyway.

He grabbed his pack, thanked Rachel, Ben, and Ethan, then faked his way through a perfunctory conversation. Then he strode toward the resort. He pushed through the back door, adrenaline surging through his veins.

"Well, hey there, Jude. How'd it go?" Mrs. McGuire glanced at him over the rim of her reading glasses.

"Great." He pasted on a smile.

She nodded. "Glad to hear it."

"Hey, could I borrow your car again? I want to go over and check on Caroline. I feel bad about how things were left this morning."

Empathy flashed in her eyes. "Of course."

She tossed him the keys. He plucked them out of the air. "Thanks. I'll be back as soon as I can."

"Tell her we'll be by with dinner shortly."

"Yes, ma'am. Will do."

He got caught behind a pack of motorcycles on the road back to town and gripped the steering wheel, the vanilla-scented air freshener hanging from the mirror making his stomach churn. How could she have done this? Didn't she think before she gave him those drugs? It would have taken a two-minute internet search to figure out that a biathlete couldn't ingest certain medications. And after all he'd been through, he'd told her the story.

An old pop song came on the radio, dragging him back to his high school days when he'd confessed to his buddy that he didn't think he could hang with the competition, that he didn't see himself getting past the qualifying round to get to the junior world championships. He'd stepped way outside of his comfort zone and expressed that he didn't think he belonged with these guys—so much so that he'd been throwing up for a day and a half. He'd felt weak and dehydrated.

He'd felt like they'd bonded, but his teammate had gone to dinner and told the whole story to a table full of athletes. They'd all stared at him like he'd brought a contagious disease to the dining hall. That was the last time he'd confessed anything to a teammate.

He parked on the street in front of the Redemption Outfitters building, grabbed the keys, slammed the door, and took the steps two at a time. Thankfully, the outside door wasn't locked. He stepped into the hallway, banged on Caroline's door. He heard the muffled *thump, thump, thump* of crutches. Pause, and then the door opened.

Caroline stood there, her hair spilling down her shoulders, damp, probably from a shower. She had on lavender scrub pants. She was barefoot, and she wore a T-shirt advertising a ski resort in Colorado, one he'd been to many times. She wore a bulky gray walking boot. Her cheeks were flushed, eyes heavy with exhaustion.

"Jude," her voice lifted, almost hopeful. Had she been waiting for him?

"Can I come in?"

"Um, sure." She scooted backward, the rubber tips on her crutches squeaking against the luxury vinyl tile. She tapped the door shut with the end of her crutch.

"I just got the results of my blood work." His voice shook. His fingers trembled, his anger barely contained. "You want to explain why there's a banned substance in my system?"

All the color drained from her face. "Wait, what?"

"You heard me. The medication you prescribed after that salmon thing—didn't you check to see if it was appropriate and permissible for competitive athletes?"

"I . . ." She blinked, her Adam's apple bobbing as she swallowed. "Yes, of course. I double-checked before I gave you anything, except for the EpiPen because I was worried you would go into anaphylaxis."

"I had to get tested in order to clear my name, and in fact, the testing came back saying I had controlled substances in my system. Specifically something called methadone, and you're the only one who has given me the medication that I've taken. So what did you give me?"

"I gave you an H1 blocker and an H2 blocker. Think of them as two cousins working together to reduce the inflammation in your system."

"These blockers." He fought to keep his voice even. "Do they contain methadone?"

She hesitated. "I-I don't think so. They're basically Benadryl and Tagamet, which are over-the-counter medications. So I don't understand. How could they be banned substances?"

"I have no idea, but they were flagged on my blood test."

"But the medications were taken for therapeutic use. Not for doping," Caroline said. "It was never my goal to enhance your performance. My objective was to reduce inflammation and treat your symptoms."

"And in the process, you destroyed my one and only chance to get back to competing." He clenched his fists at his sides. "You didn't even think. You just—"

"Oh, don't you dare." Her eyes flashed as she took a step toward him. "I did what any responsible medical professional would do. Since you've been in Redemption, I have treated your injuries and your symptoms with utmost care. Potentially, I saved your life."

"Why didn't you just check the list? Why didn't you tell me? Report it or something." His voice cracked. "Instead, you just—what—plowed ahead? Didn't think about how your actions would implicate me?"

"I documented everything. I can submit a letter to the committee explaining the dosage, the situation, your symptoms, my limited options for treating you. Isn't it true that false positives happen? Maybe a substance in one of those medications mimics a banned substance. Surely if I provide the necessary documentation, the ruling body will take a second look."

"No," he said, shaking his head. "They won't. They don't care about your explanations. They just see black and white. Positive test, already suspended athlete, permanent suspension."

Her eyes grew wide. "It can't be permanent. That's not right. I will fix this."

"You can't," Jude shouted.

She flinched. "I know what this looks like," she said, quieter now. "But you have to believe me, I would never do anything to hurt you."

He shoved his hand through his hair. "Too late, you already did."

She gasped. Her face crumpled for a split second, but then she pulled herself together, tipped her chin up. "I made a judgment call. One that, as I have said, potentially saved your life. It stinks that it had consequences. But I'm not going to apologize for doing my job."

He stared at her. His jaw drifted down. Mouth ran dry. Something cleaved wide open inside him. He'd trusted her. He'd let her get close. He'd let himself hope.

He moved toward the door.

"I can't believe this. How could you not know that your treatment would impact my blood test?" he said, whirling around to face her again. "This is medical malpractice."

"Jude." Her eyes welled with tears. "Are you even paying attention? Did you hear anything I just said? Saving you from a severe allergic reaction is far more important than your stupid race."

Unbelievable. His blood turned to molten lava. But he wasn't going to let her manipulate him. He couldn't afford to. "You're just like everybody else," he said. "You smile, you listen, you kiss me, you pretend to be empathetic. You made me think I mattered, and then the second you got a chance, you wrecked me."

Her expression hardened. "Wow, you are really emotional and unhinged right now. Frankly, I'm glad you ran away from me, because if this is who you truly are, I don't want any part of it."

He shook his head. "Good to know." He paused, his hand on the doorknob. "Thanks for nothing." He slammed the door behind him.

He raced down the stairs and climbed back into Mrs. McGuire's SUV. Redemption had been a mistake. All of it. He never should have let Braxton talk him into this. Fresh start? Whatever. He wasn't a guy who got second chances or happy endings.

He was the guy who got accused of cheating, no matter how often he tried to do the right thing. Or rooted for the underdog. Burned every single time, and he wasn't going to stick around and give Caroline or anyone else another shot at finishing him off.

Caroline stood at the living-room window, staring down at the street. Jude hopped in her mother's car, slammed the door, and then screeched away from the curb. She barely registered the way her foot throbbed inside the boot or how the crutches rubbed against the skin under her arms. Devastation bloomed in her chest. Tears trickled down her cheeks. Then a sob ripped free. Broken. Raw.

"I didn't mean to hurt you," she whispered into the empty room.

Turning away from the window, Caroline hobbled over to the leather couch and flopped down in the middle. She propped her boot up on the coffee table and leaned back, staring at the ceiling. Another wave of frustration crashed over her.

She hadn't knowingly treated him with a banned substance. She *had* done everything right, hadn't she? She'd followed the protocol. Chosen the safest, most immediate treatment. She'd been so proud of herself for identifying a bizarre reaction to fish. There hadn't been time to agonize over banned substances or committee decisions. She'd acted in good faith to treat him, and yet somehow that wasn't enough.

Evidently, swooping in when she'd only been in town for a day, making sure he got the treatment he needed when he'd fallen and impaled himself didn't mean anything to him now. This whole mess amplified what she'd always feared: that one mistake, even one made with the best of intentions, meant she wasn't good enough. That she wasn't worthy of forgiveness. And now Jude had accused her of making a poor decision with a devastating impact. Caroline McGuire, another name on his long list of people who'd let him down.

She squeezed her eyes shut, but the words he'd flung at her wouldn't go away. *You're just like everybody else. You wrecked me. Didn't think about how your actions would implicate me.* Each word was a blade slicing through the shaky progress she'd made since she'd moved home. Every word yanked her back to the insecurities, the accusations she tried to outrun. *Too high-strung. Too afraid of failure. Too worried about being perfect.*

The same feedback she'd heard most of her life mingled with the conversation she'd witnessed between her mother and Jude in the kitchen. Hot tears streamed down her face. Ugh. Good thing she was alone because she hated crying like this. The messy, ugly, loud sobbing. There was no stopping this flood of emotion.

She'd tried so hard. She'd fought to resist him. To prove she could ignore a handsome distraction like Jude. Against her better judgment, she'd trusted him with her time, her heart. That kiss. As it turned out, she was right. It had been a mistake. But this time he'd refused to listen when she tried to defend herself. Nothing she had said registered. It was almost like he'd been waiting for her to let him down, to fail him.

How could he?

The way he'd looked at her after the grizzly scare, the tenderness in his voice when he'd kissed her, the way his hands had steadied her when she limped. He'd stayed with her. She'd been dumb enough to think that she'd finally found someone who saw her, cared about the real her. But tonight confirmed that she'd been a fool. People saw what they wanted to see. And to Jude, when it really counted, she was just another enemy out to take him down.

Why did this hurt so much? How had she let him in without even realizing how much she cared about him until it was too late—and now he'd left? He'd probably have his bags packed before she fell asleep. He'd leave again, out of her life without so much as a second thought. Oh, she'd been a fool. She swiped at her tears. Part of her wanted to run after him and make him listen. Good thing she wasn't particularly mobile. Not that it would have any impact at all. He didn't trust her. He didn't believe she was good.

A knock startled her and the door eased open. Megan stepped inside holding a bag of food. "Hey, are you all right?"

Caroline shook her head.

"Aw. Care Bear, don't cry."

Megan set the food on the console table nearby and then crossed the room and sank down beside Caroline, pulling her into a hug. It wasn't much. It wasn't perfect, but somehow it brought the tears again.

"I tried to do the right thing," she sobbed into her little sister's shoulder. "I tried, Meg."

"I know." Meg rubbed her back. "This stinks, doesn't it?"

"He thinks I'm just like everybody else who's out to get him. How can I prove to him he's wrong?"

Megan leaned back, looked her in the eyes, and gripped her shoulders tightly. "You don't have to prove anything, because you're not out to get him. He's a messed-up dude, and he's hurting, and so he's lashing out. This is not your fault."

"How do you know he's messed up?" Caroline said, using the sleeve of her T-shirt to wipe away even more tears. "You don't know what it's like to be in this position, feeling like one wrong move proves you're a hot mess."

Megan barked out a laugh. "I'm kind of the queen of that. Not sure if you noticed. I've been screwing up my whole life, sis. There are plenty of days when I feel like I'm a mess and no one should waste their time on me. But you, you came back. It would have been easier to stay away. You're here to help sick people get well and to do the best you can in a small town that faces a lot of obstacles. That's not what bad people do. Come on," Megan said. "Let's eat. He's too blind and too hurt to see that you've helped him. You've done more than anybody else would."

Caroline took a shuddering breath and lifted her head. Her whole heart felt battered and bruised. Her sister was right. She had done the best she could.

"I'll be fine," she said, standing up, grabbing her crutches, and hobbling over to where Megan had spread out dinner on the counter.

Megan gave her a long look. "You will," she said, "but not tonight. Tonight you're allowed to feel wrecked."

Caroline nodded and sat down on the stool. Megan brought her a glass of lemonade, and she pressed the cold glass to her flushed skin, closed her eyes. She would move on from this. She'd heal, somehow.

Seventeen

HE HATED COMING TO VISIT HER HERE. IT HURT so much he almost couldn't stand it.

Jude sat in the front seat of Braxton's Mercedes and stared out the windshield at Mom's care facility. One-level, rambling brick building, whitewashed with cream paint. Indigo-blue planters bookended the wide double doors, varnished in a rich golden oak stain. The emerald lawn was trimmed, the edges perfectly neat. And over the tasteful wrought-iron fence, he spotted a group of people doing some kind of wheelchair yoga.

"Nice place," Braxton said. "Has your mother lived here long?"

"Five years."

"Your family is fortunate that she can stay here long-term."

"Yeah, she's lived here ever since she had the stroke and we realized she needed full-time help." Jude scowled at a bunny hopping across the grass. "Guess my father's long hours toiling away in asset management are good for something."

An awkward silence filled the car. "Anything I can do to make this easier for you?"

"Buy me a ticket to Tahiti?"

Braxton chuckled. "I don't think that's the answer to your problems, friend."

True. Three days had passed since his blowout with Caroline, and he still felt miserable.

Braxton's entertainment system hummed with an incoming call. He checked the screen on the console, then swiped to decline the call.

Jude unclenched his jaw and forced himself to breathe. A memory of his mother—vibrant, laughing, her cheeks flushed—hit him like a punch to the chest. She used to stand in the living room holding a glass of tea mixed with lemonade while Dad made up silly songs and plunked out his ridiculous made-up creations on the grand piano. A piano she had once loved to play herself . . . but probably never would again.

Those had been good times. Real. Solid. She'd been hilarious, grounded, strong. A Vermont farm girl with more grit and determination than most people ever managed in a lifetime. And Dad—he'd gotten lucky. Because he sure hadn't deserved a woman as lovely as Jude's mom.

Braxton cleared his throat. "Look, I know you don't want to talk about this, but we've got to get a plan together."

"A plan for what?" Jude fisted his hands in his lap, knuckles pale.

"The hearing to appeal your suspension is ninety days out."

Jude grunted and tipped his head back against the headrest. How was he supposed to wait another three months?

"So you're going to need a reset, my man. Go hiking. Volunteer. Stay off social media. Don't pay attention to the way the ignorant people are spinning your story."

Wow. He made it sound so simple. "A hike's not going to fix this. Neither is babysitting kids or planting trees or . . ." He trailed off, jaw tightening. "Going back to Alaska. There's no point in training because I'm not going to be able to compete again. This one-hour visit with my"—His voice broke. He swallowed—"my mother will be about all I can handle. And I don't have anything to say to my father."

Braxton reached for his expensive bottle of water in the console. Then he pulled out a piece of paper he'd clearly kept hidden.

"Here. This is a flyer from the YMCA up near Cranebrook. I know you've always enjoyed being out that way. Maybe Eli can help you get connected."

"My old coach?"

"That'd be him."

"I don't want your flyer."

"You haven't even read it yet."

"I told you, I don't want your flyer."

"Jude, c'mon." Braxton sighed, then dragged his hand down his face. "You've got to work with me here. Just take a look at it. Why don't you drop by and visit Eli? If I can't talk any sense into you, maybe he can."

"I don't need a pep talk."

"Yeah? What do you need?"

Jude's throat burned. He turned, staring Braxton down. "To be reinstated. To have Myles admit he cheated. To have the committee acknowledge that someone saved my life. That I wasn't trying to ingest any banned substances."

Braxton's eyebrows lifted. "Huh. So you're willing to admit that she tried to save you."

Jude paused, chest tight. "Yeah. Why?"

"Because I got three text messages from you railing about how she did this all on purpose."

"I was angry."

"You don't say." Braxton's voice held a dry edge, but his gaze wasn't unkind. Just calm.

So annoying.

"Look, I don't know what happened to you in Alaska other than what you've told me. But you can't control any of that. You can't change people's minds. What you *can* control is what you do next—how you respond."

He folded the flyer into a neat little square and dropped it in Jude's lap. "Go talk to Eli. Think about ways you can add meaning and purpose to your life. Got it?"

Jude took the brochure, opened Braxton's glove box, shoved it inside, then climbed out of the car without another word.

"Jude—"

"I'm going inside to see my mother. Don't wait for me."

"I'll be here when you're finished."

"I *said* don't wait for me. I'll call an Uber."

He strode up the sidewalk toward the entrance, every step fueled by frustration. He refused to turn around and look back. But he heard Braxton pull away, the engine purring as he accelerated out of the parking lot.

Good. He didn't need another lecture. Or a flyer.

Because he certainly wasn't going to volunteer with other people's kids and use them to rebuild his image. There was nothing wrong with his image.

He was not the problem.

He pressed the buzzer outside the door, and a friendly chime sounded. Then a voice came through the small speaker.

"Good morning. How may I help you?"

"I'm Jude Mercer." His body hummed with the sudden urge to flee. He forced himself to stay rooted to the sidewalk. "Here to see my mother, Madeline Mercer."

"Absolutely, Mr. Mercer. Please have photo ID and check in at the desk. I'll buzz you through."

"Thanks."

The door hummed. The deadbolt slid and the automatic door eased open. He stepped through.

Classical music played from a wireless speaker mounted on the walnut desk. A trio of potted plants stood just inside the door.

Overstuffed beige furniture and wide windows with bright light streaming in greeted him.

He stepped up to the desk.

"Hi there. Jude Mercer?"

He nodded and showed the young woman his photo ID.

"If you'll sign in, please."

She turned the electronic tablet his way. He scrawled his signature across the line with the stylus.

"Great. I believe your mother is just over there working on her favorite puzzle."

A vase of beautiful pale pink hydrangeas adorned the desk. He leaned around the arrangement and spotted his mother sitting in her wheelchair at a small table beside a window. Large puzzle pieces were spread across the table in front of her.

"She's really a delightful lady." The woman lowered her voice. "One of our favorites."

Jude gave a curt nod. "Good to know. Thanks."

His stomach churned as he approached his mother from behind. A woman in maroon scrubs stood at a mobile workstation nearby, working on a tablet. She glanced up.

"Mrs. Mercer, I believe you have a guest."

His mother twisted in her chair to look over her shoulder, her smooth brow furrowed. When her pale-blue eyes met Jude's, her whole face lit up. She struggled but managed to lift a hand. One half of her mouth tipped up in a slow, delighted smile that crinkled the corners of her left eye.

Her smile. That expression. Sudden light breaking through storm clouds, every single time.

He closed the distance and dropped to his knees beside her chair, cupping her hand between his.

"Hey, Mom."

She leaned over and brushed an awkward kiss across his cheek. He squeezed his eyes shut.

"Can I get you anything, Mr. Mercer? A soda? Coffee?"

He cleared his throat. "What does my mom like to drink?"

"Oh, she loves sparkling water. Cherry limeade is her favorite. Would you like to try one?"

"Sure, thank you."

"I'll be right back."

The woman disappeared out of sight. Madeline tapped her finger awkwardly on the tabletop and tipped her head toward the puzzle.

"This is cute," he said, scanning the project.

Puppies in the back of a vintage Chevy pickup truck, bright red of course. Beyond the truck, sunflowers in a golden field and sunshine in a baby-blue sky.

"Have you done this one a lot?"

Her pencil-thin brows furrowed. She fumbled but dragged her electronic tablet that she used for communication closer. She jabbed her finger at a few buttons and the device's electronic voice read out: "New puzzle. Too hard. Help me."

She grinned.

"Hey, I notice your assistant there has a British accent."

Her eyes lit up.

"That's clever. Can you pick the settings?"

She jabbed at a button. A voice read back, "Yes. Not many options."

"Oh, were you hoping for Hugh Jackman?"

She shook her head.

"Harry Connick Jr.?"

She shook her head again.

"Rod Stewart?"

A laugh bubbled up.

"Hmm. Colin Firth?"

She gave him a thumbs-up.

"Nailed it." He claimed a chair across from hers. Puzzles weren't really his thing—not interesting enough to hold his attention—but if that's what she liked to do, then that's what they would do together.

She tapped one of the empty spots again, then looked at him.

"I know, I know. I'm looking."

Instead of reaching for a puzzle piece, she tapped on her touchscreen. "You look sad. Why?"

He hesitated.

The woman in maroon scrubs returned with two cans of bright pink sparkling water, each with a striped straw tucked in.

"She's going to want to do this herself, aren't you, Mrs. Mercer?"

His mother nodded.

"So help her but only as needed, all right?"

"Yes, ma'am. Thank you."

He took the can, cool against his fingertips, and sipped. Mom struggled to get her can close enough. It took her three tries to get her mouth around the straw. She took a long sip.

"Great job. I'm proud of you."

It was excruciating watching her struggle to do something she used to do mindlessly. But he thought of all the times she had stood in the cold just to watch him shoot at targets or catch a glimpse of him cross-country skiing, or how she had driven him to and from countless training sessions with Eli.

Showing up for her here, even though it broke his heart, was the least he could do.

She jabbed at her touch screen again, waiting.

For what?

She could still, despite all that the stroke had taken from her, communicate with looks and body language. He drew a long breath and reached for a pile of red puzzle pieces, tried to fit them together.

"I don't know if you've heard or if Dad's been by to update you, but I got suspended. First for poor sportsmanship because I accused another guy of cheating—which he was—and then I went to Alaska to film a commercial. This woman I knew was treating me for a bizarre food reaction, but she gave me a banned substance, so now I'm suspended indefinitely."

He stared at his hands.

"I feel like such a failure, Mom. I don't know who I am if I'm not a biathlete. If I lose my identity . . . I don't know what I'll do next. It kind of seems like nothing that I do matters now if I'm just going to be accused of being a cheater."

A pause.

"And this girl in Alaska . . . I thought we had something. But I don't know. I let my emotions run the show, and I think I might have said some things I can't take back."

She took another sip of her drink and burped.

"Rude," he said, shaking his head with a smile.

She giggled, touched her fingers to her lips, then tapped out a few words. Only one of her hands worked so it took a while, but she was a determined thing. The messages came out in short bursts:

"God is still here."

Jude hesitated, his drink halfway to his lips. "Yes, I know."

"Read His Word. Talk to Him."

Jude winced, leaned back in his chair, and took a long sip of his sparkling water. "I don't know, Mom."

She pecked out a few more words.

"He loves you. So do I."

Tears stung his eyes. He blinked hard. "You still believe God loves you after everything you've been through?"

This time she didn't type anything. She pushed her tablet out of the way and awkwardly squeezed his hand tight.

That was her answer. She did.

He blew out a long, shaky breath.

Yeah. Okay. Still angry. The wounds were still raw. And he hated that she had to live trapped in a body that had failed her.

He squeezed her hand back, then let go, reached for a puzzle piece, and fitted it into an empty spot. It clicked into place.

She stabbed the air with a flailing but super adorable fist pump.

"I don't know how to fix any of this, Mom."

She pecked out more words.

"Just told you. Talk to God. Read His Word."

For the first time in days, Jude didn't get up and run from the wisdom that was offered.

The nurse reappeared just then, wiping her hands with sanitizer. "Oh, by the way, Mr. Mercer, your mother's sister came by earlier today."

"Melissa?"

"Yes! Styled her hair for her this morning. She always leaves your mom looking like she's going to a garden party."

Jude turned back to Madeline and noticed the way she patted her freshly styled hair—straight, shoulder-length, and shiny brown—with unmistakable pride.

"You look great, Mom."

She tapped on her screen again. "Melissa is busy. Owns three salons in Concord now."

"Wow. That's great. I'll have to get by and say hello sometime."

His mom nodded, pleased.

He fit another piece into the puzzle. They almost had the part with the litter of goldendoodle puppies in the back of the truck completed. The puzzle was coming together. If only he could say the same about his life.

He'd lost his footing in the sport that used to define him. Lost the girl who might've seen past all that. Now he had no plans, nothing to train for, and no idea who he was supposed to be. Frankly, he'd become a mess of broken pieces he didn't know how to fit back together.

Even if it was for the right reasons, slapping stickers on five hundred bottles of bubbles was *so* not her idea of a fun girls' night out.

Caroline shifted in her chair, stationed at the far end of Lainey's kitchen table. She pulled off her walking boot and propped her foot on a chair with a cushion under her heel. Evening sunlight streamed through the window, bathing Lainey's beautiful kitchen in a soft golden glow. Hot country hits played from Abbie's playlist on her phone to a wireless speaker on the counter. A bouquet of fresh daisies and forget-me-nots sat in a vintage glass vase, and confetti blondie bars—compliments of Lainey—cooled on a wire rack beside the oven. Emma had brought a cup carrier with their iced coffees from Copper Kettle and slid it into the middle of the packed table.

Bubble bottles. Stickers. Purses. To-do lists.

They'd thought of everything.

Distributing stickers with a Bible verse and a web address for Redemption Community Church was a clever and simple way to reach out to children and families at the upcoming festival. But did *they* have to be the ones to put the stickers on all these bottles? She was officially over it—and had only done about twenty-five. The stickers were hard to peel, and she was determined—okay, maybe obsessively determined—to line them up perfectly. So far, her progress didn't meet her self-imposed standards.

Conversation ebbed and flowed around her, but she couldn't keep up. Her thoughts kept drifting.

Where was Jude? What was he doing? Had his suspension been reversed? Was he going to reach out to her—ever?

And the one question she kept circling, no matter how hard she tried not to: Was he coming back?

Her sticker went on crooked. She blew out an aggravated breath and peeled it off, the paper tearing slightly.

Abbie passed her a clear plastic to-go cup with a neon-green straw. "Iced coffee? Double pump of hazelnut and one pack of Splenda. Is that you?"

"Yeah. Thanks." Caroline took it but didn't drink any.

"Sure, no problem." Abbie slid into the seat opposite hers.

Lainey brought over a plate of blondie bars, pastel sprinkles dotting the top. "These are good for what ails you," she said, setting them down along with adorable yellow pastel plates with scalloped edges and white napkins with—of course—yellow polka dots. "We're like a team of bubble-sticker-factory interns. I just hope they don't make us turn paper bags into hand puppets next."

"They wouldn't," Caroline said, slamming a bubble container down on the table a little too hard.

Three pairs of eyes swung to stare at her.

"I mean, I guess it would be okay if we had to. I could maybe do that. Is there a template?" She laughed, but it came out all wrong. "I'm not very useful. It's not like they're going to let me run in the race."

"If you hand out these bubbles, I'm sure you'll really win people over with your charming personality," Emma said dryly, as she ripped a sticker.

"Okay," Abbie said, tapping her phone and turning down the music. "Time-out. What's going on?"

"I'm fine." Caroline rubbed her eyes with her fingertips.

"You've been in a mood since Jude left," Emma said, reaching for her moose-track mocha.

"I am not in a mood about *him*." Caroline tugged her drink closer and shoved the row of bubble bottles aside. "I'm in a mood because I'm injured and I'm useless and everything I had planned this summer is ruined."

Lainey's brow furrowed. She propped one hip against the counter, another package of napkins in her hand.

"I don't think that's it. You typically spiral when things aren't perfect."

"No—"

Abbie held up a hand. "Remember sophomore year? Track finals? You dropped the baton and the team finished last in the relay. You wouldn't talk to anyone for a week. You acted like you'd burned down the school."

Caroline fisted her hands. "It mattered, okay? That was our shot."

"I heard that two years later, you led that same relay team to a state championship. Pretty sure there's still a picture in the trophy case and a sign on the wall." Emma pinned her with a knowing look. "Your time was a personal best, right?"

"She still made us miserable for days," Abbie said.

"It wasn't just about that race," Caroline whispered. "It was about not being able to let go of the mistake."

Lainey scooted around the chairs and rested her hand on Caroline's shoulder. "You're not broken because your plans went off the rails. Nobody's blaming you. It was an accident. I've run that trail hundreds of times. On that one measly lap, you fell. It's okay. These things happen. You work in the medical field, right? Do you berate your patients when they come in with an injury or illness?"

"Of course not."

"Well then, why is your inner critic so hard on *you*?"

Caroline ducked her head and blinked back tears. "I wish I knew."

"Oh, sweetie." Lainey bent and gave her a hug. "We love you, no matter what. We don't expect flawless execution. We're just glad you're here."

Abbie gestured toward the bottles. "Some sweet kid is going to go home with these bubbles and a verse. That's a win—even if your stickers are crooked."

Tears leaked from the corners of Caroline's eyes. "I wanted my time here to *matter*. I wanted to feel like I was doing something important. Making a huge impact. But from the minute I unpacked, people have judged me. Compared me to Dr. Wallace. Reminded me of all the things I tried to leave behind."

"That really stinks," Emma said gently, passing her a tissue. "I can relate. Some people love to dredge up the past."

"Sorry," Abbie said. "That was on me."

"No. I think I needed to hear it." Caroline dabbed at her face. "I need to learn not to be such a control freak."

The girls all paused and then exchanged amused glances.

"I'm a work in progress. Right?"

"That's the spirit."

They all clinked their plastic coffee cups together in the middle of the table. Then they passed Caroline another sticker sheet.

She grudgingly accepted it. And then she let herself place the next sticker on crooked—on purpose. Her lips twitched in a half smile as she finally glanced down and read the verse: "Be still, and know that I am God."

Be still. Was that the lesson she was supposed to learn in all of this?

Eighteen

GO SEE ELI. GET YOUR HEAD ON STRAIGHT.

Braxton's words echoed in Jude's head as he slowed his rental car around the sharp curve, turned on his blinker, then eased the vehicle onto the long, winding dirt road leading to his former coach's New Hampshire farm.

Dust kicked up around his tires, and the trees—a patchwork of fresh spring green, cedar, and cottonwood—waved in the breeze. Splashes of white and pale pink from apple blossoms dotted the field beside the road, and a few clusters of lilacs bloomed along the route leading up to a modest single-story ranch painted yellow with white trim and in a field behind a weathered red barn.

Jude smiled as a Dalmatian barked and trotted in circles, sprinting between the barn and the house, no doubt alerting Eli to his arrival.

Two huge planters filled with purple and yellow pansies flanked the open barn door. He stepped out of the car and slammed the door. In the distance, the mountains beyond the village of Cranebrook still had snow lingering in the highest elevations. The lower slopes, though, were lush and alive, blanketed in emerald carpets of fresh growth. A stream burbled somewhere nearby, and the warm sun heated his back as he headed up toward the barn, his sneakers leaving tracks in the soft dirt. The dog barked and raced ahead while a bumblebee hummed around the blooming flowers.

He stepped inside the barn and stopped, breathing in the old familiar smells of wood shavings and some kind of varnish, and maybe a hint of ski wax. The light streamed through a high, dusty window, and dust danced in the golden shafts of light. Eli McAllister sang off-key to an old Johnny Cash song as he stood at his workbench, hunched over a jelly cupboard or a pie safe, stripping something from the wood. His neat white beard hadn't changed a bit, although his hair had thinned some.

Eli paused, straightened, and turned. "Well, well, if it isn't my favorite biathlete, Jude. What are you doing?"

Jude smiled. "Hey, Eli. It's good to see you."

"You too, son. Been a long time." Eli set his tools aside, then reached over and lowered the volume on the old radio-cassette-player combo coated in a thick layer of dust. "What brings you by?"

Jude exhaled hard. "Braxton told me to come see you. He's my agent now. I didn't want to. But . . ." Jude shoved his hands into the back pockets of his jeans. "To tell you the truth, my life's a mess."

"Aw. It's probably not as bad as you think, son. Thirsty?"

"Sure."

Eli crossed to a vintage refrigerator, opened the door, and pulled out two bottles of orange soda. He uncapped them both with a bottle opener and tossed the tool back on the bench.

"Here you go. If you're hungry, we can go up to the house. I'll fix you a sandwich."

"No, no." Jude took a sip of the soda, letting the sweet, bubbly liquid coat his dry throat. "I tried to do the right thing, Eli. Can't stand it when people cheat. I reported one of my competitors. I know he was using an earpiece to talk to his coach. I just know it.

But I got slapped with a temporary suspension for poor sportsmanship." He quoted the air with his fingers. "Then I got to Alaska, filmed this commercial for the sponsor I needed. And everything just went off the rails. A stick impaled in my leg. Food poisoning. And the woman who helped me. She gave me something that had a banned substance in it. Now I'm officially suspended. For good."

Eli scratched at the beard on his chin. "Huh. That's a lot. When did all this happen?"

"Just in the month of May."

"Yikes."

"I tried to be strong. I tried to fight through. Stay in control."

"How'd that go?" Eli sipped his soda and waited.

"Not great. That's kind of why I'm here. What should I do?"

Eli palmed the back of his neck. "Well, as long as I've known you, you've been a power-through kind of guy. You just muscle your way past the pain, the politics. Most of the time, you win. But . . . I'm proud of you for admitting you're in a pickle."

"Thanks, I think."

"This woman in Alaska who helped you. Mean something to you?"

Jude shrugged. "Thought so."

"And are you interested in doing anything about that?"

Jude took another sip of his soda. "I don't know. She . . . I'm not sure I belong in Alaska. And she just moved back home there. She's not leaving. The thing is, we crossed paths once before and had a moment. And this is the second time I screwed up."

Eli's blue eyes sparkled. "You're not sure she's going to give you a third chance?"

"I wouldn't give me a third chance."

"Well, that's the thing. We don't get to speculate on what other people aren't going to do. Look. I know you have reasons for thinking that the only way to survive is to be untouchable.

But untouchable people end up lonely. They don't get to fall in love. They're reckless in ways that cause harm, and they never let anybody close."

Jude shook his head. "You don't understand. You don't know what it's like to watch your mother, who's so full of life, who prayed over you every morning, be reduced to a wheelchair and using a tablet to communicate. Meanwhile, my dad," Jude started to pace, "he just gets to keep on going, making money, only looking out for himself. Why did God let my mom suffer, but my dad doesn't seem to suffer at all? I feel like God kind of made a bad choice there."

Silence stretched between them, and then Eli spoke, his voice low, even. "God's not fair, Jude. God is just. There's a big difference. Our definition of fairness isn't really in our best interests. God seems to be more in the business of giving you what you need in ways that will shape you into who you're meant to be."

"So my mom had a stroke because I needed to learn about adversity and hardship and justice?"

"Maybe," Eli said, shrugging. "More than likely she had a stroke because we live in a broken world. And your dad—don't cut him off completely. He's providing for her. And I know he's proud of you, even if he doesn't know how to tell you. But your job? Your job is to stand back and let God do His work in you. That's where you will find meaning. And it will have far more value than a medal or a trophy or getting reinstated."

"I don't know about that," Jude scoffed. "My career is literally on the line here."

"So it seems," Eli said. "And you're angry about it. I get that too. You've got a right to be. But you can't use that anger as armor. It won't work. If you don't mind my saying so, you're living a lie."

"Oh yeah, what's that?"

"Only the strong survive. But that's not true. That's your fear leading you astray."

Jude shook his head. Scraped his sneaker along a dusty path on the barn floor.

"So this woman—what's her name?"

"Caroline."

"Sounds like she saw something in you."

"Maybe."

"Maybe a wound that's deeper than an allergic reaction or a flesh injury?"

"I don't know about deeper, but she definitely heard me say some things I wish I could take back."

Eli stepped forward, clapped Jude on the shoulder. "Son, we've all been there. Maybe it's time to redefine your definition of winning. Be the kind of man who's strong enough to be vulnerable, to forgive, to ask for help. That kind of strength won't come from inside you. You can't get it by yourself. You're going to have to let the Lord carry what's too heavy for you. And in my opinion, that's when you'll see genuine and lasting change."

He'd rather climb to the top of the nearest mountain—twice—than redefine the singular thing he'd been about for most of his life. Jude examined the glass bottle of soda. "I don't know, Eli. You're asking a lot. I'm not sure I even know how to go after that."

"You don't need to know how. That's the juicy secret." Eli winked. "Just say, 'God, help me.' That's it."

Outside, a bird chirped and hopped along the ground, pecking at the dirt.

"I don't like being weak," Jude said.

"Then you'll never be strong."

"What?"

"I think you define strength as the absence of weakness. But what if it's choosing to keep going, to keep loving, even when you feel like you're teetering on the edge of a cliff?"

"Huh." Jude polished off the rest of his soda. "That's a lot of truth."

"Remember, it's not condemnation." Eli patted his back and stepped away. "Just my two cents."

"You need any help? Anything I can do while I'm here?"

"Nope. But I'm always around if you need me."

"I know. Thanks." Jude raised the empty bottle in the air. "Appreciate you."

"You betcha. Anytime. Don't be a stranger."

He stepped outside into the warm sunshine, looked up at the mountains, their peaks etched against the blue sky. The emptiness that had gnawed at him for weeks had relented. He closed his eyes, turned his face to the sun.

"Lord, help me," he whispered.

So much for finding a quiet place to read and journal. A line spilled out the door of the Copper Kettle coffee shop. Thankfully, Megan had been kind enough to accept the order Caroline had sent ahead via text and had her iced coffee waiting for her when she arrived. Perks of having a little sister as a barista.

Caroline wedged her napkin under her drink so it wouldn't blow away, then scooted the wrought-iron chair closer to the small table under the pergola. The table wobbled slightly, so she pulled a medical journal from her bag—one she honestly had no intention of reading—and tucked it under the leg. She ditched her crutches, although her foot already throbbed, and used the sneaker on her uninjured foot to push the chair opposite hers out—it scraped on the concrete as she winced—and finally, she elevated her foot, propping it on the chair.

Exhausted already, she pulled her favorite pen and notebook from her bag and set them on the table, then trailed a finger down the condensation on the outside of her cup.

Staring out over the bay in the distance, her thoughts drifted like a charter fishing boat bobbing over the whitecaps. Why did she feel so adrift? She'd been home all of five weeks, and with the town's summer festival looming and her foot slowly healing, maybe she should feel grateful for a slower pace. Instead, she rubbed at the hollow ache nestled behind her sternum.

Her friends' words from two days ago at Lainey's house spilled through her head on repeat. Had her worth always been tied too tightly to her performance? That was an uncomfortable truth to wrestle with.

A shadow passed across the table.

"Is this seat taken?"

Caroline glanced up, squinting into the sunshine. Dr. Wallace stood, coffee in hand, wearing a ball cap and a vintage Redemption High T-shirt and khaki shorts. Like a blend of fit grandpa and doctor on a weekend outing.

"Not at all," she said, clearing her throat and straightening. She lowered her boot to the ground.

"No, no, keep your foot up there. I'll bring a chair over."

He turned and politely requested to borrow a chair from a table nearby. The customers agreed, and he sat down to Caroline's right, facing the water. Releasing a contented sigh, he pointed toward the harbor.

"I never get tired of this view."

She nodded. "What's your coffee of choice here?"

"Well, your sister, Megan, makes a mean moose-tracks mocha, but my wife says I'm not supposed to drink too many of those, so today I'm just drinking an oat-milk latte. A little sprinkle of cinnamon on top. Kind of boring."

"Well, I'm sure Mrs. Wallace—and the rest of us—are glad you're taking care of yourself. I didn't expect to see you out today. No fishing?"

He chuckled. "No. Speaking of Mrs. Wallace, she had a bit of a honey-do list. I'm off to the hardware store after this."

"There's still plenty of time left in the day for you to do something heroic."

He chuckled. "Heroic's a bit of a stretch. Just doing the work the Lord has laid before me. Which reminds me . . ."

She hadn't noticed until now that he carried a small Bible with him.

"I'm on a mission."

"Oh? What's that?"

He set the leather-bound Bible in front of her. Honey-brown. Rich. With the words *Holy Bible* embossed in gold. He slid it closer.

"This has belonged to me," he said, "since I was about your age. A gift from my mentor after I finished my residency."

She picked it up. The pages crackled when she opened it. The spine felt tight. The gold leaf on the book edges didn't have a single imperfection.

"It looks untouched."

"Yeah, that's the problem," he said, leaning back. "Because it was. Caroline, for years I relied on my own skill, my excellent training, good instincts, if you will. I thought that would be enough."

"Dr. Wallace, your career here has been remarkable. You've built an amazing clinic. This town adores you. You treated my injuries more than once as a kid—and probably half the people in this town. Not to mention, if you hadn't referred my dad to that specialist in Seattle, I don't know—"

He reached over, gently cut her off with a kind smile and a gentle pat on her arm.

"What you see is only a small part of the picture. If I could go back, I'd do a lot of things different. There were countless times I should have prayed before I took action. I'm grateful and humbled by kind words and the relationships I've made here in Redemption. There are dozens of people who sing a different tune, and they all have every right to step forward and tell you about the times I tried to fix things myself and ended up making a mess."

She shifted in her chair. "It all worked out, though, didn't it?"

His eyes softened when he reached for his coffee. "Not without cost."

She couldn't explain, but his three words—so simple—stirred something deep.

"I don't know how to not do that," she said, using her straw to jab at the ice in the bottom of her cup. "Fix everything, I mean. Just . . . It's how I'm wired. If I'm not solving problems or checking things off a list, I feel like a failure."

He didn't answer right away. Just nodded. And stared out at the water. Then he turned and faced her again.

"I can relate," he said. "But if you're anything like me, maybe that means you also wake up in the middle of the night and feel like you're holding the whole world together. With duct tape and willpower. That's exhausting, Caroline, and it's not what God asks of you."

She looked away.

"I'm here to make a difference," she said. "I came back to prove that I could be someone worthy of respect. Someone who wouldn't let people down. I want people to talk about me the way they talk about you."

He leaned forward and rested his elbows on the wrought-iron table.

"Caroline, when you were a little girl with scraped knees and wild ideas, you already had our respect. No matter what you do—your kindness, your reputation, your actions, and the goodwill your family has earned in this town—those are all good things. But the most important thing is that God loves you. Despite your blemishes, your shortcomings, His love for you hasn't changed, and it won't change, ever. You're not in competition with me or anyone else."

She blinked fast, trying to keep her tears from spilling over. "But I still feel like I'm constantly falling short. Why?"

He reached into his shorts pocket and pulled out a small package—something from a sporting-goods store. He handed it over. It was a sleek pair of stainless-steel tweezers, the kind only a doctor—or somebody deeply entrenched in wilderness rescue—would have.

"These were given to me when I first moved to Alaska," he said, "by a midwife who'd delivered more babies in Arctic villages than any OB I'd ever known. She said, 'You'll be surprised which tools you reach for over and over. But true wisdom comes from knowing when *not* to use them.'"

He set the tweezers on top of the Bible.

"I won't part with mine, so I got you your own pair. Not because you need fancy equipment or a new tool to carry in your pocket. It's more of a symbol, really. I just want to remind you that sometimes simple tools—like simple faith—change lives."

She swallowed against the lump in her throat.

"But what if I mess up?" she said. "I've already messed up so many times. And every time I just feel worse. What if I do more harm than good?"

"You *will* mess up," he said, nodding. "It's not really a matter of *if*, more like *when*."

Her stomach dropped. "Thanks so much."

He grinned. "That's why I'm trying to tell you that if you walk with the Lord, He can use even your mistakes for something redemptive." He winked. "See what I did there? It's not your job to be perfect. We are called to be faithful."

A long silence passed between them, broken only by the sound of laughter and conversation spilling through the open doors of the coffee shop. She could hear the comforting rumble of the espresso machine steaming warm milk in the frother. She looked down at the tweezers and the Bible in her hands—hands that were her best tools most days. She'd already stitched wounds and written prescriptions and staunched bleeding, injected an EpiPen into a handsome man's thigh.

She banished the thought of Jude before the pesky intrusion derailed her conversation.

"I've spent a long time trying to be someone else's version of *enough*. This is hard—letting go."

"It is," Dr. Wallace said, reaching over and tapping the Bible with his finger. "But it's also the most freeing thing you'll ever do."

A soft breeze picked up, carrying the scent of salty air and fresh flowers blooming in the nearby terracotta planters.

"So . . . if you're not reading *this* Bible, what Bible are you reading?"

He laughed. "Good question. Valid point. Every morning I read the same Bible that my wife does, because she writes in the margins and leaves notes I'd never think of. I learn something every time."

"Aw, that's really sweet." She tucked the Bible and the tweezers carefully inside her bag. "Thank you—for the talk, and the tweezers, and the Bible."

"Well, you can do what you want with the pep talk, but I want you to use that Bible and those tweezers every chance you get."

He rose, tipped his hat, and patted her on the shoulder before walking away.

She looked back toward the harbor and took another sip of her coffee. Maybe it wasn't about proving anything. Maybe she did need to learn to be still—and trust that even her crooked plans and fractured pieces could be used for something good.

She pulled out her journal and uncapped her pen. The tip hovered over the blank page.

Then she wrote down Dr. Wallace's advice, word for word.

Nineteen

"HERE GOES NOTHING," JUDE WHISPERED, THEN tugged open the glass door of the Twin Lakes Community YMCA, less than two miles from Coach Eli's farm.

He stepped into the air-conditioned, chlorine-scented lobby. His trail runners squeaked on the gleaming linoleum, and he paused, surveying the welcoming space. They'd remodeled since he'd been here last. Navy-blue love seats and club chairs now sat in the middle of the room with an arrangement of fresh flowers in the center of a basic blond-wood coffee table. At the round tables near the windows, people sat and talked. The muffled sound of basketballs bouncing in the gym at the end of the corridor reminded him of weekends spent playing here as a kid.

You need something that grounds you, gives you a sense of purpose while this suspension plays out.

Braxton's last text looped through his head.

"All right, here we go. Volunteering. I'm on it," he said.

At first, he'd balked. Sounded like a cheesy publicity stunt—an easy way to polish the dumpster fire of a reputation he'd earned. But the more he'd sat alone in his empty condo, stewing in what-ifs and regret over how he'd treated Caroline . . . well, the more he'd embraced Braxton's advice. And Eli's pep talk had spurred him to action. Time to stop thinking about what he'd lost and start figuring out who he wanted to be—even if he never competed in a biathlon again.

The front-desk attendant looked up from her computer and squinted. Her face lit up in recognition. "Well, I'll be," she said, coming around the L-shaped counter and striding toward him. "Jude Mercer. Haven't seen you since you terrorized me in tenth-grade chemistry."

He couldn't stop a smile. "Mrs. Daly?"

"Yes, sir," she said with a chuckle. "Retired from teaching though."

"Cranebrook High isn't the same without you, I'm sure."

"Probably better, actually. I was getting feisty. Now I run this front desk like a boss." She patted the counter. "What brings you by? Trying to find the weight room? Or did you get lost on your way to Vermont?"

"Ha." He palmed the back of his neck. "Um, neither. I, uh, want to volunteer."

Her dark brows lifted. "You? Hmm. That's not the headline I expected to see today."

He winced. "Yeah, local news has had a field day with me lately. I need to stop thinking about myself, Mrs. D. I've got to keep busy. Do something useful."

"Well, good. You're an answer to prayer. We are *desperate* for help with our soccer camp this week."

"This week?"

"The guy we had lined up had a family emergency. Now I've got about forty-eight first and second graders in cleats, two teenage counselors, and a grouchy retired coach from the community college."

"Hmm. You do sound desperate," he teased, "but is it really that bad?"

"Worse. You ever herded cats?"

"Not lately. But I don't have a background check or a résumé or anything."

She grinned. "I've been here a while, son. I know people. Don't you worry. We'll fast-track whatever you need."

He glanced out the huge picture windows toward the soccer fields. Lush green grass. Colorful cones. Kids running in every direction.

"Okay," he said. "Why don't I take a look?"

"All right. Give me your number before you go. I'll text you a link to the form."

"Um, shouldn't I go out there first?"

"I'm confident you'll fit right in. If you like what you see, let me know and I'll set up orientation online. By Thursday morning, you could be Coach Jude."

"Oh boy." He cringed. "That sounds terrifying."

She went back around behind her desk, ruffled through some papers, wrote the date, and handed him a sticker. "Here's your visitor pass. Super official. Just observe for now and proceed with caution." She winked. "Good to see you, Jude."

"You too, Mrs. Daly. Thanks."

He peeled the sticker and slapped it onto his T-shirt, discarding the backing in a trash can as he headed for the double doors leading to the fields.

Outside, humid air wrapped around him. The smell of fresh-cut grass and sunscreen filled his nose. Kids were everywhere. Some kicked soccer balls. Others wrestled on the ground. One little girl chased a butterfly. A frazzled-looking teenage girl in a blue YMCA T-shirt blew a whistle, but nobody paid attention.

Jude stood near the edge of the field, hands tucked into the pockets of his cargo shorts, smiling as a little girl scored a goal—except for the wrong team. Her teammates cheered anyway. Her coach clapped.

Chaos. But there was an odd sort of comfort in it. No expectations. No fans. No pressure. Just kids, grass stains, sunshine, and laughter.

Maybe this *was* exactly what he needed.

"Hey," a woman said behind him. "Aren't you Jude Mercer?"

He turned. She was about his age, stood with her phone in hand. She wore a Red Sox T-shirt, cutoff denim shorts, and a ball cap.

"I am," he said.

"May I have a quick photo, please? My husband's a huge fan. And my kid's on the field too. He's going to lose his mind when he hears you're here."

He hesitated. Part of him wanted to say no. But the part that had dragged him here—and genuinely wanted to heed Eli and Braxton's advice—pasted on a smile and stepped closer.

"Absolutely. As long as I don't have to autograph a soccer cleat or anything, I think we're all good."

She laughed, stood respectfully beside him, lifted the phone, and took a selfie.

"Want to check it? Make sure you like it?" he asked.

"Yeah, I should." She touched the screen with two fingers, enlarged the photo, and nodded. Then she turned the screen toward him. "Is this okay with you?"

"Looks good."

"Is it okay if I post?"

"Wow. I appreciate you asking that. Sure. But please—no controversial comments. Nothing political. No jabs."

"Oh, I would never," she said. "Just a regular mom post, I promise."

"Thanks. What did you say your name was?"

"Cheryl."

"Nice to meet you, Cheryl." He gave her a polite nod and then turned back toward the field. He rubbed at the tightness in his chest.

That photo would be out there now. What if his kindness came back around to bite him? Thoughts of social media made him think of Caroline.

The guilt twisted his insides. He hadn't been fair to her. Not even close. He'd been scared. Angry. Cornered. And he'd lashed out, accused her of terrible things.

Oh, the look on her face when he'd said those words.

He would never forget it.

As he watched the soccer game, something shifted inside him. He wanted to be better. Not just so he could get back to competing. Not to prove the press wrong.

He was just . . . *tired*. Tired of being the guy who pushed people away.

One of the YMCA employees blew a whistle, then motioned for the kids to huddle up. A mom stepped forward and handed out a cooler full of juice boxes and Goldfish crackers.

Jude walked back inside, found Mrs. Daly at the front desk.

"Well, sign me up," he said.

She grinned, then clapped her hands. "Seriously?"

"Seriously. I'll fill out whatever forms you need."

"Aww, you're a good man, Jude," she said. "A lot of people would not show up like this."

He didn't say anything for a moment. Then he nodded slowly. "I didn't used to be a good man, Mrs. Daly. But I'm trying."

"I think you're doing just fine."

As he headed out to his car, his phone blipped and buzzed. He glanced at the screen—over a dozen notifications. Cheryl had posted the photo.

He hesitated . . . then tapped the screen.

Comments. Likes. Mentions. Shares.

He didn't read a single comment. Because for once, he just didn't care.

Caroline adjusted the Velcro strap on her immobilizing boot, wincing slightly as she stood up from the desk chair at her cubby in the clinic. The dull ache in her foot had become part of her daily routine, a constant reminder of a misstep she wished she could rewind, in more ways than one. Thoughts of Jude floated through her head—how he'd showed up for her that night, stayed with her, helped her stay safe while that huge bear prowled around outside the yurt, made sure her brothers got home safely.

How could that guy be the same one who had hurled such terrible accusations at her?

Shaking her head, she reached for the tablet with her patient's schedule and tapped the screen. Next up: Amanda and Brian Kessler with baby Noah.

Her stomach clenched. The Kesslers. She hadn't seen them since that horrible day they were airlifted out of the ER. Amanda's skin clammy and pale. Brian terrified. Their baby on the verge of not surviving. It had been gut-wrenching making the call to get them airlifted out. It had been a risky move. One she tossed and turned and overanalyzed many times. She'd felt like a total failure that day.

Drawing in a deep breath, she knocked on the door to exam room three, then stepped inside. Amanda sat in the recliner that Connie had ordered for moms and well-baby checkups. She held a baby swaddled in her arms. The white blanket with cement trucks printed on it made Caroline smile. Brian stood by the window, hands shoved in the pockets of his jeans. They both looked up as Caroline entered.

"Caroline." Amanda offered a tired smile. "We were hoping we'd see you today."

Caroline closed the door softly. "I didn't expect to see you all on my schedule. I'm so glad you're here." She glanced at the newborn. "And this little guy—is this Noah?"

Brian nodded. His smile so wide, a dimple on his cheek popped. "Noah James was born with a strong set of lungs and hasn't quieted down much since."

"Oh, stop." Amanda laughed, reaching up to squeeze Brian's arm. "He's perfect. Hardly cries at all. And we owe you and Dr. Monroe everything."

Caroline swallowed hard. "You were both in real trouble, to be honest. I'm so relieved to see you're doing well."

Amanda reached for Brian's hand. "Thankfully, you stayed calm and saved both of us." Amanda blinked, her eyes glossy with tears. "We're forever grateful."

Brian cleared his throat, stepped forward, and handed Caroline a bouquet of gorgeous roses. Yellow, wrapped in purple paper and tied with a twine ribbon. "These are for you. We've got a bouquet for Dr. Monroe too, but your admin says she's on vacation. We hope you like them."

Caroline took the flowers, sniffed them. "They're gorgeous. Thank you. This means more than I can say." She carefully set the flowers on the counter by the sink, along with her tablet, then washed her hands and worked through the exam.

But this time, she felt lighter somehow. Steady, confident, she checked Noah's vitals, asked about feeding.

"His lungs are strong," Caroline said, entering data into the baby's chart on her tablet. "Healthy as can be. You're doing an incredible job."

Amanda sniffed and wiped at the moisture on her cheeks. "I was terrified that night, but we still talk about it all the time. We can't believe how calm you were. My memory's a little fuzzy, but I feel like you showed up and restored order, and we can't thank you enough."

Caroline ducked her head. "I did my job. I did what I thought was right."

Something blossomed inside her, a feeling she hadn't felt in weeks. Pride. Not the kind that came with self-aggrandizing behavior or making headlines or proving yourself to skeptics. The quiet kind. The kind that made her feel like maybe she belonged after all.

"Congrats again on bringing a healthy baby into the world. It was a pleasure to see you both. I hope to see you again soon, and I hope you get some sleep."

"Thanks." Brian leaned down, kissed Amanda on the forehead, then re-swaddled Noah.

Caroline stepped out into the hallway, the bouquet of flowers tucked in the crook of her elbow. She closed her eyes, savoring the moment. For the first time since Jude had left town, she felt like maybe she wasn't a total disaster. Maybe the part of her that had felt incapable of hope wasn't completely trashed after all.

She went to her cubby, found her phone and her purse. Dr. Monroe needed to hear about this. She had to share the joy with someone who'd totally get it. But before she could start a new message, her phone buzzed with a group text alert from Emma.

Emma

You GUYS. Look at this.

An image filled the screen. Jude standing on the edge of a soccer field. The summer sun glinting off his hair. He wore shorts and a T-shirt with some kind of sticker affixed to the chest. In the background, little kids kicked soccer balls. One adorable little boy clung to Jude's leg like Jude was his personal hero. Jude's eyes crinkled with laughter. Hard angles of his jaw relaxed. He looked charming, handsome, heartbreaking.

Abbie

Is this real? He looks happy, like actually happy.

Lainey

Okay, but also sweet. Look at the way that kid is clinging to his leg. My word. Caroline, are you seeing this?

Caroline, biting her lip, clicked over to the original post. Someone had tagged Jude's name and written:

@3GirlsSoccerMama: Look who showed up to help at camp today. #volunteerhero #soccerstar #yesplease

The picture had already racked up hundreds of likes and comments. People praising him for getting back to the community. Women asking if he was single. Mentions of how good he looked.

Oh, she wanted to be happy for him. Really, she did. But it was hard to breathe. She rubbed her fingers against her sternum. Then, with her thumb hovering over the screen, ready to close it, she stared at the photo again.

This was also the same guy who had lashed out, kissed her and broken her heart, hadn't bothered to reach out. Had everything that they'd shared been just another part of an image he had to protect?

Oy, she wanted to scream. Instead, she sat down slowly on her chair, flowers on her lap, her phone still in her hand.

She scrolled through the comments again, absorbing the way strangers talked about him as if he could do no wrong. Maybe he was changing, growing, doing all the things he needed to do to become a healthy person. But he still hadn't apologized, not once. Not for the accusations, not for walking away when she needed him to trust her. Not for the way he made her question every instinct she'd followed in the wake of his blood work.

She swiped away the image and set her phone on the counter. Oh, she should move on. She really wanted closure. Instead, the jagged hurt of unfinished conversations twisted her insides.

Just for a minute, she let herself feel bad. She let the hurt seep in. Basked in the afterglow of the way his smile made her feel so good.

Yeah, all right, so he looked good volunteering with kids. But that didn't erase what he'd done to her—and the fact that he hadn't reached out or tried to make things right told her more than any social-media posts ever could.

She drew a ragged breath, then picked up her phone again. Not to scroll through the comments or stare at his photo anymore. She didn't even reply to her friends yet.

Instead, she texted Dr. Monroe, the only person who would truly relate to the way a newborn baby and grateful parents reminded her of why she showed up and kept doing her job every day.

Caroline

Just saw baby Noah, Amanda and Brian Kessler's newborn. He's perfect in every way. Amanda and Brian say thank you for saving their family. We did good, Dr. M. We did good.

She hit Send. Her fingers itched to look at Jude's picture again. But she didn't.

Instead, she whispered, "I hope you find what you're looking for, Jude Mercer."

Because she did still care about him. Deeply.

But she wasn't waiting around for him to choose her.

Twenty

HE COULDN'T RECALL THE LAST TIME HE'D spent twenty hours traveling anywhere.

Man, what a slog. Jude stepped off the ferry in Redemption, Alaska, his stomach still sloshing, thanks to the six-hour ride from Whittier. Had he known he wouldn't be able to get any flights out of Anchorage into Redemption, he might've rented a car and driven five hours. But instead, he'd gone with the ferry, thinking he'd be able to catch up on his sleep and rest before he ran the Redemption Ridge Race.

Except he hadn't accounted for the ferry traveling through a storm—or for spending most of the journey battling seasickness.

The salty air hit him first as he walked up the metal grate on the gangway. Folks milled about in the sunshine outside the ferry terminal, pausing to take selfies and photos of the gorgeous mountains with just a hint of snow on their jagged peaks. Jude trailed after the other passengers, his legs stiff.

He'd barely slept since he'd left New Hampshire. Rough seas weren't the only things to blame. Too many thoughts, too many regrets pummeled him. Adrenaline made a great mask for his exhaustion though. And he had one purpose—okay, two. Run this race. See Caroline.

This would be a grueling test of his endurance and grit, but every minute would be worth the struggle if it meant he could make things right. Because he never should've said those terrible things to her about the medication she'd given him. Or accused her of getting him permanently banned from competition. Now he was banking on her giving him one more chance.

The route had been posted online. He'd studied the map multiple times. The course wound through town, into the forest, and up a mountain that would make most people want to turn around and go home. He found a locker in the ferry terminal, swiped his card, paid the rental fee, and stowed his belongings. Then he grabbed a snack and tucked his ID and credit card into the small pocket in his shorts, along with the key to the locker. He'd use the three blocks to the starting line as his warm-up.

He unwrapped a peanut butter energy bar, eating it slowly as he left the terminal.

Heading for Main Street, Jude broke into a slow jog. Bright banners flapped from every light pole, and gorgeous fuchsia flowers spilled from hanging baskets. Spectators lined the sidewalks in their canvas camp chairs. Cool wind blew off the water. Many people wore hoodies and jackets, ball caps pulled low to shield them from the chilly air. Kids darted up and down the sidewalks, laughing, chasing one another.

Volunteers set up water stations. A red-and-white flag hanging from a canvas tent over a table advertised first aid and medical treatment. He ducked behind a crowd of onlookers—only on the off chance that Caroline was manning that tent. He didn't want her to know. Not yet.

He found his way to the check-in desk, pinned on his bib, then waited at the starting line. Not that he could blend in for long, but he hoped to run the race—at least the first leg of it—without her seeing him.

He jogged in place, stretched, shook out his legs, the energy of Redemption seeping into him. This town had been through a lot. The tidal wave had left scars. There were still faint watermarks on the outside of a few buildings. Construction tape fluttered around two orange cones in front of the hardware store. A couple of windows in a building on Main Street were still boarded up, but the place felt alive again.

Maybe he wasn't the only one staging a comeback.

Music spilled from large speakers near a makeshift stage. A few people in the crowd sang along, clapped with the rhythm.

"All right," he whispered, adjusting his number one more time. "I'm really doing this thing, I guess."

Racers of all ages filled in around him, talking and laughing. A few snapped last-minute selfies.

A man with a megaphone stepped up on a ladder and got their attention.

"Ladies and gentlemen, boys and girls, welcome to the Redemption Ridge Race. May the most resilient human win."

A cheer went up from the crowd. Air horns honked. People clapped. Adrenaline spiked.

And when the starting horn blasted, Jude surged forward with the pack. The thump of hundreds of feet on the new pavement on Main Street echoed. He kept an easy pace, stuck with the crowd. As they trotted down Main Street, flower boxes burst with color and chalkboard signs read *Welcome runners.* Even the kids had gotten in on the fun, holding up signs cheering people on.

His quad was still healing from his debacle with that trail marker. And his hamstrings were tight, probably from being curled up in a fetal position on the carpeted floor in the ferry's passenger lounge. Every ache or twinge drew his attention.

Stop. Focus on breathing. The slap of his sneakers against the road.

As the route led into the forest, where the sunlight filtered through the towering evergreen and cottonwood trees, racers thinned out, each adopting their own pace. Birds chirped, and the aroma of damp earth filled his lungs.

Up ahead, the first obstacle in the course loomed—two long rows of huge tires laid out on the ground.

"Oh boy," he whispered.

Jude lifted his legs high, stabbed the toe of his shoe through each of the holes. The guy ahead of him wasn't so lucky. He yelled, stepped on the edge of the tire, twisted his ankle, and went down hard.

"You okay?"

The man winced, clutching his ankle. "No, man. I think I rolled it."

Without hesitation, Jude crouched, offered an arm. Another runner paused, and the two of them got the man off the course to two volunteers standing under a canopy beneath the trees.

"We'll take it from here," the woman said, smiling and adjusting the navy-blue visor she wore over her salt-and-pepper curls.

"Thanks, man," the injured runner breathed as he collapsed into a chair.

"Take care," Jude said.

The delay had cost him minutes, but it didn't matter. Caroline would've done the same. Not that he'd done this to impress her.

He'd simply wanted to do the right thing.

The course twisted again, breaking out of the trees toward a brand-new zipline platform. Runners strapped in one at a time, gliding over the creek burbling over rocks below, shouting. Jude jogged in place, waiting his turn. Then clipped on his harness, double-checked that it was secure, and a beat later—he soared. Wind rushed in his face, the blue water of the creek flashing in his peripheral vision, and then a jolt as he landed in a crouch on the opposite plywood platform, grinning.

"Wow. What a ride."

He unhooked, hung his harness on a tree branch, and bolted toward the next stretch of the course.

There was water and an aid station just before the next obstacle. Thankfully, about a dozen runners were ahead of him, lined up, waiting to grab a cup of water. He spotted her before she saw him.

Caroline stood in khaki shorts and a white T-shirt with the Redemption logo on the front. Her hair was pulled back in a sleek ponytail, her cheeks flushed, her mouth set in concentration as she offered a paper cup of water to a passing runner.

She still wore her walking boot. Poor thing. He hated that her injury hadn't healed.

Then she looked up.

Their eyes met.

He didn't stop. Grabbed a cup of water from the volunteer assisting her.

Surprise registered on her face. The widening of her eyes. The parting of her lips.

He saw it all. Recognition. Shock. Something else he dared to hope for—interest.

He tossed her a smile even as his muscles and chest burned from exertion.

She blinked.

He downed the water, tossed the cup in the trash, and jogged away.

This would be a tricky part. Log bridge across another shallow creek. His shoes slipped on the wet wood and squelched in the muddy creek bank.

Gross.

Every obstacle tested his stamina. Mud splattered on his calves. Tree branches scraped his arms. His lungs burned, but he wouldn't stop. He pressed forward. And when he reached the steep incline at the end of the trail, he paused, stared down the brutal climb up Redemption Ridge.

Runners slowed to a walk. Some bent over, clutching their knees.

He wasn't giving up. He planted one foot, then another, his quads screaming.

You trained for this. You can do this.

Sweat rolled down his back. The sun warmed his neck. The crowd noise along Main Street had faded.

Near the summit, the path narrowed, and they had to go one at a time. He heard a cowbell clang in the distance.

Somebody made it. He planned to be next.

He reached the top, lungs burning. Grabbed the bell. It was tied to a crooked pine tree with a bright red ribbon.

He rang it hard. The sound echoed down the mountain.

Finally. He'd made it. Then he turned and ran back down.

Downhill burned—just as much as the uphill climb. Different though. His knees protested. His leg muscles trembled.

Redemption spread out below him like a postcard. Rooftops bright in the sun. The bay shimmering beyond.

The finish line, marked by a festive arch of white, blue, and silver balloons beckoned in the distance. He was going to make it. He could do this.

The final stretch was a blur. Not just because it was an easy run through a residential neighborhood. But as he passed houses with newly mowed lawns and the library getting a facelift, smiling faces and cheering fans rose like a wave.

He'd done it.

He crossed the finish line, limping slightly and struggling to catch his breath.

A volunteer handed him a cup of water and clapped him on the back. "Well done, man. Well done."

"Thanks." Jude forced out the word, but really, the only praise and recognition he wanted was from one person.

And one person only.

He was here. Running the race. How could that be?

Caroline climbed out of the golf cart that Dave had used to transport her from her first aid station on the course to the one closest to the finish line.

"There you go. Thanks again for all your help today, Caroline. We appreciate you."

She smiled. "Not a problem. Great race."

She joined the other volunteers at the folding table, handing out cups of water as runners jogged toward the finish line, panting and their faces flushed. The salty air swirled around her, carrying the scent of kettle corn and something delicious—french fries, probably—wafting out of the open doors of Homeport nearby.

A cheer erupted from the crowd as another runner crossed the finish line, darting under the balloon arch. She swiped her hand over her forehead, dabbing away the sweat, then passed a cup of water to a young boy as he dashed past her table.

"You want to sit down?" one of the volunteers asked, offering her an empty folding chair. "Put your foot up?"

Caroline waved her off. "Thanks, but I'm okay." She glanced down at her boot. Oh, how she'd wanted to run today. But Dr. Wallace had repeated her X-ray a few days ago and gently but firmly told her no. The bone in her foot's fracture still hadn't healed completely. Not only could she not run, she couldn't ditch her boot. Not yet.

She sighed and scanned the crowd. Frankly, she still couldn't believe it that he'd appeared at her water station on the trail. And that smile—ugh. As much as she'd wanted to glare and ask what in the world he was doing, his appearance had stolen her breath, stolen her words. All she could do was stare as he'd grabbed a cup of water, pounded it, and disappeared into the forest.

It was fine, she'd told herself for the rest of the time she'd spent at that station. It was fine that he hadn't called, hadn't bothered to tell her he was coming back to Redemption. He didn't owe her any explanation.

Oh, but the truth wouldn't let her go. And how she missed him. His witty comments, that handsome smile, the way he looked at her when she challenged him.

A flurry of movement near the makeshift stage outside the community center got her attention. They were ready to announce the winners for each age group. Dave took the mic, offered a few introductory comments, and then started with the youngest runners.

Caroline handed out a few more cups of water. A young runner looked like she'd pushed herself a little too much and stumbled over to the station. Caroline kept an eye on her as another volunteer guided the girl to a seat nearby.

Then Jude—tall and lean, his hair damp with sweat, that familiar easy stride she'd memorized—moved across the stage. She blinked. What was he doing? Yeah, okay, so of course he'd probably won in the thirty to thirty-five age group for men. It would've been bizarre if he'd lost.

His fingers trailed along his jaw as he stood beside Dave, and her breath caught in her throat. What was he doing?

She shifted her weight to her good foot. Her mom appeared at her side.

"You all right?" her mom asked, grinning. "Don't hurt yourself trying to leap into his arms."

"Ha! Funny." But her pulse sped. "I can't believe he's here."

"Let's hear what he has to say," Mom said.

"And the winner of the thirty- to thirty-five-year-old men's division, all the way from New Hampshire—Jude Mercer!"

Cheers erupted. Jude accepted the medal, offered a sheepish smile.

"Could I have a few words? Just—I'll be quick, I promise."

Dave grimaced and handed over the mic. The crowd quieted. A few balloons bounced down the street, caught and swept up by the breeze.

Jude cleared his throat. "I know I have no right to take the stage, but if you would allow me, I'd like to say a few words. Please."

A few people clapped. Someone rang a cowbell, and a man yelled, "Go for it, dude!"

Jude's eyes swept the crowd, and she nearly sank to the ground when the full weight of his gaze locked on hers.

"To be honest, I came to Redemption to hide," he said, his voice steady. "It's been a rough year for me. Nothing compared to what you all have been through, of course." He hesitated. His cheeks flushed. "I told myself I was here to heal and recover, find a new normal. But what I didn't realize until recently is that it wasn't just my body that was injured. Something else needed healing. It was my heart."

Gasps and murmurs rippled through the crowd.

"Oh my word," Caroline's mother whispered, linking her arm through Caroline's.

"Redemption gave me more than a place to rest. It helped me embrace a new perspective. People here genuinely care about one another. And you gave me a second chance in your own unique way—and that's something I didn't know I needed."

He paused. Caroline's vision blurred with tears.

"And one person in particular . . . she saw me—the real me—when I was disgusted with myself. Caroline McGuire."

Several heads swiveled toward her.

"Caroline, I pushed you away because I was scared. Scared of failing, scared of not being good enough. Frankly, I was afraid I couldn't be the man you deserved."

"Oh, honey," Mom whispered, touching her head to Caroline's.

"But the truth is, you made me *want* to be everything you deserve—and more. Not for cameras or for empty praise, but for *you*. Even though I haven't deserved your grace, you saw the parts of me I kept buried and you still stuck close . . . until I pushed you away. I was dumb enough to think that running would somehow protect me. But it doesn't. It just ensures that I end up alone."

A woman nearby dabbed at her eyes with a napkin.

"So I'm done running," Jude said. "I'm standing here in front of all the people who matter, asking for a fresh start. I'm so very sorry. I hope that you can forgive me. Like I said, I don't deserve another chance. But I *would* like one . . . because I love you, Caroline. And if you'll have me, I want to fight for this. For us."

The woman crying into her napkin leaned closer and whispered, "If you don't forgive him, I will."

Caroline let out a shaky laugh, then clasped her hand over her mouth and burst into tears.

"Thanks, Dave." Jude handed the microphone back.

"You betcha." Dave put his hand up to his forehead to shield his eyes from the sun. "Caroline? Where are you?"

Oh boy.

Warmth heated her skin and the crowd parted as Jude jogged down the steps from the stage. Then walked. Then broke into a jog again—limping slightly—straight for her. Heart hammering, she swiped at the tears running down her cheeks.

When he reached her, he stopped.

"Nicely done, Jude." Mom squeezed his arm, then stepped away.

Jude inched closer, then cupped her cheeks with both hands. "Hi."

"Hi," she whispered.

"I meant every word."

"I know," she said, her voice cracked. "I believed in you. I still believe in you. I always will."

"Caroline McGuire, will you give me another chance to make you laugh every day?"

Instead of answering, she kissed him—long and sweet—until the crowd erupted.

"It's about time!" somebody yelled.

And there, in the middle of a town still rebuilding, surrounded by neighbors and family, in the aroma of second chances, she knew she was right where she belonged—home, in Jude's arms, ready for their next adventure.

Together.

Epilogue

THE CLINIC WAS QUIET FOR A MONDAY IN THE summer. Too quiet. The kind of break in the action that only seemed to happen when Dr. Wallace was about to leave town. Caroline leaned against the counter in the reception area while Connie handled a phone call with an insurance company.

Caroline glanced up when the door to the break room opened and Dr. Monroe and Wendy came out.

"Dr. Wallace still wrapping things up?" Dr. Monroe asked, stepping up to the counter beside Caroline.

Connie hung up the phone and spun around in her chair. "Oh, that man. He acts like he's going to the moon every time he takes a vacation. He's probably adding final notes to his charts just to keep us all informed."

Caroline shook her head. "I'll believe it when he actually walks out the door."

Almost as if he'd heard her, Dr. Wallace emerged from his office. A battered duffel bag, the kind that looked like it had survived one too many outdoor adventures, was slung over his shoulder.

He wore a T-shirt under a fleece vest, along with cargo pants and hiking boots.

"Okay," he said, locking the office door behind him. "This is it. I'm officially off duty for the next two weeks. Don't text. Don't call. No smoke signals. I'm out."

"Noted," Caroline teased, a smile tugging at her lips.

"Caroline?" His tone shifted slightly. "You're in charge."

"Huh," she said, her stomach doing a little flip. "That's cute."

"No, seriously," he said, holding her gaze. "You've got this. Take the wheel."

He wasn't serious. Was he?

Connie's chair squeaked as she rolled closer. Caroline stole a glance at Dr. Monroe. How would she feel about this?

The older woman gave her a thumbs-up.

"All right," she said. "I'll do my best."

"I'd expect nothing less," he said.

Wendy clapped him on the shoulder as he moved past. "Have a great time," she said. "Enjoy your family."

"Tell Mrs. Wallace she needs to keep an eye on you," Connie added with a grin. "We know you think you're a seasoned fisherman, but please be safe."

"Of course." Dr. Wallace headed for the front door. Then he paused and turned back, his expression softening.

"I mean it, Caroline. You've done more than enough to prove yourself here. Redemption is blessed to have you."

Her throat tightened and she cleared it quickly. "Thank you," she said. "That means a lot."

"All right, enough of this sappy stuff," Dr. Monroe said, offering a teasing smile. "You're going to miss your flight if you don't hit the road for Anchorage."

"Fine, fine, I'm going," Dr. Wallace said, but his hand lingered on the doorknob. He hesitated, looking around the waiting room.

"Go," Connie said with a gentle shooing motion. "And don't

come back early. We don't want to see your face until you've had at least two solid weeks of vacation."

"Fine," he said, feigning exasperation. "Consider me gone." And with that, he stepped into the bright summer light.

They all lingered, staring at the door. Caroline glanced at her coworkers. Were they all expecting him to come back in? Say he'd changed his mind?

She glanced at her watch. "Let's get back to it. Doctor's orders."

The others nodded and dispersed, returning to their duties. Caroline stayed at the counter, giving the afternoon's schedule a careful once-over.

"You okay?" Connie asked.

Caroline looked up, smiled, and nodded. "Of course."

"You're gonna do great. I just know it."

"Thanks," Caroline said. "I think I'm finally starting to believe that."

The rest of the day passed in a blur of activity. She treated her usual patients, sneaked in a quick coffee break, and even managed to handle stitching up an injured tourist who'd walked in after lunch. By five o'clock, she had treated her last patient and straightened the waiting area with Connie.

As Caroline stood near the window, organizing the flyers on the community bulletin board, she caught sight of movement in the parking lot. A familiar truck pulled into a spot near the front door, and her pulse quickened when she saw Jude climb out.

He was carrying a paper bag in one hand and a tray of drinks in the other. Her pulse sped. How could he look so good in black joggers and a gray T-shirt? He glanced up at the clinic's windows, caught her watching, then grinned.

Caroline opened the door just as he reached it. "What's all this?" she asked, stepping outside.

"Dinner," Jude said, holding the bag up. "Figured you might enjoy a picnic down by the water."

She smiled. "You didn't have to do that."

"I wanted to," he said simply, shrugging. "Besides, I heard it's your first day officially running the show around here. That deserves a little celebration."

Her cheeks warmed. "How did you hear about that?"

Jude pinned her with a look. "Because this is Redemption. And your mom is low-key bragging about you at Homeport."

She laughed. "You didn't have to, but . . . I'm glad you did."

"Anytime," he said, his voice soft. "Ready in five?"

"Be right back."

Inside, she shut down her computer, then grabbed her purse and stepped out into the cool evening air, the breeze tugging at her hair. "See you," she called to Connie, who was locking up behind her.

"Have a good one," Connie called back with a wave.

Caroline lingered on the steps, then glanced back at the clinic. There would probably be a few surprises while Dr. Wallace was away. She might even make a few mistakes. But along with her coworkers, they'd figure it all out.

Smiling, she followed Jude to his truck. For the first time in ages, she felt like she belonged.

Thank You!

Thank you so much for reading *The Last Mile Between Us*. We hope you enjoyed the story. If you did, would you be willing to do us a favor and leave a review? It doesn't have to be long—just a few words to help other readers know what they're getting. (But no spoilers! We don't want to wreck the fun!) Thank you again for reading!

We'd love to hear from you—not only about this story, but about any characters or stories you'd like to read in the future. Contact us at www.sunrisepublishing.com/contact.

Read on for more of the

WELCOME TO
REDEMPTION, ALASKA

series

Return to Redemption for
Tate and Scottie's story in
The Echo of Your Heart.

Where broken hearts come to heal.

He's been in love with her for fifteen years. She's never noticed. Until now.

He made her mix CDs. Drove her home in the dark. Idled at the curb through an entire Alaska winter just so she'd have a ride after practice.

She called him her best friend. Then she left.

Scottie Sheridan has spent seven years proving she doesn't need Redemption — or anyone in it. She films reality survival shows in the Alaskan wilderness, runs camera on heaving fishing boats in driving rain, chases the perfect shot in every dangerous place her boss can find. The job is her whole life. The adrenaline fills the gaps.

It's also going to get her killed. And Tate McGuire knows it.

When a last-minute assignment pulls Scottie back to Redemption — back to her ailing father, her complicated stepsister, and the man she never let herself really see — Tate is done pretending he's fine with "just friends." He's watched her take every risk but the one that matters. He's prayed over every dangerous gig she's taken. And now she's here, filming on the same wild waters he pilots for a living, and every instinct he has is screaming.

When a violent collision on Prince William Sound puts Scottie in the water and Tate in after her, fifteen years of silence finally breaks the surface.

She left because staying hurt too much. He stayed because leaving was never an option.

One

JATE MCGUIRE LIVED TO KEEP PEOPLE SAFE.

Some might call him hypervigilant. But what was so wrong with being aware of his surroundings? He relished peering around corners and developing backup contingency plans. Besides, today had reconfirmed what he'd always believed—if everyone followed the rules and obeyed regulations, fewer people got hurt.

Too bad not every captain embraced his perspective.

He slung his backpack over his shoulder and climbed down the fiberglass-and-rope ladder draped over the side of the cruise ship. Rain sprayed his face and wind buffeted his back, flipping the hood on his GORE-TEX jacket up around his ears. He gripped the bright-orange ladder rails, gritting his teeth as it swayed from side to side.

One step at a time.

Had the ship sped up? He'd instructed the captain and the officer on duty to hold at twelve knots until he'd fully disembarked. But given the attitude he'd encountered on the bridge from the older captain with the thin smile and territorial approach, it wouldn't surprise him if they'd ignored his guidance.

He descended the last few rungs, then hopped onto the wet deck of the *Silver Bullet,* the water taxi that ferried maritime pilots to and from the vessels they guided in and out of Prince William Sound. If they remained on call, they went back to their home base—a houseboat anchored in Shelter Cove. But when their shift ended, they caught a ride back to Redemption.

"Hey, thanks for the lift." Tate greeted Anthony, a lifelong Redemption resident and today's driver on the *Silver Bullet.*

"Not a problem." Anthony shook Tate's outstretched hand. "It's gnarly out here today."

"Sure is." Tate double-checked the buckles on his life jacket, then followed Anthony toward the cabin's door on the starboard side. The boat dipped and swayed on the waves as it rode its own wake alongside the massive cruise ship.

"There's hot coffee in the thermos." Anthony pointed to the moss-green canister on the ledge under the window. "We'll be back in Redemption ASAP. I've got to pick up the new pilot."

"Looking forward to meeting him." Tate tugged the cabin door shut. "We could certainly use the extra help."

Anthony raked a hand through his tousled silver hair, then resumed control of the vessel. Faint lines pleated from the corners of his blue eyes as he looked at Tate. "You're going to be a busy guy if you decide to fill that empty seat on the town council."

Steam curled from the thermos as Tate poured coffee into a Styrofoam cup. "I suppose so."

He hadn't definitively accepted the nomination yet. Word must've spread anyway.

Anthony pushed the throttle forward and then peeled away from the Norwegian cruise ship. Picking up speed, they cut across the choppy blue-gray water of Prince William Sound, leaving the departing ship behind. Wispy fingers of fog hugged the dense green hillsides along the bay.

Anthony adjusted the volume on his Bluetooth speaker, and the guitar solo from "Free Bird" filtered into the cabin. Tate settled into the bench seat on the port side and tried not to spill his coffee on his gray cargo pants.

"Nothing against politicians, but are you sure that's the role for you?"

"Not exactly." Tate stared through the rain-speckled windshield. "But now that Jason Walters moved away and Sarah Goldsmith declined the nomination, someone needs to step up. We need stronger safety protocols. Better emergency planning. Redemption could be a lot . . . safer."

"Protecting people and looking out for your community are excellent reasons to serve." Anthony paused, letting the boat ride over a swell. "Keep in mind it's not always your responsibility to worry about safety."

Tate's fingers tightened around the cup. But if he didn't, who would? Because he'd lost way too much sleep over the years, slogging through his guilt from his own missteps. His failure had nearly cost his father everything. Tate had had one job—to change the batteries in the smoke detector—and he hadn't done it. Now Dad paid the price.

"Tate?" Anthony's voice tugged him back before he relived the gut-wrenching panic of that horrible night. Again.

Tate swiveled in the chair and met Anthony's steady gaze. "I heard what you said and I appreciate your advice. But I can't sit back and let this town coast without trustworthy leadership."

"That's fair." Anthony nodded. "Especially after what happened with the reality TV folks."

"Oh no, what happened?"

"A guy broke his femur. Had to call on your brothers to help get him out."

Tate shook his head. "That's why those people shouldn't be here."

"What people?"

"The Hollywood crowd. It's time to stop giving those folks opportunities to film here."

"It's income. Maybe even some tax revenue? Perhaps our town council could look into that. Or you could campaign on that very issue. Make it part of your platform—no more TV shows and movies made near Redemption." Anthony grinned. "You know I'm just messing with you. We've been friends a long time. Happy to hear your opinions."

"Glad somebody is," Tate said. "Will the guy with the broken leg be okay?"

"Hope so. I heard he was transferred out of state though. Wanted to be closer to family."

"Makes sense."

Twenty minutes later, Tate spotted the pastel clapboard houses built on the hilly streets of Redemption, his hometown. He'd grown up fishing, hunting, living here, and only left for a few short years to attend the Merchant Marine Academy. And now, every time he went to work, he vowed he'd do his job to the best of his ability. He'd made it his mission to protect the water, the people, and the livelihoods of the men and women who were counting on him to escort ships safely in and out of Redemption.

Anthony slowed down when he hit the no-wake zone at the harbor's entrance. Tate grabbed his backpack, drained the rest of his coffee, and tossed the cup in the trash. He stepped outside. As the bow of the boat glided up along the dock, Tate hopped off and tied the lines to the cleat. There was no one else around, and a steady drizzle fell from the thick white clouds draped low.

"I don't see anybody here. I'm a little early though," Anthony said. "Pilot's not due for another hour."

"Can I give you a ride somewhere?"

"Nope." Anthony smiled, a dimple forming in his ruddy cheek. "I'm good. Gonna gas this baby up, then kick back and relax for a bit."

"All right. Thanks again for the ride."

"You bet. See you next time."

Tate fished his keys from the pocket of his backpack and headed for the ramp. It was steep due to low tide, and his shoes squeaked on the metal grates. The briny scent of the water lapping against the wood pilings under his feet brought him comfort. Smelled like home.

The truck sat where he'd left it across the street from Dockside Pizza Company. A low rumble in his stomach reminded him that breakfast had been a banana, an energy bar, and scrambled eggs several hours ago. The aroma of yeasty dough baking tempted him to pop in and order a pizza, but Gary Sheridan came first. Tate wanted to stop by his place and check on him. Make sure he had his meds and his oxygen. Lainey wouldn't appreciate him feeding Gary junk, anyway. And he had promised her that he'd look after her stepfather while she was out of town for a couple of days.

The rain pattered against his windshield as he drove through the main intersection, his wipers thump-thumping the moisture away. An RV cruised down Main Street, slower than molasses, so he cut through on a side street in front of the café, then drove one block over and parked in front of Redemption Outfitters.

He waited for two kids on scooters to ride past, then he jogged across the street to the Copper Kettle. The place hummed with activity and conversation. Shiny green plants drooped from macramé hangers, their trailing vines curling along the shiplap walls. An older couple had claimed the deep upholstered armchairs in the far corner. A family he recognized from church had crowded around the big table in the center, the kids' mouths ringed with chocolate as they hoovered down their donuts. A long line snaked back from the counter and bakery case. He breathed in the buttery sweetness of pastries mixed with the sharper edge of fresh-ground espresso. The grinder rattled like stones in a metal pail, followed by the hiss of steaming milk.

Tate shifted forward. Two chairs scraped on the laminate floor, and conversation from a table near the window filtered toward him. He cut a quick glance at the two men hunched over steaming mugs, their camo ball caps pulled low.

"You see those TV people setting up again?" one asked, his voice gravelly.

The other snorted and shook his head. "If their cameras get in the way this weekend, they'll be fish bait. Pinks are running, and I'm not missing out because somebody wants to stage a fake TV show."

"And they better not mess with deer season either," the other guy grumbled. "Some things are off-limits."

Tate looked away, pretending to study the menu. But the complaints lodged in his head, underscoring what he already feared. Not everybody in Redemption was thrilled about *Ultimate Alaskan* filming here.

His sister Megan had taken the day off, and he didn't recognize the barista filling in for her. He got himself and Gary two green smoothies, yogurt with granola and fresh fruit, and a chocolate chip scone. Maybe Gary needed at least one treat.

A few minutes later, he parked in front of the Sheridans' house, a gorgeous mint-green Craftsman-style home on a coveted plateau carved out of the hillside overlooking Redemption.

As he climbed the three wide steps on the front porch, the last one felt a little loose and squeaked under his weight. He stopped and tapped it with his toe. He'd have to come back and fix this later.

He knocked softly on the door, then turned the knob and stepped inside.

"Gary, it's me."

The place smelled faintly of cigarette smoke. *Uh-oh.* Gary was not supposed to be smoking. Tate took off his boots and left them on the faded linoleum in the entryway. The muffled sound of a television game show hinted that Gary might be in his usual spot in the living room.

Pausing, he gave the framed photos in the entryway a brief glance. The wall was a gallery of Gary's life. Interesting how he hadn't taken down any photos of either of his former wives. There were plenty of photos of Lainey and her stepsister, Scottie, throughout the years. Tate let his gaze linger on his favorite—Scottie standing on the bank of the Copper River, grinning at the camera and proudly holding up a salmon. She wore a trucker-style ball cap, with her dark brown curls tamed into two chunky braids. Nobody else looked that good in a vintage ABBA T-shirt, with faded jeans tucked into rubber boots.

She was gorgeous.

She'd turned sixteen that summer and conveniently hadn't bothered to get her license yet. She'd persuaded him to take her fishing. He'd pretended to be exasperated. Honestly, though, spending a whole day with Scottie had been his idea of heaven.

Another fun fact he'd kept to himself.

Tate scooted past a stack of boxes, then peeked through the wide cased opening and found Gary sitting in the brown leather recliner facing the television, his oxygen tank wheeled up next to the cracked armrest. "Hey, pal. Are you awake?"

"Hi, Tate." Gary's craggy face creased even more as he smiled. "How are you doing? What brings you by?"

"I thought I'd check on you. Just came back from work. Have you had breakfast yet?"

"Not yet." Gary eyed the bag. "What you got there? Croissants, I hope."

"How about some yogurt with granola, and a smoothie?"

"Hmm." Gary's smile faded. "Did Lainey put you up to this?"

"Not exactly."

Gary reached for the remote, clicking off the game show. He pressed the button on his chair and lowered the recliner's footrest.

"You want to eat right here?"

"No, no." Gary waved his hand. "Let's go into the kitchen. I was taking a catnap. You're my second visitor already today."

Tate helped him up, and they walked together as Gary wheeled his oxygen to the kitchen. "Oh yeah? Who else was here?"

"Make yourself at home, but get some plates, please. And how about some coffee?"

Tate eyed the dark brew sitting in the well-loved coffeemaker on the Formica countertop.

"Did you make that?"

"Yep, this morning."

"Got it."

Tate poked around the kitchen. A few minutes later, they had their breakfast spread out on the square wooden table, with hot coffee between them.

"So, I guess you heard the big news." Gary removed the lid from the yogurt parfait, added three blueberries, and took a small bite.

"Been at work. What's the news?"

Gary paused, a spoonful of yogurt halfway to his mouth. "Damian Michaels dropped by. He wants Scottie to come home."

What? Tate choked on his smoothie.

Gary smiled, then dipped his spoon back into the container.

Tate plucked a napkin out of the bag, then wiped his face and the speckles of smoothie on the table. "Really? Huh. Wow, I hadn't heard that."

"He left a few minutes before you got here. Wants her to be a camera operator on that show. The one they're filming out at Port Frisco."

"I thought somebody just got hurt out there."

Gary peeked inside the bag, then fished out the scone. "Broke his leg or something. That's why Damian needs Scottie."

"How do you think this is going to go over with Lainey?"

Gary shook his head. "Lainey's gonna blow a gasket."

"You're not wrong," Tate said.

Selfishly, Tate wouldn't mind seeing Scottie again. And he wanted Gary to have his daughter back, even if she only stayed for a few weeks. He knew how old wounds festered though. Part of him was already bracing for impact.

Scottie Sheridan never backed away from a challenge.

Wiping the sweat from her brow with the back of her hand, she dug her toes deeper into the warm sand and shot her partner, Violet, a "we've got this" look. The California sun warmed Scottie's bare shoulders as she stared through the volleyball net at their opponents, a feisty pair from Santa Cruz. The match was tied 1–1. Scottie and Violet were down by two points—11–13—due to a pair of vicious ace serves.

"She won't land a third," Scottie whispered.

The woman, a willowy blonde with her hair twisted in a long, intricate braid and her tan sculpted arms glistening in the sun, tossed the ball in the air and executed a flawless jump serve.

"Mine," Scottie called out and hustled backward. She made contact, but just barely. The ball smacked her forearms, then arced toward the net. A beautiful pass, really. Violet got under it and offered up a fantastic set. Scottie sprinted, grunting as she leaped into the air, then spiked the ball.

Blocked.

Violet dove into the sand, but the ball landed just out of reach.

Shoot. They were about to lose. Scottie helped Violet to her feet, then gave her a double high-five. "It's all good."

Doubt flickered in Violet's hazel eyes.

"We're still in this, girl." Scottie patted Violet's sweaty shoulder and returned to the back of the court, ready to defend the serve.

This one took them by surprise though. The woman served a

gentle lob that barely cleared the net. Violet had to scramble to dig it. Scottie hustled to make a clumsy set, but it was off-balance and sloppy.

Violet spiked the ball into the net.

"Rats," Scottie said. This was not going well. "It's okay, Vi. We're gonna rally."

Violet turned away without saying a word.

But the next serve sailed over the net with such force that Scottie barely had time to respond and shanked the ball out of bounds. Applause rippled through the crowd sitting in the bleachers. Their opponents cheered, high-fived, and hugged. Scottie stood, hands on hips, her chest heaving.

"It's all right. Good match." She slapped Violet's outstretched hand and then moved toward the net to congratulate the winners. After shaking their hands and offering polite praise, she trudged in the sand to the bench where they kept their water bottles, towels, and string bags.

"No worries, we'll get the next one," Scottie said.

"Double elimination," Violet said, uncapping her water bottle. "That was our second loss."

Oh. Scottie buried her face in her pink towel. What a bummer.

"I'm supposed to be in Vancouver next week," Violet said, tugging her auburn hair free from her yellow scrunchy. "We're shooting a Christmas movie in four weeks, so I won't be here for the next tournament."

"Understood," Scottie said, then chugged half of her water. "Want to grab lunch? At Beach Street Grille?"

"Sure," Violet said. "Let's do it."

The Pacific Ocean roared its way onto the Southern California coastline, waves ebbing and flowing and leaving trails of white, foamy lattice on the golden sand. Their raucous Saturday morning game of beach volleyball had ended, but that didn't mean they had to go home.

Scottie packed her free time full of beach volleyball, hikes, and eating out with friends. She hated being still, especially since she spent so much time traveling. When she was home in Carlsbad, she liked to soak up every minute, making memories. Because stillness was dangerous. Stillness forced her to think.

A young couple walked past, following their curious toddler down the beach toward the waves. The woman wore a baby wrapped in a snug blanket against her chest, her fingers twined through the man's.

Scottie's heart pinched. She looked away.

Nope, can't get distracted by regret.

The what-ifs and the maybes would take her out. Sure, in her weaker moments, her thoughts circled back to her life in Redemption and what might have been. She hadn't been back to Alaska in ages. Other than her five-year class reunion, she conveniently avoided her hometown. Ever since her stepmother divorced her dad and moved to Montana about ten years ago, things hadn't been great at her dad's house. And frankly her relationship with her stepsister, Lainey, had always been dicey.

But she'd heard from Damian, one of her friends from Redemption who'd helped her get her first job in LA as a production assistant, that her father's health had declined. Would Lainey tell her if things got really bad?

The notion sent her stumbling, and she took three awkward strides to regain her footing.

"You all right?" Violet shot her a concerned look. "Need more water?"

"Nope, I'm good." Scottie pasted on a smile. "Just got distracted."

"I get that," Violet said, digging in her string bag for her keys. "Sometimes I have the attention span of a gnat."

Scottie laughed. "Same."

Her dad's chronic health issues made it challenging for him to work. His settlement from the oil company provided a comfortable life. At least that's what she'd been led to believe. She wasn't eager to return to the place that had been the source of so much heartache. Besides, her career as a camera operator kept her busy with its long hours and intense demands.

Except her latest gig had wrapped last week—ten episodes of a true-crime show filmed in Studio City. Now she had a break, which should've felt good. But ever since that crane malfunctioned three months ago on set in Arizona and nearly crushed her during a tracking shot, something inside her had shifted. Yeah, she said she wanted the big assignments. Claimed she could work as hard as her male counterparts. But on the inside, she quaked with fear. That freak accident had pulverized her confidence.

Her watch hummed with a text. She couldn't resist reading it:

Damian

Call me when you have time to chat. Something's come up.

She frowned. *Tempting.* What if he offered her an assignment she couldn't turn down? An ideal location with perfect weather, interesting culture, and plenty of places to hike on her off days. Like New Zealand. She'd even take rustic accommodation. That wasn't a deal-breaker. Thanks to her nomadic existence, she'd learned to be content staying in basic cabins, yurts, or old-school roadside motels.

Violet and Scottie were almost to Violet's white Prius when Scottie spotted a blue pacifier lying in the sand. She bent down and picked it up, brushing off a few grains of sand with her fingers. Looking up, she spotted the people she'd passed earlier—the young couple with the toddler and baby. They were scanning the ground, the toddler tugging at the man's hand.

"Excuse me," Scottie called out, holding up the pacifier. "Is this yours?"

The woman's face lit up. "Yes! Thank you. We've been looking everywhere for it."

"No problem," Scottie said with a smile. She uncapped her water bottle and gave the pacifier a quick rinse before handing it back. "Here, good as new."

"Thank you so much," the man said, his voice warm with gratitude.

"You're a lifesaver," the woman added, adjusting the baby against her chest.

Scottie waved it off. "Happy to help. Have a great day."

Before she joined Violet, waiting by the car, Scottie's phone hummed with another text.

Damian

Hey again. I know it's your day off, but this situation is evolving quickly. Chat in 10?

Sighing, she tapped the screen and called him. He answered on the second ring.

"Scottie, hey. Sorry to interrupt your Saturday."

"No problem." She paced in a small circle in the parking lot. "What's up?"

"One of my camera operators in Alaska fell and fractured his femur."

"Oh no." She stopped walking. "Is he all right?"

"They flew him to Anchorage and then on to Seattle. He's having surgery, and he'll recover, but he can't work. I need to fill that spot ASAP."

A knot formed in her stomach. "Is that why you texted me?"

"We need someone who won't flinch when things get unpredictable."

Ha. She was not that girl. Not anymore.

"You grew up there," Damian continued. "You know the terrain, and you can handle the weather. So you're the perfect person for this role."

"Is it reality TV? Unscripted?"

"Yes. *Ultimate Alaskan.* You'd be finished by mid-October, or by Halloween at the latest."

Less than two months. Maybe she could handle it. "Where at exactly?"

"That's the best part. Port Frisco and Redemption."

No. She pressed her palm to her forehead. "Damian, I-I can't go back there."

"You're perfect for this, Scottie. And you'll be able to see your dad."

"Yeah. That's the problem."

Damian hesitated. "Listen, I'll sweeten the deal. You take this and I'll give you first pick of next year's assignments. Including New Zealand."

She kicked a pebble across the asphalt. "Wow, you know the way to a girl's heart."

"I need an answer by tomorrow."

"Twenty-four hours?"

"Can't afford to wait, Scottie."

"All right, I'll let you know. Thanks." She ended the call. Violet met her gaze over the roof of the car.

"Everything okay?"

"That was Damian."

"Oh?"

"He wants me to go to Alaska."

Violet's eyes widened. "Home sweet home. Did you say yes?"

"I didn't, and I don't want to."

"Why not?" She clicked her key fob and unlocked the car. Scottie climbed into the passenger side, dropping her string bag at her feet.

"I'm never ready to go back there."

"Oh, come on. You're usually so adventurous. What's wrong?"

"For one, my dad's health isn't improving. I've let my stepsister handle everything. We've never been close and it's . . . a whole thing."

Violet shot her a look. "Sounds like now would be a good time for you to visit, then."

"They're filming a reality show on location."

Violet raised her brows. "What kind of show?"

"It's a competition. Haven't watched yet, but I saw a story online. Eight contestants fighting to be crowned the ultimate Alaskan. Damian wants me to film while they slog through survival challenges. Then after each episode airs, viewers vote, week after week, until the last one standing wins."

"Sounds brutal."

"Exactly."

Violet started the car, then adjusted the AC. "You can handle it though. You're always so brave."

"I used to be." Scottie buckled in. "But not anymore."

"What does that mean?"

"Remember that Arizona shoot? A few months back?"

Violet drove toward the lot's exit. "Yeah, the western movie."

"The crane almost dropped a rig on me. I could've died. I haven't told anyone, but I'm not the same. Even though I say I want the hard jobs, I'm scared to death."

Violet eased to a stop, then glanced over, her eyes filled with empathy. "Scottie, I'm sorry. I didn't know."

Scottie turned and looked out the window. "But part of me wonders if I need to prove to myself and to Damian that I can still do hard things . . . except I don't want to learn that lesson in Redemption."

"Sounds like Damian believes in you or he wouldn't have reached out."

Scottie finished off the last of her water. "Is belief enough when you're stranded on a remote location in pouring rain with reality TV stars who have probably never been to Alaska before? And the fog is so thick you can't see ten feet in front of you?"

"That does not sound like a super-fun time," Violet said. "But maybe this job is the catalyst that gets you where you need to be."

"Uh, you don't understand. My family has this weird streak. And not the good kind. My great-grandfather passed away fighting a fire, my grandfather passed away in the '64 earthquake, and my dad is on permanent disability after cleaning up the oil when the Exxon tanker ran aground. Three generations of my family have been impacted by some terrible disaster."

"Well, that doesn't mean you'll be the fourth."

"It's still nerve-racking."

"I get it. But like I said, maybe you'll go, have a fantastic experience, and be so glad you said yes. You can't let your fear hold you back, Scottie. This is so unlike you. Trust that there's a bigger plan for your life."

"I'm so not a fan of that."

Because trusting in bigger plans meant confronting her fears. Wading through pain. And frankly, she'd rather run.

Acknowledgments

I'm so grateful for the many people in my life who make this writing journey possible. I spend a lot of time working at home by myself, writing day after day, one word at a time. But the production of a book requires a team effort, so this novel wouldn't exist without the following:

To my husband Steve, I couldn't write a single word without your unconditional love and support. For years, you have graciously shared me with a lot of fictional friends and never complained. And you've cheered me on when I was certain I couldn't keep going. Thank you. I'm blessed to call you mine.

To our three sons, thank you for the laughter, the hugs, and most of all, your love. I hope watching your mom chase her big dreams inspires you to chase your own.

To my mom Nancy, I'm certain you're my biggest fan. Thank you for always being in my corner, helping me find new readers, and praying without ceasing. Your faith journey and commitment to the Lord is my inspiration. Thanks for the many memories made in Alaska. I wouldn't trade my childhood for anything.

To my sister Heather and her family, thank you for being loyal readers and telling your friends about my books. I know how much Alaska means to you, and I hope you love this story as well.

To Lisa, Wendy and Linda Jo, our chats are the best! Thank you for the laughter and the prayers. I'm so glad we've been able to encourage each other week after week and month after month. You are a blessing.

A big thank you to my awesome extended family for supporting my writing dreams and celebrating my successes.

Steve Laube, you're an extraordinary human and an awesome literary agent. Thank you for your tireless efforts, encouraging words, and your sense of humor. Your professionalism is unmatched, and I'm proud to be a part of your agency.

Susan May Warren, a thank-you hardly seems adequate for all you do. You've invested tirelessly in the lives of other writers, set an incredible example for us to follow, and challenged us to put forth our best effort every time we write a book. Thank you for helping me make this story shine!

To everyone at Sunrise Publishing, thank you for your phenomenal efforts to get our books out into the world. You rock!

About the Author

Heidi McCahan writes uplifting inspirational romance novels set in small towns. She is the bestselling author of sixteen books, including *Her Alaskan Family* and *A Baby in Alaska*. A perfect day for Heidi includes a cup of good coffee, dark chocolate, and reading stories with happy endings. She makes her home in North Carolina with her handsome husband, three amazing boys, and the world's greatest Goldendoodle.

Heidi enjoys connecting with writers and readers, so please visit her website at HeidiMcCahan.com.

It's time to come *Home* to *Heritage*

"A heartwarming and inspiring story of second chances, renewed faith, and the enduring power of love."

—SUSAN MAY WARREN

USA Today bestselling author

We solve the problem of what to read next.

YOU MAY ALSO LIKE...

When Noah Hebert inherits the struggling Blue Pirogue Inn, he must solve a puzzle left by his grandfather to save it from his family's nemesis, Isaac Bergeron. Teaming up with Elisa Bergeron, the café manager and his rival, they must navigate family feuds—and unexpected sparks—while racing against time.

***Where I Found You* by Besty St. Amant**

Working together to keep Fox Bakery from going under, Robin and Sammy find that something more than friendship is simmering between them. But will Robin follow her old dreams back to the glamor of Paris, or will she discover how sweet it is to be loved in Deep Haven?

***How Sweet It Is* by Andrea Christenson**

Dani Sullivan is determined to revive Jonathon Island's fading charm and reunite her fractured family. Her plan? Reopen the Grand Sullivan Hotel. But without the funds to restore the hotel, Dani's forced to accept help from Liam Stone—a big-city hotel developer whose sleek, modern vision is everything she's trying to avoid.

***Meet Me at the Grand* by Lindsay Harrel**

We solve the problem of what to read next.

www.ingramcontent.com/pod-product-compliance
Lightning Source LLC
Chambersburg PA
CBHW020919060726
47591CB00004B/1320

* 9 7 8 1 9 6 6 4 6 3 8 8 7 *